FORTUNE FAVORS THE CRUEL

KEL CARPENTER

Fortune Favors the Cruel

Published by Kel Carpenter

Copyright © 2019, Kel Carpenter LLC

Contributions made by Lucinda Dark

Edited by Analisa Denny

Cover Art by Trif Book Cover Designs

Map Art and Graphic by Zenta Brice

Some people bring out the worst in you, others bring out the best, and then there are those remarkably rare, addictive ones who just bring out the most. Of everything. They make you feel so alive that you'd follow them straight into hell, just to keep getting your fix.

Karen Marie Moning, *Shadowfever*

The Sirian Continent

N

THE CRYSTAL
CONTINENT

TRITOL

NSKARA

LIPH

JIBREAL

ILVAS

VUSUT

CISEA

CISEAN MOUNTAINS

BANGRATAS

DUMAS

ZYBURN

SARI SARI ISLANDS

NORCASTA

TRIENE

LEONE

IAMONT

Marketplace Meeting

"If luck were left to fate, then it would indeed be a cruel thing."
— *Quinn Darkova, former slave*

Silver strands whipped around her face as an errant wind brushed over her bare forearms, raising goosebumps in its wake.

Quinn shivered, then paused.

The southern market of Dumas was alight with happy faces and playing children. The sun shined, and the sand drifted in the breeze. It was the same as it always was.

And yet it wasn't.

The scent of smoked meats and salt water filled her nostrils, but there was something else there too. Something subtler. A shadow in an otherwise peaceful scene. Quinn glanced down the row of brightly lit tents, pausing for only a moment longer before someone bumped into her.

"Sorry," she breathed as a stranger hustled by with a muttered curse.

Shrugging off the strange feeling, she turned and ducked into the tent to her right.

"Quinn," the middle-aged woman said in greeting. "Is it that time again already?" The woman stood and the colorful swaths of her patchwork dress fell loosely to her feet. Quinn pressed her lips together in a tight smile as she reached around to the back of her neck and lifted the leather drawstring.

"So it seems, Jada," Quinn answered. Her fingers brushed over the black opal stone that dangled off the end. It flashed for a brief second, and Jada frowned.

"I renewed the barrier just two weeks ago…" she began, her brown eyes filling with concern and trepidation. Quinn's fingers tightened around the amulet, her neutral expression going cold as tendrils of fear wafted from the other women's rust-colored skin. It was cloying, sinking into Quinn's pores as though attracted to her own power.

"It's not working."

Jada swallowed for a moment, her eyes moving from the pulsing stone to Quinn's face.

"If it's not working then it's not because the spell weakened," Jada said, treading cautiously. "That renewal should have lasted at least two more weeks…"

Quinn bit the inside of her cheek as the shadows under Jada's skin stirred further. Riling her up more, the smell of midnight weeds and damp petals grew stronger. Why was it that they always feared her?

Was it the marks on her skin from all her past masters? Perhaps it was the quiet tone she used; accented, but without emotion. Or maybe, just maybe … it was the look in her ice blue eyes—the crystalline color tinged with darkness.

"The amulet isn't working and you're the only apothecarian that will see me." Quinn took a step forward just as Jada took a step back. The flap of white material behind her shifted as a child came bounding through and ran around the rickety wooden table.

She stopped short at the look on her mother's face. Jada pulled her to the side and spoke soft warnings under her breath about disturbing her while there were clients about. Quinn pretended not to notice the way she shielded the young girl with her body, or how she sent the child to the back of their shop instead of back out into the streets.

"My apologies," Jada said. "As I was saying, though, I want to help you, Quinn. I really do." She opened her mouth to continue, but Quinn looked away, a familiar tingle spreading through her limbs as she clenched her jaw shut to keep herself in check.

"You're telling me there's nothing you can do to make this work properly again?" she asked, wrapping her knuckles in the leather string and holding it up. The colorful veins running through the black opal sparkled as beams of light shined through the cracks in the tent.

"Magic is not easy, Quinn. It's even difficult for those of us who have ancient scrolls and potions to go by. There's not much known about your type, and—"

"Can you do *anything*?" Quinn asked. It was the last time she would. She didn't come here for excuses. She came here for a fix. A solution for her problem, if only temporary. A barrier.

"No … I—maybe," Jada said, clasping her hands together. "The best I can do is renew it, but if the current one hasn't lasted, I don't know if that will do you much good at all."

Quinn dropped the stone on the table with a heavy thunk. "Do it."

"It'll still be fifteen pieces of silver…"

"I know," Quinn snapped. It was expensive and would drain most of the small sum she'd saved, but she was at the end of her wits. If she couldn't keep her magic under control it was only a matter of time until another accident happened, and she couldn't afford one of those or there would be a noose around her neck before the week was out.

Quinn counted out the fifteen pieces requested, and not a copper more. Jada swept them from the table into a leather pouch and set to work. Her spindly fingers grasped for some herbs that she ground into a fine powder. Quinn stood off to the side, arms crossed and expression pinched as she listened to the bustling market beyond.

"Blood," Jada said. Quinn pulled the knife she kept sheathed under her oversized burlap shirt and came to stand over the onyx bowl of dark sludge. The slice of the razor edge pressing into her skin only briefly registered before red droplets fell into the waiting solution. The moment it touched the mixture, it molded into a semi-clear fluid, growing more translucent with each passing moment. Quinn pulled away, wiping her bloodied knife on her pant leg before stowing it as Jada murmured an incantation in a foreign tongue under her breath and dipped the black opal thrice.

The lacquer hardened and then broke away, leaving the veins of color glowing.

She held it out and Quinn took the amulet back, frowning slightly when the usual blissful silence of magic didn't immediately fall over her.

"You did it?" she asked.

"I did," Jada answered, more tepid than usual. "But I can tell by your face it was not the results you were hoping for." She went about dumping the odd concoction into an unmarked jar and seated herself again before Quinn. "You're coming into your full power, and soon even this spell will do nothing for you."

"How long?" Quinn said quietly. "How long do I have?"

"It's hard to say," Jada murmured. "But at this rate I wouldn't bother coming back to me again. You're going to have to learn how to control your powers and the"—she paused, a twinge of sympathy in her expression as she said—"side effects."

Quinn pressed her lips together and looked away as she slipped the string around her neck and stuffed the amulet down her shirt. The black opal sat snuggly between her small breasts, cool against her skin, and not nearly as oppressive as it should have been.

"Thank you," Quinn whispered. "It may not save me from the gallows…" She swallowed and looked to the top of the tent. "But you've bought me time these last few months." She didn't look back at Jada as she departed, not wanting to see the pity in her eyes. Quinn simply lowered her head and swept out her arm, stepping through the gap. The flap fell shut behind her and she was alone once more in a crowd of people.

The sun sat high in the sky, its fever bearing down on the bustling marketplace. Fresh flowers wilted in the scorching heat of Dumas as a mirage danced on the horizon. Quinn pulled her gaze away from the enticing illusion and turned down the nearest alley.

Her worn boots were near silent as she stuck to the shadows, but not all was quiet.

The sharp sound of a whip meeting flesh rang in her ears like an echo from the past.

Quinn stopped in her tracks. Her hands limp at her sides as she blankly stared straight ahead. A second crack split the air, and Quinn shuddered.

A woman screamed. A baby began bawling. All the while the muffled grunts of a man and harsh bite of the whip flooded Quinn's senses.

Her hands balled at her sides as she tried to resist the call. Tried to defy the compulsion.

Tried to do something—anything—other than what she knew she could not resist.

Without realizing that her choice was already made, Quinn turned on her heel and began tearing through the marketplace, following the sounds of disparity. Another wayward wind slammed into her, blowing the long strands away from her face. Her teeth grazed her bottom lip, biting down when the sound of the whip rang out again. The scent of copper and tang of metal in her mouth made Quinn pause before the courtyard. She reached up and pressed a finger to her lips.

It came away red.

Crack.

She looked beyond that bloodied finger to the man in the street. He wore a tattered burlap shirt not all that different from her own. Dark brown hair hung

7

from his head in sweaty locks, and on his cheek—smudged, but visible—was the brand of a slave.

Quinn's heart began to pound so loud it was all she could hear as the slave master's whip came down again. Tendrils of black that only Quinn could see snaked up the slave's arms as he used them to attempt to cover his face from the brutal assault.

"Stupid. Pathetic. Weak." The master spat one-worded insults with every blow as a woman in a slave shift stood behind him, screaming with silvery streaks of tears running in rivers down her face. The baby in her arms, swaddled in dirty rags, bellowed its own outrage.

Quinn didn't think as her feet moved towards the man. She didn't register what she was doing as cold calming clarity settled deep within her bones. She hadn't known how much the man's fear—the woman's fear—the baby's fear—all called to her.

All she knew was a whip and blood and silence.

The master struck once more, turning his head to look at the crowd, the end of the thin leathery weapon falling into the sandy streets in front of her. Quinn's boot came down on top of it, holding it in place as he yanked his arm again. He turned when he realized it would not budge. Sweat slicked his skin, cheeks red from anger and exertion, tan skin rough and darkened in uneven patches. He had a finely trimmed beard and black eyes, but these things were all trivial to Quinn as she followed the path from the whip being jerked about beneath her boot to the handle that he gripped tightly.

"I detest whips," she said quietly. Her voice was abnormally distant, the roaring in her head louder than her words. The sound so consuming that it blocked her from hearing or feeling or thinking about anything else. It stopped her from seeing the shadowed figure in her periphery.

"Who do you think you——" the slave master started.

"It doesn't matter," Quinn answered softly. She knelt down, her fingers reaching for the smooth leather vice. She picked up the thin end of the whip, trailing her nails along its bloodied exterior.

Without any warning, her left-hand wrapped around it.

Her right reached for her dagger. The one she always kept on her, its sheath resting over the brand of a master from long ago. A master that had the same detestable urge as this man. To beat her to the edge of death. She never went anywhere unarmed after that. Even when she became as much a weapon as the sharpened bit of metal that she kept on her person.

With a flick of her wrist, the dagger soared true. A crunch of tendons snapping and bones splintering. An anguished scream as he dropped the whip's handle.

The dagger protruded from his hand, sticking out the other side. Red smeared the open wound, dripping down the gleaming steel and into the sandy streets.

Quinn didn't even blink at the mess she'd made. Violence was in her bones. Brutality in her blood. She swung the whip and the thick end veered straight into the man's face.

A deafening crack rang, and shadows gathered beneath his skin.

Fear. The very thing that called to her.

She licked the copper taste from her lips and swung again and again and again.

The leathery end pummeling his face into a bruised and broken pulp. The blood vessels in his eyes burst, turning them a grotesque shade of pink. The skin over his cheekbones split, and when he spat, a wad of crimson and mucus came out, two of his teeth landing in the puddle of fluid.

Even still, Quinn didn't stop.

Not when his breathing grew shallow or the stench of piss ran in the streets.

Not when the thick end of the whip coiled around his neck, choking the life from him.

Not when she ripped the dagger free, only to raise it—

"Stop."

Quinn blinked.

The roaring quieted.

All at once, the bubble of silence around her popped

and she heard it: the screaming, the sobbing, the shouting, the chaos. The cracks of the whip had lulled her into a state where there was only rage … only pain.

And the sound of a man's voice—dark as a shadow, deep as the ocean, powerful enough it reverberated through every bone in her body—was what pulled her out.

Warm fingers stilled the hand where she clutched the dagger.

Quinn paused and raised her eyes, taking in the man that had stopped her.

Backlit by the sun and sky, a creature of savageness and sensuality stared down at her. His eyes, they were unlike anything she'd ever seen. Smoldering coals they were, burning from within, without a speck of color in sight. Her lips parted and her breath caught, but only for a moment.

Those eyes were so … fierce. There was a wildness to him that Quinn had not found in others. Ever. She took a step back and he paused, waiting, before he released his hold on her wrist.

She composed herself, a mask of indifference falling over her as she allowed her eyes to travel the length of him. Long dark hair—the color of black skies—hung in thick strands surrounding a face that had seen more than its fair share of fights. His skin was tanned, but an off-white scar spanned from his left eyebrow to his cheek. Other smaller flecks of old healed wounds dotted his face, making it all the more striking.

Quinn found it a strange sort of beautiful.

He wore the fine fabrics of a nobleman that was worth his weight in gold, and two rings adorned his left hand. None graced his right, Quinn noted as she took a step away, slowly coming back to her full senses.

"Who are you?" he asked her. The shouts grew louder as a crowd began to form around them. Quinn didn't spare the slave master a look. She'd never killed before, though she'd come close. Despite her slipups with that cold impassioned madness that sometimes took hold, the honor of her first kill was reserved for someone who owed her restitution, and therefore she didn't want or care to know if he was dead or alive.

Quinn took a step away, slowly lowering the dagger to her side. She didn't put it away. Not yet.

"No one," came her reply as she moved back towards the crowd. There was a ringing in the square, and the occupants of the market scattered in confusion and fear.

The bells meant only one thing.

Soldiers. City guards, to be exact. She froze.

"No," the man said. He didn't move. Neither of them did, even as the people in the streets scattered like rats around them. "You're someone." She began to shake her head, and he stopped her with a calculated look. "You're someone like me."

That made her pause.

Did he mean…

The streets thinned as the pounding of hooves against mortar thundered through the city. She needed to get out of here. If they caught her with the evidence of her actions bleeding out behind her, she would never even find out if Jada's latest attempt at keeping her magic under control would work. She'd be hanged before the end of the morrow.

Quinn turned to leave when something stopped her. It was startling; a whisper of air blew across her face. The cold chill of winter that didn't belong.

"I'll find you after I take care of this," he told her. She didn't have to ask what *this* was. Nor did she want to know what he meant. As much as he intrigued her, Quinn just made herself a wanted woman one too many times.

Still, she looked over her shoulder. With a frown, she replied, "Unlikely."

Then she disappeared into the shadows where people like her belonged.

Where she should have stayed.

Dark Masquerade

"Mirrors reflect the monsters no one else can see."
— *Quinn Darkova, former slave, possible murderess*

Quinn stared into the shimmering reflective surface of her dressing room mirror. Just outside, she could hear the distant bustling noises of the rest of the night's acts getting ready. Lifting the opal stone from between her breasts, Quinn examined the cracks in its surface. Although not by much, the magic Jada had enchanted the stone with had already faded since that morning. Sighing, she slipped it back under the collar of her dress.

A knock on the door echoed throughout the small room just a moment before it swung slightly inward.

"Are you ready?" a familiar voice asked. The top part of a sandy blond head peeked around the wood.

"Almost," Quinn said. "I will be shortly."

"Good," Caine replied, his dull brown eyes looking her over before sliding away. "Hastings is looking for you."

Quinn narrowed her gaze on the young man. He rarely looked her in the eyes when he delivered bad news, meaning that whatever Hastings wanted—it wasn't good.

"Fine," she snapped. "I'll be there in a moment."

He nodded and then quietly backed out, letting the door click shut behind him. Quinn turned back to her mirror and snatched up a container of white powder. If possible, the dusty mix made her appear even paler. That was what she needed tonight. On nights when she was the primary act of the show, she needed to look like a ghost—not that it was difficult to do. Cool, glassy eyes stared back at her as she smeared the powder over her cheeks, forehead, and down her nose. Just before she was done, she dabbed a bit over her lips so that even there, she was void of all color.

Laying the container back in its place, she picked up her white skirts and headed for the hallway leading out to the main stage. Several stagehands saw her coming and veered away. She could hear Hastings shouting at someone in the main theater as she entered from behind a tall musty curtain.

The theater was falling down around them. The

roof leaked, the walls were thin, and it rarely held any cool relief from the eternal summer Dumas seemed to be in, but it had given her sanctuary when she had none. It may have not been home to her, but it was useful for the time being.

"You needed me?" Quinn asked.

Hastings, a ruddy-faced man with a curly red beard, turned and fixed her with an irritated look. "I heard there was an incident in the market today," he said.

"Was there?" Quinn stared back at him, her face impassable.

"Mmm hmm." He stroked his beard. "You wouldn't happen to know anything about that, would you?"

"Why would I?" Quinn replied.

Hastings stopped and dropped his fat sausage fingers away from his face, squinting at her with a dark look. "If I find out you've done something to interrupt my business, I'll—"

"You'll throw me out," Quinn cut in dryly. "So you've informed me. Many times now, I might add."

Hastings grumbled his response before brushing past her. "Just make sure you're ready for your act. The doors open in twenty." And off he went, yelling at passing stagehands as Caine—his ever-present assistant—came slinking out from behind the curtain and trailed after him.

Quinn watched them go before turning towards

the open room where rows upon rows of benches were anchored to the hard floors. In just under a half an hour, the room would be filled wall-to-wall with people of all shapes and sizes and colors. All of them wanting to see a bit of themselves that so rarely came to light. And she was more than willing to give it to them.

For a price.

As the lamps dimmed, Quinn removed herself from the stage. The echo of hushed whispering began to fill the air as Hastings, dressed in his ragged coat, took center stage. His booming voice ricocheted up the walls, silencing the crowd.

"Welcome, faithful citizens, to the Dark Masquerade. If you've been with us before, then perhaps you've seen some of our acts. Perhaps your curiosity has brought you back. If you're new and not sure what to expect, then just hold onto your seats, ladies and gentlemen. The show you're about to experience is like no other…"

When the warning reverberated into the silence of the theater and then teetered out, Hastings raised his thick fist and threw a small vial to the floor at his feet. It shattered against the wood, and a large plume of smoke appeared. A moment later, his big body slipped behind the curtains and he rushed the first act out on stage—a pair of fire-breathing twins with dark black masks covering their faces.

Quinn stood to the side, her own mask—retrieved

from her dressing room vanity—clutched in her hands. She watched as act after act approached the stage, wowing the crowds with their strange talents. Near the end, Hastings stepped up alongside her.

"You're almost up."

She nodded, raising her hands and tying the soft strands of fabric around her head. The mask wasn't to conceal her features—merely to accentuate her eeriness to the crowd as she played her role in Hastings' Dark Masquerade. He glanced down at her as she stared between the curtains, eyes fixed on a point in the distance beyond the crowd.

With a shake of his head, he strode out from behind them as the latest act moved backstage and then off towards the hallway. Something was different about the crowd tonight. They fell in a hush as Hastings lit a single candle in the middle of the dais. His voice carried throughout the room as dark figures moved several large mirrors in front of the curtains, spanning the length of the stage. People's reflections stared back at them.

"Tonight," Hastings said, "we have something special for you."

Quinn closed her eyes as he spoke, listening to the wind whistling through the cracks of the doors at the back of the theater, and the breathy excitement humming from the crowd.

"From a distant land, the Dark Masquerade brings you something"—Hastings paused, his words catching in a melodramatic tone—"unique," he finished. "A phantom from the in-between. Please welcome to the stage—*Mirior*."

The curtains parted slightly, and the crowd's breath nearly stopped as Quinn rounded the wall of mirrors. Absolute silence greeted her as Hastings faded into the background, stepping away from the light of the candle.

Moving with grace-like beauty, Quinn glided across the stage, her footsteps making no sound. That was when the whispers began. It started low, a dark tingle in the audience. But as Quinn stepped up to the candle, allowing the dim fiery glow to flicker over her features, it grew.

Black tendrils, like rising smoke, lifted from individuals in the crowd. The more opaque the strands, the more fearful the person. Quinn closed her eyes, reached out, and extinguished the flame with her thumb and forefinger. The strands of fear turned into rivers, flowing out and around her as darkness descended upon the room.

Stagehands hurried to light the candles placed on the top edge of each mirror. Quinn turned her back on the audience and lifted her pale hands. She pointed the tendrils towards the mirrors, and they followed.

The reflections of the audience rippled before her and there were several gasps at her back. Quinn's expression did not falter. She lowered her hands and moved forward, passing one mirror, and then another, until she was on the other end of the stage. She glanced at the audience, noting the people were enthralled with what they saw before them—then she moved across the stage, skimming the tips of her fingers across the glass as she passed it by. The tendrils she controlled were brought to life inside the mirrors.

Images appeared. People began to whimper and cry. Some gasped for breath but found no relief. Several turned their faces away, clenching their jaws as they prayed that what they saw was not real.

As Quinn came to a final stop at the end of the stage, at the very last mirror, she met a pair of glittering eyes in its reflection. With a frown, she turned and followed that gaze to its owner and a shock of recognition seized her.

It was the man from the marketplace.

He had found her.

The candles above the mirrors were snuffed out before the crowd became too agitated, and Quinn disappeared behind the curtains as the mirrors were removed and Hastings hurried out to calm them with the last act of the evening.

Quinn had no clue what the people saw in the mirrors, only that it showed their deepest, darkest fears. Each person's fear was different, but in the mirrors, it was expounded upon and brought to life.

Tonight, though, one of her own fears had come to life.

She had never expected to see him again, much less here. But there he had sat, his eyes fixated on her, watching her every movement. She wondered if he knew. She wondered if he would look for her again. If he would tell Hastings about today.

Quinn strode quickly through the backstage area, ripping her mask away from her face. Caine scurried after her, attempting to stop her, but she waved him away with an irritated scowl. Quinn stormed into her dressing room and slammed the door in his face, leaning heavily against the wood as she stared at her pale image in the vanity mirror across the room.

As much as she worried over the stranger, she didn't detect fear in her own eyes. No. Instead, she saw something far more dangerous.

Curiosity.

Stranger in the Night

"There's no such thing as coincidences. Only unknown motivations."
— *Quinn Darkova, former slave, possible murderess, and reluctant performer*

The dull roar of the crowd trickled to a comfortable silence as Quinn stripped away her stage persona and the amphitheater emptied out. With a sigh, she hung up the white gossamer gown with care and cleaned away every trace of face paint from her skin.

Clad in nothing but her undergarments and a loose burlap shirt, she grabbed one of the three books she owned and an apple with its skin already beginning to pucker. It was a day past ripe, but it and the hunk of bread were all the free room and board Hastings was prepared to give his performers. He needed them alive, but well-fed wasn't a requirement.

Quinn padded over to the rickety ladder at the back of her dressing room and climbed up to the small loft where a lumpy bed and old blanket resided. She sighed softly, not happy, but content for the moment. Tonight would be her last night here after the stunt she had pulled in the market. It was only a matter of time until the guards came looking for her, and while Hastings might not rat her out, she wasn't so sure about Caine. The boy was an opportunist if there ever was one. Regardless of whoever's expense his small gain came from. Then there was the fact that she had seen the man in the audience tonight. But there was no way he would be allowed back here. Hastings never let audience members meet the performers.

She settled into her makeshift sleeping area and struck a match, lighting the oil lamp at her bedside. Picking up her book, she let it fall open to wherever she had left it last and began softly reciting the story aloud in her native language. The one she had not spoken to another in over ten years, but she refused to forget.

Because one day she would need it again.

A knock came and Quinn frowned, her eyes snapping up to the door. When it didn't immediately open, her lips pressed together. No one bothered her after a show, not when fear was still running so rampant in her system. It didn't affect her as it did them, instead acting as a drug that lowered the barriers containing her dark power as the magic tried to rise.

No one who knew better would disturb her right now.

Quinn closed her book and set it aside, clambering down the ladder.

There was another knock, and she braced herself as her fingers curled around the wobbly handle. Standing partially behind the door, she twisted the knob and opened it a crack.

A hand paused before the door, obviously raised to knock again, then lowered.

Her heart pounded faster as the dark eyes of the stranger from the market settled on her.

"Who are you?" she asked, her fingers curling around the doorframe as he slipped his boot into the tight space to stop her from possibly slamming it shut on him. *How had he been allowed backstage?*

"That remains to be seen," he murmured. Quinn cocked an eyebrow, tilting her head. She'd met some determined ones in her time. Silver hair and cream-colored skin made her an oddity in Dumas. One considered exotic, beautiful even, if not for her brands.

Never had there been a man that could find her when she didn't want to be found.

Nor one that had the audacity to stop her from shutting him out.

"Why are you following me?" she asked quietly, not as perturbed as she should have been. Quinn was paranoid by nature, but she'd be leaving tomorrow.

There would be no finding her after that.

"Because I'm intrigued by you," he replied, as though that meant something to her.

"And do you regularly follow women and knock on their doors in the middle of the night if they intrigue you…" She trailed off, searching for the name he clearly wasn't going to give. "Sir?"

"You aren't like most women…" He left it open-ended, waiting for her to give her name first.

"Mirior," she obliged, offering him the only name he currently knew her as, "and if that's the best you can come up with, I'll have to pass. If you're looking for a quick fuck, the brothel is two doors down." Quinn stepped back, prepared to force his foot through the door when a large, gloved hand closed around the frame. He pushed, and try as she might, she was forced to yield with a scowl.

"I'm not looking for the brothel," the stranger said. There was no hesitation in the man's expression, no apology on his lips as he barged in. Quinn crossed her arms as his eyes dropped from her face to her bare legs. She didn't blush or even reach for her robe. Modesty, after all, was for the privileged.

"If you lay a hand on me, I'll make what

happened in the square look gentle," she said with a narrowed look. Her hip smacked against the side of the door, and it swung shut. He lifted an eyebrow, the makings of a smirk ghosting across his mouth.

"You sound very sure of yourself."

"I am," she answered without hesitation. "This world isn't kind to women or slaves, and at one point, I was both. You don't survive that without developing a few skills."

The stranger seemed to consider her words as he moved about the room. He came to a stop in front of her mirror and turned around to face her. His hands rested on either side of her vanity, his fingers curling around the aged wood as he leaned back against it, taking in the rest of the nearly barren room before returning his unsettling gaze to her face. "Is that what made you do it?"

There was no need to ask him what he meant. She knew. He had seen her bludgeon a man with his own whip today. Gods, she might have actually beaten the slave master to death. She had no clue, but if she had … well, she still felt no remorse.

"No," she answered honestly. "Not entirely."

"Then why did you?" There was no admonishment in his tone. No judgement. No condemnation. Only curiosity and something else … eagerness, but for what, she couldn't tell.

Her gaze strayed to the other two books on her shelf. They were written in the language of her homeland, their spines worn and letters faded. If the stranger noticed her wandering eye, he didn't mention it as he waited for a reply she wasn't going to give him.

"If you came here for answers on why I did what I did, you're going to be sorely disappointed," Quinn said. There was something strange about him that made her suspicious of his motivations.

"You didn't kill him, you know," the stranger replied with a tilt of his head. He eyed her. "In case you were wondering, that is."

"I wasn't," she said.

"He could still have you hanged."

Quinn narrowed her eyes, uncrossing her arms to reach up. Absently, she tugged on a lock of her silver hair. Fidgeting wasn't a fault she really had, but people were so often disturbed by her stillness. As a result, she had taught herself tricks to make her habits seem more normal, things that gave no bearing to what she was actually thinking or feeling.

"He'd have to find me for that to happen," Quinn said softly.

He tilted his head to the side. "I found you easily enough," he pointed out.

Scowling, Quinn dropped her hand away from her hair. "A coincidence," she replied through gritted teeth. Quinn didn't believe in coincidences, but she didn't want the man to know just how disturbed she was by the fact that he *had* found her—quickly too.

His full lips twitched. "Possibly." He said it in such a way that it was clear he was merely humoring her.

"He won't find me," Quinn snapped.

"What makes you think I wouldn't tell him," the stranger asked, not quite threatening … but testing. Learning. It would seem that he was cataloguing her responses and trying to piece together the enigma before him.

"If you wanted me arrested then there would be guards here now. You've had ample time to call them if that was the route you wished to take." Quinn paused. "Which brings us back to my original question. Who are you?" Quinn did better and asked another almost immediately. "Why are you here?"

The stranger nodded as if hearing her words, but he didn't jump to reply. She huffed, glaring at him. Against the peeling paint and sparse furnishings of her dressing room, he looked so very out of place. The rich fabric of his tunic, a vibrant red just a shade lighter than blood, was adorned with golden thread that gleamed in the low light, drawing Quinn's attention as she waited for his reply.

"I'm here," he started, "because a very dear friend of mine died not long ago and left me a letter. Unfortunately, I was out of the country at the time of his death and I didn't get it until it was too late. It was about a woman—a very special woman."

The stranger stopped perusing her belongings and leveled her with a powerful look. With a push away from her vanity that left the mirror shuddering against the wall, he stalked forward.

"I'm here," he continued, "at the twilight hour in this dingy, disgusting amphitheater because I'm fairly certain you're that woman." Quinn's heart began to beat faster, but her hands didn't tremble. Instead, they went still. Her whole being froze. Where most people experienced shock and tended to unravel, Quinn stiffened with resolve.

"I think you need to leave," she said, reaching for the door.

His fingers wrapped around her forearm.

So warm, she thought. *So very … warm wasn't the right word.*

He wasn't warm.

He was burning hot.

"Olivier Illvain told me—"

"Olivier Illvain is dead," Quinn said flatly, ripping her arm from his grasp while sending a tendril of fear his way. Surprisingly, though, he didn't react the way she had come to expect.

There was no panic in his gaze. No worry. No fear.

He stood still, his hand still outstretched and nostrils flared as his eyelids slid closed. Almost like he might have known what she'd done, but that wasn't possible.

"You…" His jaw tightened and his neck craned, cracking, as he opened his eyes and dark glittering pools looked down on her, "shouldn't have done that."

What little color she possessed drained from her face, and she truly looked like a ghost in that moment. Colorless. Ethereal. A mere reflection in the mirror.

She gripped the knob of the door tightly, thrusting it open. She stepped to the side and pointed.

"It's time for you to leave," she said, brokering no room for argument.

The stranger took a single step towards her, and two men appeared in her doorway. The fire-breathing twins—Nix and Nox. Out of all Hastings' performers, they'd taken a liking to her, but chose to respect Quinn's boundaries better than most others living in the amphitheater.

"Problem here, Q?" one of them asked, likely Nix.

"No problem," Quinn replied curtly. "My guest was just leaving, weren't you?" All three sets of eyes fell on the man that Quinn still couldn't figure out. Something was off about him. It wasn't just the way that he held himself or the noble clothes he wore. There was a sense of *otherness* to him that all other men she had met, noble or not, didn't have. Something she couldn't quite put her finger on.

He took two steps towards her, towering like a god, larger than life. Quinn didn't flinch as his lips came only a hairsbreadth from hers and he whispered, "This isn't over. Until next time, Quinn."

She didn't let it show how much it unsettled her

that he knew her name. His presence was all consuming, seeming to steal the very air from her chest until he stepped away. The twins parted to let him through, and he started down the narrow hallway. The stranger paused and turned back, the look in his eyes seeming to scream of something dark and dangerous and violent.

Quinn waited for him to disappear through the musty curtain before inhaling deeply.

The twins looked at her with concern and she simply shooed them away, closing the door firmly. Her fingers moved to click the lock shut, not because she was afraid he might come back … but because she was afraid she might go after him.

One thing was certain. It was time to get out of Dumas.

Even if the soldiers didn't find her, Quinn had no doubts in her mind that he would be back.

And she wanted to be long gone when he returned.

Cruel Opportunities

"Everyone has a weakness. It's always the same thing. Power."
— *Lazarus Fierté, nobleman and master manipulator*

Lazarus stood on the edge of the street, the door to the decrepit amphitheater swinging shut behind him. The building should have been torn down years ago. The roof leaked. The floors were stained and wobbled under him. It had the smell of poverty sunken so deep into the walls, the only way to get rid of it was to rip it all apart. He knew because Gulliver had given him a report on the establishment that the girl called home not three hours before.

The dim light of a coach rounding the corner of the street swayed back and forth as it came to a stop in front of him. Gulliver stepped out, holding the door for his master.

"You're late," he said as he used the bottom rung to step inside and then turned, sitting and resting his back against the seat cushions.

"I apologize, my lord," Gulliver said. "We were waylaid by…" The man's eyes darted to the driver.

"Get inside," Lazarus said with a heavy sigh.

Gulliver nodded. As soon as he had closed the coach door behind him, the driver snapped his short whip at the horses and they jerked the carriage forward.

"What happened?"

"There was a notice for you at the inn, my lord." Gulliver's dusty gray eyes met his with trepidation.

"Go on," Lazarus pressed the young man. "Who sent the note?"

"That's the thing, sir," Gulliver said. "I don't know. The innkeeper refused to give it to me. I've been arguing with the man for the better part of an hour. He says that he was told to hand it specifically to you. I assume he was paid handsomely for his promise to make sure it was delivered appropriately."

"It's fine," Lazarus said, holding up a hand as the man leaned forward, preparing to launch into an apology. Gulliver settled back, casting a concerned look his way, but thankfully he didn't say more. "Did you do what I asked? The boy?"

Gulliver nodded. "I did, sir."

"Good."

Lazarus turned his gaze away, letting the carriage fall into silence as he watched the city's passing scenery. Dumas was older; the buildings tall but worn, the streets cobbled and sinking. The people were old-fashioned as well, both in their clothes and their culture. But the girl ... the girl was new. New to this city, he assumed, but perhaps not new to this country. Her voice had the briefest lilt to something foreign. If her features were anything to go by, he'd say she was a native N'skaran. How she'd ended up with Olivier and now in the Dark Masquerade ... it puzzled him.

The coach lurched around a corner and came to a slow stop in front of the Iron Queen Inn and Tavern. Gulliver exited first, holding the door for him. Lazarus' boot splashed into a small puddle as he stepped out of the carriage and towards the dwelling.

Inside the boisterous tavern almost all conversation stopped. He had a way of silencing a room without a word. With a harsh squeak of the innkeeper's wide frame against the smooth wood of the bar, the short, rotund man made his way over to Lazarus.

"My lord," the innkeeper began.

Lazarus didn't let him continue. "You have a message for me," he stated.

The innkeeper nodded profusely, reaching into his stained and frayed apron to produce a letter. Lazarus took it, and without a glance back at the innkeeper, walked off towards the stairs leaving Gulliver to hurry after him.

The Iron Queen Inn's rooms left much to be desired. The windows were thin. The bed hardly long enough to fit a man of his size—not that he would be sleeping much in this place—and the noise below was a constant dull roar in the back of his mind.

After dismissing Gulliver for the night, Lazarus sat down and began to remove his boots. He leaned back in the wing-backed chair, reaching for the decanter of spirits he'd had delivered. Pouring himself a hefty serving, Lazarus lifted the glass to his lips and sipped, letting the burn of the alcohol slip down the back of his throat and he considered his options.

There was no doubt in his mind that the girl—Quinn—was the same girl that Olivier had wrote to him about. She had skin paler than the moon and eyes the color of ice crystals. He saw more brands adorning her body this evening than had been clear in the market earlier in the day. The marks of many masters, and yet none had tamed her. Something about that amused Lazarus, as if any human master could bring her to heel. No. It would take someone with a finer touch and a might of their own. Someone that she couldn't strike down in a rage when her magic would get the better of her.

Quinn was something more than just a pretty face, though she tried to hide it. There was a darkness that didn't simply cling to her, it came *from* her and she embraced it … to a certain extent.

Lazarus thought about the black opal around her neck. A cheap trinket crafted by those without magic of their own in an attempt to control the torrent that wreaked havoc inside her. It wouldn't last her long if she lost control again.

He sipped his drink as thoughts of the woman in white held him.

A soft knock brought Lazarus to his feet. He closed the distance between his chair and the door in several long strides. One click of the latch and a twist of the handle and the wooden panel swung open.

"You called for m-me, sir?"

Lazarus stared down at the thin man that had been following the stage master all night, waiting in the wings. Lazarus nodded and stepped to the side, allowing the other man entrance. Caine's gaze darted around the room before he hesitantly moved inside, his left leg dragging a bit behind him.

"Take a seat," Lazarus said, gesturing towards the chair he had just vacated next to the fireplace.

Trembling as though he were a newborn calf, the man did so. His eyes continued to dart around, one of them not quite as fast as the other, giving him a rather dull look.

"Would you like a drink?" Lazarus didn't wait for a response as he poured another glass and handed it over. Without much of a choice, Caine took the amber liquid and stared at it with wary trepidation, then sipped until he gagged.

Lazarus hid a smirk behind the rim of his glass as he took a long swig. "I called you here, Caine, because I know you're a smart man."

"Sir?"

"Were you aware that you had a criminal living at the amphitheater?" Lazarus asked. Caine's eyes stopped bouncing, and Lazarus nodded. "Yes, just today I saw a girl that nearly beat a man to death in the marketplace."

Caine's trembles lessened the more he sipped his drink. "Oh?" he said, less shaky this time.

"I was quite surprised to see that same woman in *your* show tonight," Lazarus stressed the word 'your,' watching for the other man's reaction. "They're offering quite a sum for the person who gives them any information regarding her whereabouts."

"It's not m—" Caine stopped himself, pausing as he thought something over. "They are?" he asked instead.

Lazarus nodded. "I assumed you didn't know," he said slowly. "That you hadn't heard." Lazarus knew he had. Everyone had heard about Quinn's little episode.

"No, I had no clue," Caine lied. "Who did you say this was, again?"

Lazarus couldn't stop the cruel smile that graced his lips for a brief moment. But he needn't have worried. Caine was too busy thinking of the monetary opportunity Lazarus knew he would take full advantage of.

"I believe she was introduced as Mirior." He laid the groundwork to see that the right chain of events happened. To do what he saw as best for all parties involved.

Caine nodded, draining the last of his spirits and teetering on his feet as his stood up too quickly. "Thank you, sir, for the information. I will make sure to pass this on."

Lazarus stood as well and led the man to the door. "I'm sure you will," he said as he turned the knob and showed the man out. "I'm sure you will."

The door clicked shut and Lazarus' eyes glanced towards the envelope sitting on his bedside table. It carried the seal of one of the only men he still respected in this world. But Lazarus didn't have time to respond to Claudius at the moment. He knew what that letter contained and if he opened it, solidifying his suspicions, he would have to leave before he could procure what he came to Dumas for.

And Lazarus wasn't willing to leave without the girl.

Cimmerian Skies

"Never leave anything to chance. Few Gods are as fickle as Lady Luck."
— *Quinn Darkova, former slave, wanted fugitive*

Quinn woke with a startle. Morning light poured through the small window that hovered over the loft. She blinked twice and stretched her tired limbs. Sleep hadn't come easy after her encounter with the strange man from the market. Dreams of black tendrils and dark desires mixed together in a hazy recollection that she was rapidly forgetting the longer she laid there.

Wasting no time, she slipped out of the lumpy bed and half slid, half climbed down the ladder to the main area of her dressing room. She pulled on her worn leather pants, bending at the knees to work them all the way up. A quick glance in the mirror told her that her mass of silver-white hair needed to be tamed. Left wild and unruly, she'd attract too much attention. Braiding the strands back as quickly as possible, Quinn searched for her discarded boots and began to ready herself for the coming journey.

Three books, a black opal, the papers that proved she was a free woman—despite her remaining brands —and ten pieces of silver were all the worldly possessions she held. If it wouldn't draw so much attention, Quinn may have considered taking the stage clothes she performed in and selling them off in the market. But as it was, she was running late, and the amphitheater would be too packed to sneak out something so large. She'd have to make do.

With her items stowed away in her handmade satchel, Quinn walked out of her dressing room and didn't look back. All she could do was go forward.

"She has silver hair and blue eyes—you can't miss her," Caine was saying to someone. Approaching the curtain that opened up to the greater amphitheater, she paused.

"She's in the door at the end of the hall, you say?" another voice asked, one she didn't recognize.

"Yes, just through that—" He made a sound of protest. "Where's my payment?"

Dread settled in Quinn's stomach like a lead weight.

She was right to leave, but she'd acted too late. *Myori's wrath!* Caine had already run his mouth to the city guards.

The amulet between her breasts pulsed as a sliver of power snaked up her arms. Fear. Black and potent. She didn't feel afraid, though, oh no. She felt powerful. Strong. It was a heady thing, this emotion that motivated so many. To Quinn, it was the ultimate drug. The very thing that brought her clarity … and also stole it away.

The barrier tried to contain it, tried and failed as the darkness slithered along her arms.

She took two steps back and bolted for the other exit. Her body was just disappearing around the corner when the curtain at her back swished aside.

Shouts rang out as footsteps trampled in her wake.

She flung herself at the back door, using her momentum to open it. The wood splintered apart at the lock and the door swung wide, banging against the side of the old amphitheater. The sound ricocheted through the southern market of Dumas as Quinn took to the streets, guards hot on her tail. She sprinted down the narrow alleyway and veered left, running away from the slums and into the thickening mass of people.

Bells rang out, coming from the square and the crowd grew frenzied. Confused looks followed her as Quinn raced down the sandy streets as fast as her legs would carry her.

She was quicker than the guards. She was more motivated than them.

But they had one thing that Quinn did not.

Strength in numbers.

The end of the street was blocked off with more soldiers dressed in the Norcastan uniform of white and gold. Not just city enforcers then, but the army as well. If she got out of this, it would be by the skin of her teeth and the goddess Fortuna's blessing.

"Stop!" Their shouts echoed all around. On either side tents and city walls surrounded her. There would be no running.

With every exhale of her breath, black wisps drifted from her mouth like smoke from a dragon's lungs.

She reached inside her shirt and pulled the stone from her chest. The veins within it pulsed unnaturally bright. She knew her body's own response to fear was blowing through what was left of the barrier meant to help contain her powers.

"Quinn of House Illvain, also known as Mirior, you are under arrest for the intended murder of Earl Houche of House—" The guards pretty speech broke off as Quinn started laughing, cackling like the maruda they thought her to be.

Quinn was not yet a dark Maji gone mad, even if she did dance with Mazzulah, the god of the dark realm, in her heart. Being wicked and being insane were two different things, though they often went hand-in-hand.

The sky dimmed with pewter and charcoal clouds tinged red. Hysteria crept into her thoughts as she clutched the black opal.

Too much…

It was trying to funnel too much…

Quinn pulled the knife from her sheath and held it in one hand, the stone in the other. Her arms didn't shake. Her breath didn't quiver. The makings of a wicked smile ghosted her lips, because she felt far too confident and that only meant one thing.

The guards advanced on her from all sides, swords in hand and armor glistening beneath the nightmarish sky. Apprehension thickened the air, and Quinn took an intoxicating whiff.

The black opal cracked down the middle and exploded. In that instant, every flicker of power it had been holding back fell over Quinn with a quiet hush.

She gasped for breath, air leaving her body but nothing coming in. The pieces of the useless amulet fell to her feet.

The guards took another step forward, their over-whelming anxiety leaking into the air around them and fueling the cataclysm sinking into her bones.

Dark shadows thickened and swirled around her. They clung to her skin as if attracted to the very power inside that fueled them. An aching abyss of despair and promise opened up inside her. Too much power. Too many people. So many feelings that were tied to her very being. They swarmed her.

Her confidence wavered as her power consumed her.

Black tethers snaked around her arms, snapped out, wrapping around the guards. Screams reverberated through the market as, one by one, men began to fall around her. Their internal struggles now as overwhelming as her own.

Panic clawed its way through them as terror coiled around their hearts, sinking sharp vile claws into their deepest, darkest fears and squeezing the organ that beat rhythmically, trying to keep them alive. She couldn't control the onslaught. She didn't know how.

For most of her life, she'd worn some sort of barrier—chains or stones meant to mute it, to cage that darkness inside her. The trouble with cages is that eventually the beast breaks free.

Those chains of silence that allowed her to control it in small bursts had completely fallen away with the shattered opal and left to her own devices, Quinn did the only thing she knew how.

She lashed out.

In a burst of power, she detonated. The entire southern market fell into utter chaos. People dropped where they stood—men, women, children—as their nightmares consumed them. No longer could she contain it to just the guards. Some fell to their knees and sobbed. Others simply stood. Stared. Catatonic.

And at the center of it all was Quinn.

The girl with more power than she knew what to do with.

More men came and the bells rang in the square. A horn sounded, and in Quinn's turmoil, a soldier not yet obliterated by her powers stepped up. Brandishing his sword, without pause, the man brought the decorative pommel down on her head.

Like a candle snuffed out, the market fell eerily silent as Quinn crumpled in the dirty streets without any barrier—magical or otherwise—to protect her. And finally, the nightmares ceased.

Blood Contract

"The price of freedom is greater than all but one—survival."
— Quinn Darkova, former slave, prisoner, possibly deranged

Quinn opened her eyes and stared at the slowly dripping ceiling—the very thing that had awoken her—as another water droplet fell, splashing her forehead and sliding down her temple. An echoing silence greeting her and a slight ringing in her ears that slowly ebbed. Her throat was parched, and it hurt to swallow. She wiped the back of her hand across her face, and it came away slick with sweat, water, and grime.

Where in the dark realm am I? Quinn wondered.

A creaking hinge nearby alerted her to people and stirred her into action. She struggled to sit up just as a wave of nausea threatened to send bile up her throat. Groaning, she leaned forward, head on her knees with her arms wrapped around her middle as she waited for it to pass.

"She's awake," a low voice whispered, just at the edge of what she could hear past her own beating heart. "Go notify Fierté before someone's head ends up disconnected from their shoulders."

Quinn perked her ears upon hearing a name. She wasn't sure who exactly this Fierté was, but a niggling in her gut gave her a suspicion.

"Where—" she choked, her mouth salivating. She swallowed twice, trying to settle some moisture in the back of her throat before trying again. "Where am I?" she called out, blinking and turning her head to the other side so she could take in her surroundings.

Dirt floors and a bucket to piss in. Metal bars surrounded her on three sides, just tall enough for her to stand if she desired. She didn't.

The guard at the end of the hall outside her cell didn't reply. He wasn't wearing the gold and white of the capitol. Nor the blue and silver of Dumas's city guards.

He wore red and gold. She frowned. "Who...?" she started.

Her lips parted when it hit her. She *knew* exactly whose footsteps were coming down the corridor. The guard said nothing, made no move to reply to her unfinished question. His eyes were cold as they settled on her.

"Thank you, Dominicus," that voice said. The one from the market. The one from her dressing room. He turned the corner, and Quinn inhaled sharply.

"You," she spat. Her voice gravely and dry. She lifted her head as her nausea finally settled.

"I told you it wasn't over, Quinn," he said. There was a hard edge to his voice that spoke of control. Restraint. "Did you really think I'd let you go after your little threat?"

Quinn remained silent as she stared at him through the bars of her cell. The guards behind him watched her with an anxiousness she had expected. She couldn't quite remember how dried blood had gotten on her hands, but she clearly wasn't getting out of here any time soon.

"If you wanted me dead, then why bother trying to talk when they'll hang me all the same?" Quinn asked with a rasping cough.

"Who said I wanted you dead?" the man replied.

Quinn blinked, confused.

"You don't?"

"No. I don't want you dead." He paused for a brief second, giving her a moment for thought. "I want you to work for me."

Quinn drew a stuttered breath. "To—work for you?" she asked, not entirely sure what that meant …

Work for him doing what? He simply nodded. "Why?" she asked, eyes narrowed as a thought occurred to her.

"You have gifts I'm interested in."

Understanding sparked in her eyes as she said, "Ah, I see."

"You're a fear twister," he said quietly, stepping up to the bars.

Quinn stilled for a moment, sinking into deep thoughts. Silence descended as the last vestiges of his words echoed in the nearly empty imprisonment block.

Fear twister.

She hadn't heard that term in a long, long time. Certainly not spoken with such assuredness. Fear twisters were a thing of legend. While theoretically they came about in every age, dark Maji such as these could rarely hold themselves together through adolescence. Even fewer into adulthood.

They were scarce; some of the rarest Maji of them all, and yet here he stood completely assured. Completely certain that he had indeed found such a unique and powerful Maji.

Quinn's chuckle was low as it slid between her cracked lips. She tilted her head back and let the sound carry out, racking her body as it built to a hoarse laugh.

She cackled until tears ran down her face and her stomach cramped with pain. The roar of laughter died out as quickly as it came, leaving Quinn gasping for air as she continued to snigger under her breath. She watched the man, noting the tick in his jaw as she became unhinged.

"Who told you that?" she asked. "Because it wasn't Olivier." She was quite certain of that. While the old man had figured out she was a Maji, he never asked what kind and she never volunteered.

"What makes you say that?"

"People don't allow dark Maji to live with them, not even Olivier. They're too unstable. Too volatile. Too … prone to delusions of grandeur …" Her voice trailed off as she pointedly looked at him.

"I suppose you are fortunate then that I am not most people," the stranger said.

"Forgive me if I don't trust who you are or what you want when you show up looking for me, touting the name of a dead nobleman that didn't know half the things you seem to think you do," Quinn replied icily. She turned her head the other way, searching the gaps between the bars and the cracks in the wall for even an inch of wiggle room. This place was a prison, though, made for men far larger and physically stronger than her. Quinn let out a slight huff when the man spoke again.

"Olivier was one of my oldest friends. One of my only friends, really." She narrowed her eyes, glancing back at him. Waiting for him to continue. "He knew that I've been looking for—" He broke off, hesitating for only a fraction of a second, but it was a fraction enough to notice the change. "Someone like you," he surmised.

Quinn raised an eyebrow. "Someone like me?"

"A fear twister," he supplied. Proclaimed. He was so sure, it made her want to know how exactly he'd been able to pinpoint that in less than twenty-four hours when not a soul had figured it out in the past ten years.

"Olivier was my master. My *last* master," Quinn stressed. "He pulled me from a post, still bleeding from a whipping that might have killed me had he not brought in healers. He bought me from the monster that did it. He gave me food, and clothes, and a place to stay." Her lips pinched together as she took a breath to push past the brief flashes of memories so debilitating that they had more in common with nightmares. "Do you know what he asked of me in return for my freedom?"

His dark eyebrows came down as he narrowed his eyes slightly and shook his head.

Quinn smiled bitterly. "He asked that I have breakfast with him every morning and read to him for one hour every night. Willingly. Until he died." She paused, swallowing hard on the dusty, stale air. "Olivier Illvain was a kind man. One of the only I've ever known. Even if he had somehow figured out what I am and let me stay, he had no reason to betray me."

There was a short silence before he spoke again. "Did you know Olivier had a daughter once?"

Quinn squinted in confusion for a brief second and then narrowed her eyes in distrust. "Many years ago. Why? What does that have to do with anything?"

"His daughter was a dark Maji." Quinn blinked, biting the inside of her cheek to keep from showing surprise. "She died when she was thirteen."

Expression unreadable, Quinn said, "I hadn't realized."

The stranger nodded once and said, "Olivier couldn't help his child when she lost her mind and hung herself. He blamed himself for her death, but he also knew he had no idea how to help her. As you pointed out, he was a kind man—and kind men don't understand dark magic. They don't realize how deeply it is ingrained in one's soul, or that simply telling them to be different won't make it so."

Quinn's lips parted. "And you do?"

His voice carried as he said, "Olivier knew I was looking for you and that you would be better off with me. That's why I'm here."

She stared at him wondering if this seemed as far-fetched to him as it did to her. She wondered if he saw his own manipulations.

"You weren't looking *for* me. Just someone like me."

"Semantics." He raised his eyebrows when she glowered at him.

"This isn't going to work the way you think it will," Quinn replied. There was a tremor of ire in her inflection, a note of warning, but above all else there was a blunt honesty.

"I can get you out of the jail cell, that won't be a problem." He spoke crisp, coolly. His eyes may be burning coals, but his voice rang of complete and utter control.

"I wasn't referring to my imprisonment," she replied tepidly. "Given it's hard to employ those that are dead, I assumed getting me out of this blasted cell was the minimum."

He stepped closer to the cage, just inches away if Quinn were to try to reach through the bars. "Then what?" he asked softly, but firm, his words brushed over her skin leaving a trail of gooseflesh in their wake. Quinn shook her head and slowly got to her feet, wavering as she reached out to steady herself against the bars.

"Suppose that I am a fear twister"—she paused when his eyes flashed—"You saw what happened in the marketplace. You likely heard of what happened when they came to arrest me. I have very little control."

"I can train you."

Quinn blinked. That wasn't the response she'd been expecting, but it had her attention all the more now. "What makes you think that?" she asked.

"You and I are … alike."

"You're a fear twister?" She had never met another before.

"No." That was all he said. Just 'no.' They stared at each other for another moment before Quinn let her gaze drop to his clothes again. He was definitely a nobleman. Some merchants often made enough to buy noble cast-offs, but this man was dressed in a fresh pair of breeches and a new tunic. He was wealthy, there was no doubt.

"Why are you here?" Quinn finally asked.

"I told you," he replied. "I want you to work for me."

"And if I don't want to?" She threw it out flippantly, testing his responses while running through her options. She wondered if she could escape before they planned to execute her. Because there was no doubt that after what had happened in the market both times, they would.

The gods' honest truth of that didn't sit well with her.

"Then I suppose I'll see you at the hanging they have planned in a few hours."

Quinn jerked her gaze back to the man. "A few hours?" she repeated, her pulse picking up. *How long have I been out? Weren't there trials for these things? Or am I too dangerous to put on trial now ... that was more than likely accurate.*

He really may be her only real option out of this, and while she was curious about what he meant ...

that wasn't enough to make her want to work for this man. He intrigued her far too much.

"So, what will it be then? Work for me and live, or stay unemployed and die?"

"I don't even know your name," she countered, a trickle of sweat sliding down her back.

"Lazarus Fierté," he replied.

"No *Lord* with that name?" She lifted an eyebrow as she leaned forward and grasped the bars.

His expression didn't change. Lazarus remained silent as he waited. She scoffed, turning her face away.

"Do we have a bargain?" he asked.

"I'm not a slave," she said, fixing her eyes back to his face. "Let's get that straight right now. I'd rather die than go back to that, so if that's what you're wanting, then leave. I hear hangings are nice this time of year."

Her irreverence managed to score a slight twitch on the right side of his mouth, but she couldn't say for sure if it was a frown or a smile, or perhaps it was just her imagination because it was gone before she could fully appreciate it.

"You will not be a slave, I assure you," he replied. "Now, do we have a deal?"

"Sure. Fine. Yes. Get me out and we have a deal." Lazarus didn't move to open her cell door or call for a guard. She slapped the bars. "What are you doing? You asked if we had a deal, I agreed. Get me out."

"You didn't really think it would be that easy, did you?"

Quinn growled low in her parched throat.

"A contract," Lazarus said, reaching into his pocket and withdrawing a feather.

"A contract?" she repeated, staring at the strange jagged edges of the feather. He didn't produce paper, nor did he produce ink. He simply held the feather out for her to examine.

"There is an inscription on it," he stated.

She noted that, but she couldn't read the language it was written in.

"When you sign your name with this, you will bind yourself to me in service of ten years—"

"Hold on." Quinn pressed her hands flat against the bars and leaned closer. "Ten years?"

"Yes."

She shook her head. "No. Five."

"I'm saving your life," Lazarus reminded her.

"And I'm sure you're doing it out of the goodness of your heart." Quinn lifted a brow before dropping it and continuing. "You're offering me this deal—this *contract*," she corrected herself, "because you need me —even if you won't tell me why just yet. I will not be bound for ten years to someone I don't even know."

"You will have to live with the disappointment," Lazarus replied coldly, "or you could die with your freedom."

"You. Need. Me," Quinn repeated, emphasizing

her words. "You wouldn't even bother if you didn't, would you?" She didn't wait for him to reply. Quinn pulled her hands away from the bars and folded her arms across her chest. "I'm a translator. I know languages, and I can quickly learn more."

"I can hire other translators," he replied, but he didn't keep talking, allowing her to continue.

"Sure, you could. But why when you would have me? I have more to offer. You've already made that clear," she pointed out.

"For five years?"

She nodded. "For five years."

"Or I could have you for ten," he replied, "and you could thank me for saving your life."

"I've never met another fear twister," Quinn said, catching his gaze. "Have you?" When he didn't reply, she smiled. "You haven't," she deduced, "and dark Maji aren't very common."

He nodded. "Not with their sanity intact, no," he acceded. That she knew. Gods, did she know.

"Five years, then." She pressed a bead of sweat dotting her brow.

Silence descended as he looked her over. She didn't know what he was looking for, but when his eyes met hers once again, she held still, refusing to break away first. Finally, he took a deep breath and held the feather out to her.

"Five years," he said. When she reached for the quill, he held it back slightly. "But," he warned, "if I am not satisfied at the end of those five years, you will be in my service for ten more uninterrupted years, understood?"

His tone was hard, his gaze cold—eyes devoid of any sympathy she may have attempted to prey on. Not that she would have. Quinn wasn't one for taking people's sympathy. And since she didn't have many options, she nodded and agreed to the terms. He handed it over.

"Okay, what do I do with this thing?" she asked.

"You will write your name on my wrist." Lazarus moved the sleeve of his tunic up and her eyes widened. Dark scales of something peeked out from beneath the fabric. It wasn't completely uncovered, but it was strange looking. Her eyes were drawn to the edge of whatever was etched into his flesh, but he leaned forward and tapped the strip of bare skin at his pulse point.

Quinn looked from the pen to his wrist. "There's no ink," she pointed out.

"You won't need any. Write," he commanded.

Quinn was surprised. When she reached out to do as he bid, her hands didn't shake. She was signing her life over to a man she knew little to nothing about, and there were no trembles. It was then she realized that she wasn't afraid. Her fear had dispersed. She quickly wrote her name on his flesh and after a brief moment, her eyes widened as drops of blood and scratches rose where the end of the pen had pressed into him. He whispered something in a low language she vaguely recognized, but couldn't place, and the tanned surface around the scratches of her name began to glow before the name sank deep beneath his skin, turning black.

"Now you," he said.

Quinn handed the pen over and jerked her sleeve up as well, sticking her arm out. Lazarus' gaze landed on one of the many slave brands. This would not be the first unwanted symbol etched on her body.

Lazarus took her hand in his, twisting it so that he could press the end of the pen to her wrist. When he stroked it over her, she didn't feel a thing. It wasn't until he removed it that she gasped and snatched her hand back, turning it so that she could watch the process as a fire blossomed under the skin and spread.

"Myori's wrath!" she hissed under her breath as it reached her veins. "You didn't say it would hurt," she snapped as she wiped away the blood.

Lazarus tilted his head to the side. "You didn't ask."

She glared at him as he recited the incantation again. Once it was done the scratches of his name— *Lazarus Fierté*—settled under her skin and rose once more in curved black lettering. Quinn stared at the name. It was one thing to have a noble seal branded on her, it was quite another to see someone else's full name there. It was odd, to say the least.

"So, what now?" she asked, rubbing her wrist.

"Now, I make sure you understand that should you attempt to break this binding, you will die."

Quinn jerked her head back and gaped at him. "*Die?* If I break this I would die?" Her voice rose an octave and shadows flickered. "Shouldn't you have mentioned that earlier?"

His eyes tracked those brief flickers. A slow smile curling around his full, masculine lips with amusement. The darkness in that smile struck her silent.

"What's done is done, Quinn," Lazarus replied as he raised his hand and one of the guards approached with a set of keys. "In the future, however, I would make sure that you understand the fine print of a contract with someone before signing it."

As the cell door swung open, Quinn stared at the man in shock. He turned around and headed down the hall, towards what she presumed to be the exit.

Just who in the dark realm have I signed my life over to?

The Weeping Eye

"Pain is the body telling you that you're alive; that you survived to make whoever hurt you pay."
— *Quinn Darkova, former slave, ex-prisoner, definitely deranged*

The carriage shuddered along the road as Quinn stared at the man across from her. When she had first climbed inside there had been another person waiting. Lazarus hadn't introduced them before he had sent the man away. She had to wonder if he was planning on keeping her away from his other vassals.

"Where are we going?" she finally asked after several minutes of mind-numbing silence.

Lazarus looked up from the small booklet he had

pulled out from beneath his clothes earlier—first a magical quill, then a booklet—Quinn wondered if he had secret pockets under his garments. He glanced down at her bare arms and then to her neck. Quinn stiffened, but didn't cover the slave brandings.

"We're going to get those removed," he stated before going back to the pages of his booklet.

Quinn frowned. Not that she didn't want to get her slave brands removed—it was an expensive process that she hadn't been able to afford—but it was interesting that removing her brands was the first thing he wanted to do. She wondered if they bothered him. "Why?" she asked.

Lazarus sighed and closed the book before tucking it away once more. "Because," he said, "as my vassal you will be in front of people of nobility. I have not and never will approve of the slave trade in Norcasta, nor any other country. You will be expected to attend certain functions with me and the clothes you will be provided for those functions would reveal them. I cannot have a vassal of mine running around wearing the slave brands of a dozen masters."

Her eyes widened for a brief moment before a snort overtook her. Quinn looked away, amusement still twitching at her lips. *Someone thinks highly of himself,* she thought. "It's actually seventeen," she corrected him. "Not a dozen."

His expression didn't alter. "Either way, I cannot have you representing me looking like that."

Quinn wondered if she would meet his wife. If narcissism ran in the family.

The coach turned a corner and came to a wavering halt alongside the road. Quinn moved to stand. "Wait," Lazarus commanded.

"Aren't we here?"

He shot her a dark look. "When you are in a carriage, you wait until the driver has descended to open the door."

"I don't need anyone to open my doors for me," she said brazenly. "If you're too delicate, I can surely take care of it for you."

Not even a muscle moved in his face. He didn't reply. Quinn sat back with a huff and waited. The door opened not long afterwards, and Lazarus gestured for her to get out. She did so with pleasure— anything to get away from his condescending presence.

Quinn stood on the cobbled sidewalk and stared up and down the alley they had parked in. There was a sign above them, swinging back and forth on squeaky iron hinges. The sign read "Oculi Flere." Across the way, a street beggar hobbled onto a nearby doorstep and collapsed, grunting and groaning. An empty bottle of spirits rolled away from him.

Lazarus strode towards the door to the shop and pushed it open, holding it for her. Instead, Quinn pointed to the sign. "What does that say?" she asked.

He looked up. "It says Oculi Flere," he replied. "Let's go."

"What does it mean?"

He sighed. "It means 'The Weeping Eye,'" Lazarus said. "Now, come. We have a schedule to keep."

"We do?" Quinn asked as she entered the small, narrow shop, but Lazarus didn't reply.

The interior was just as rundown as the outside. The wooden floorboards creaked under their feet, several spots rotted through and sagging inward. The shelves surrounding the front room were dusty and the baubles and bottles that lined them all appeared as though they held some strange substances—like animal livers and eyeballs. As Quinn wandered farther inside, the bottles appeared newer, lighter.

She stretched out her hand to touch one of them when Lazarus stepped up and grabbed her wrist. "Do not touch anything," he commanded, quickly releasing her as if her skin had burned him. She wished it had.

Quinn rubbed her wrist as she took in the rest of the room. A crusty older woman with a hunched back and protruding lower jaw hobbled in from a doorway leading deeper into the shop.

"Ma' lord, so good ta see ye' again. 'Ave ye' come fer a solution today?" she asked politely, her voice hoarse from age.

Lazarus nodded. "I was wondering if you had any sanitatem in your shop, Driselda."

The woman's eyes turned to Quinn and then trailed down. "We do, ma' lord. Fer bran' removals."

Quinn didn't move or flinch as the old woman examined her from across the room. She crossed the creaking floorboards to stop before Quinn and lift her sleeves. "I suspect ye 'ave more?" she inquired, releasing her.

"Yes," Quinn said through gritted teeth, readjusting the sleeves of her shirt.

Driselda nodded thoughtfully before turning to Lazarus. "T'will not be cheap," she stated.

"I didn't think it would be," he replied coolly.

The old woman nodded again. "Follow me."

Lazarus eyed her for a moment, watching for Quinn's response. She didn't spare a glance in his direction as she followed the apothecarian into a back room. It was tiny. The back wall was made up entirely of shelves, each filled with a strange assortment of bottles that mostly appeared to be collecting dust. In the center of the small space was a water bin used for animals, with a short stool beside it.

The wooden door swung shut and a boney hand prodded her in between her shoulder blades towards the tub. "Strip an' get in, girl."

Quinn tugged off her dusty brown shirt, streaked with grime and dirt. The leather pants took a bit more finagling in the small space as they clung to her bare skin. With some awkward bending and enough persistence, they came free. Stripping away her undergarments Quinn climbed into the makeshift tub and settled with her knees together and her chin propped over them. Her arms wrapped tightly around her legs while she waited for Driselda to begin.

"Ta get rid'er bran's, we usually just smear tha area of skin wit' sanitatem, but—" the old woman glanced back over her shoulder as she began pulling dusty bottles off the shelves. "Ye' 'ave so many. Ye' need a bath."

Quinn said nothing as Driselda began dumping the contents of each bottle into a large bucket. The liquid hissed and crackled with each new ingredient added. She was fairly certain there was a light steam coming from the liquid in the tub when the older lady clicked her tongue and nodded. Without any explanation she walked out of the back room, closing the door firmly behind her. Quinn could make out Lazarus' low voice on the other side as he inquired about something. The woman's voice was harder to discern as she replied. There was some shuffling about, and a few minutes passed before the door cracked open and in came the stern-faced old woman with her back locked tight, a massive bucket of water swishing side to side. She hefted it up to the ledge of the tub and heaved it over, letting the chilly water fall over Quinn.

She let out a small sigh at the blessed moisture,

chancing a quick drink, she scooped some up in her hands before Driselda slapped her palms away. "Tis a 'ery delicate balance. Could melt ye' insides if ye' drink it." The woman turned to the second smaller bucket full of a grayish-green goop. She picked it up and quickly tossed the contents in. Quinn yelped at the nip of burning heat before it settled into the water, staining it a soft mint green.

"Now what?" Quinn asked.

"Now, we wait. Tha sanitatem will take an hour ta remove tha bran's, but t'won't take away ye' scars," the women said, plopping down on the short stool. "Sink down an' let it reach 'verywhere, girl. Ye' 'ave quite a lot—yes, all the way up ta tha back of ye'r neck—'ere ye' go."

"Will it remove this?" Quinn asked into the silence. She lifted her hand where Lazarus' name was written in black.

"Is' it a bran'?" she asked.

"Of sorts. We signed a contract."

Driselda nodded once. "Looks ta me like tha work o' a firedrake feather. 'At's not a bran' o' iron, but o' magic. Neither tha sanitatem nor anythin' but tha dealer o' tha contract an' their desire ta break it will remove 'at."

Quinn looked at the inky letters under her palm. The other woman fell silent, leaning back against the wooden panels. She crossed her ankles and interlaced her hands over her lap as Quinn laid all the way back in the sanitatem bath and let her hand fall to her side. Initially the pure stuff had burned like an open flame, but now it was a subtler sort of burn. The kind that slowly ate at a person, moving from lukewarm and a bit tingly to being stimulated all over.

She closed her eyes against the small zings that went through her as the top layer of skin was eaten away entirely.

"'Ow's tha burnin'?" Driselda asked some time later.

Quinn cracked an eye open. "I've had better days."

The older woman nodded and smoothed her hands over her wrinkled skirt to rest on her knees. She leaned forward and said, "Folks ten' ta yelp 'er cry like children when I remove a bran' 'er two. Only had ta do a full body once." Quinn didn't say anything, and the woman continued. "He was like ye'. Ne'er made a soun'."

"There are worse pains a slave endures, particularly those of us that never stopped fighting against it," Quinn said, recalling the crack of a whip before the shredding started. She'd been beaten so brutally by some of her masters, she'd come to the edge of death more times than she could count. She didn't want to die. She wasn't searching for a death sentence. Quinn had accepted the life she led, and was prepared for if or when the day came when she couldn't outrun it. It seemed that with Lazarus, today was not that day—and while she would never tell him —she was thankful, despite the price he'd asked.

"No'one is really free," the old woman answered. "We're all a slave ta somethin'. Whether tis a person, a past, our own fears…" The woman rocked forward, and her joints popped as she came to stand. "Freedom's a myth, one use'ta keep us all 'n line. E'ry now an' then, there'll be one like ye' that sees tha invisible bars an' searches fer a way ta break them." She motioned for Quinn to stand. She did as was requested and reached out, grasping both sides of the tub as she got to her feet. "A word from tha wise, girl. Breakin' tha bars be 'mpossible. Decidin' who holds tha key, though…" She pointedly looked sideways to the closed door that led out to her shop where Lazarus waited. "Lord Fierté's known fer protectin' 'is own, so lon' as they're loyal. Jus' somethin' ta think 'bout." Quinn's lips parted, trying to think of a response while the weathered shopkeeper dried the mint-colored liquid from her skin.

She felt fresh, cleaner than she had in a long time, when she dressed again in her dirty clothes. Now that she was newly employed, she would be inquiring about what exactly that entailed, and if a second set of trousers was asking too much.

She thought back to his fine-tailored tunic with gold embellishments and snorted.

On second thought, he has the money. I'm asking for undergarments too.

Driselda opened the wooden door and pushed her out, following behind. Quinn looked up, expecting to see Lazarus sitting and instead finding him standing only a few feet away with a grimace on his face. In his fist was a crumpled letter written on fine parchment.

Quinn quirked an eyebrow. "Everything alright?" she asked, testing the waters.

Lazarus pulled a small pouch from his pocket and tossed it to the woman beside Quinn. Driselda reached out with knobbly fingers, catching the coin purse in one hand and tucking it away in one of the pockets of her cloak.

"Pleasure doin' business, Lord Fierté."

"Until next time," Lazarus nodded and turned for the door. Quinn followed after, hot on his heels, only briefly stopping at the doorway to the alley.

"Thank you," she said over her shoulder, happy to be free from her past—even if she wasn't sure what the future held.

Judging by Lazarus' mood, if nothing else, it would be interesting.

Secrets and Shadow Men

"If you're going to pull a knife, plan to use it."
— *Quinn Darkova, former slave, ex-prisoner, definitely*
deranged, currently employed

Quinn was wrong. So very wrong.

Apparently, the future didn't hold anything interesting. From the moment they'd stepped into the streets, they were loaded back into a carriage where they rode all through the night and into the next day, only taking stops to relieve themselves. Throughout it all, Lazarus hadn't said a word or made any move to explain himself, and when she asked, all she was met with was vague notions of danger or silent looks of annoyance.

Quinn settled back into the seat with another huff

of annoyance at the crick in her neck and the brooding man across from her who was the cause of it.

"So," Quinn huffed. "Where are we going?"

"I must stop by my manor in Shallowyn and then we will be on our way," Lazarus replied gruffly.

"On our way to…?"

He didn't reply.

Gritting her teeth, Quinn turned and peered out at the passing scenery. Land, land, and more land. A few chickens. A few cows. A country cart filled with marketable wares passed by every once in a while, but for the most part, Quinn and Lazarus were alone on the road. Two days and two nights trapped with this man, they had only stopped to change out horses and drivers once.

"Can we talk about my employment?" Quinn asked, returning her gaze to Lazarus.

"You may talk about whatever you want," he stated. "You are a free woman."

She narrowed her gaze on him. "If I'm to be your vassal, then I assume you'll want to inform me of my wages at some point."

"Life. Survival. Freedom," Lazarus replied. "You're welcome."

Quinn didn't respond to his dry comments. "New clothes would be nice. Thicker fabrics for the winter. Coin for food and provisions—"

"Anything you need will be provided. That

includes clothing and food. I haven't let you starve yet, now have I?" Lazarus quirked a brow.

"It's only been two days," she replied. "I have no clue what the future will bring." She paused. "Especially since you've refused to answer my questions about where we're going."

"I told you—"

"Yes, yes," Quinn cut him off with a wave of her hand. "You've told me we're going to Shallowyn, but I mean after that."

Lazarus scowled. He did not appreciate being cut off, and she knew it. "You will know what I need you to know and nothing more," he stated with finality.

Quinn rolled her eyes, crossing her arms over her chest as she glanced out the window once more. The sun continued on and her vision grew blurry. She blinked, clearing away the haze. Quinn focused on the coach's outline, tracing it with her eyes as she pressed up against the side of the carriage when her sight fell on a strange lump.

Flicking her gaze up to Lazarus and then back to the odd shadow, Quinn's eyes narrowed as it moved. She opened her mouth. "Laz—" The shadow jumped, vaulting over the top of the coach and a thump followed as something large and heavy hit the road. Lazarus jerked upward and looked outside.

He growled. "Stay here," he commanded, reaching for the handle.

"But—"

"Stay." He was gone in the next moment. It didn't matter if the carriage was still moving along, he was outside and she was left staring at his empty seat after his quick exit, wondering how a nobleman had learned to move like that. Quinn slipped out of her cloak quietly and moved towards the door as the coach came to a shuddering halt. Quinn slid forward, stopping herself from falling by putting her feet against the edge of the seat across from her that had just been vacated.

The horses let out a cry of dismay as a man shouted. Another thump came from outside as something hit the ground.

A body, Quinn assumed. Maybe all Lazarus' mutterings of danger weren't just paranoia after all. She reached under her shirt and pulled the short knife she had retrieved from her satchel before they set out. Quinn let her hand fall back to her side as she flattened her back to the wall of the carriage.

Footsteps sounded outside. Large. Heavy.

Men's footsteps, she decided. Men *attempting* to be stealthy.

The first traces of fear whispered to her, calling her from outside the carriage. She held firm to her sensibilities, waiting for another cry to ring out. The door directly across from her swung open and a man dressed in black peered in. He wore a dull wooden mask over the upper half of his face, covering his features.

Quinn acted without hesitation. A flick of her wrist was all it took, and the knife went flying.

His lips parted beneath the mask as the dagger hit him square in the chest, sliding between two ribs with precision. It wasn't a direct hit to his heart—but it was close.

A hiss of breath was all that escaped him before Quinn brought her boot up and smashed it into his face. The wooden mask cracked beneath the impact, and his fingers released their hold on the edges of the doorway. The attacker teetered mid-air for a brief second before a heavy thud sounded as he landed, a plume of dirt particles drifting around him in the evening light.

Quinn wasted no time, jumping from the carriage to land on his prone form, pinning him beneath her as she grasped the dagger and ripped it free from his chest. The pieces of his mask fell to the side. He gasped for breath. She didn't care. Using the hilt of her dagger, she slammed it down on the top of his head, easily knocking the man unconscious as she watched his eyes roll back.

Shadows twisted and twined against her, obscuring her in shadow as Quinn backed against the carriage. Two men came around the side of the coach and the tethers of darkness wove a barrier over her form. She didn't notice the dark strands as they moved to circle her body. She watched as the two attackers didn't seem to realize she was there when they turned their attention to their unconscious friend.

"Did you see that?"

Quinn could only see the outline of the men as the first turned to his partner.

"There's no one there," the other said. He, too, was dressed in dark clothing. Both wore the same mask as the man she'd stabbed.

The corners of her lips turned up in the slightest of smiles. The man before her was slowly bleeding out and giving off tendrils of fear. There were only a few of them, and in the obscurity of evening light, Quinn wasn't as overwhelmed by the darkness that called to her.

Two more muffled cries made the men jump into action, pulling away and turning towards the sounds of distress.

They both moved to the front of the carriage where Lazarus had disappeared. While she couldn't see much more than their figures, Quinn could feel the apprehension coming from them, the way it slithered into their hearts.

"You don't think…" the first began, a trickle of unease trembling in his voice.

"There's no way he beat Krone—that man's a beast. He's—" An almost inhuman roar split the air, filled with a savage fury. Quinn had little doubt who it was.

The two in front of her whirled as he appeared

behind them, seeming to materialize out from the shadows.

"Who sent you?" Lazarus asked, a ruthless kind of malevolence working its way into his voice, unlike anything Quinn had ever heard before. She craned her neck forward, finding herself drawn into his deep predatory gaze. Though she wasn't the one locked under his stare, she could feel the power behind it and it sucked her in.

The two masked men flashed terrified glances at each other and took hasty steps back.

"N-no one..." Quinn didn't know who had breathed the answer, but Lazarus was obviously not mollified. He took a step forward, and in unison, they took another back, coming within an arm's reach of Quinn.

"Then you acted on your own and will suffer the consequences," Lazarus growled, sounding more beast than man. Their fear bled off them in terrible but tantalizing rivulets. Quinn leaned forward and breathed it in heavily. A face flashed before her eyes— an image of a man with a cane. The distinct impression of previous fear hit her. Before anything more could happen, the man's image faded and in its place was the scene in front of her.

A flash of metal gleamed in the low light as a knife slid down the second masked-man's sleeve, jutting out from beneath the jacket's armhole.

Lazarus moved impossibly fast, raising an arm to

strike the first man just as the second moved to do the same to Lazarus. All the while, none of them had yet noticed Quinn.

She slashed in a wide arc, running the blade clean through the weak tendon and bone that connected the back of the second man's foot to his ankle. Blood splattered, and the armed assailant faltered. Lazarus struck down the first man, grasping his head between two enormous hands. He didn't even have time to beg before a crack rang out.

Lazarus released him and the body dropped to ground, entirely limp.

Quinn blinked as wide unseeing eyes stared back at her.

The man with the sliced tendon collapsed forward onto the road, blindly swinging his dagger in an attempt to protect himself, tendrils of fear sprung from his skin as his heartbeat thudded in his chest with wild abandon. Lazarus moved faster than the eye could see, and just like that day in her dressing room, he caught the man's wrist. Both of them fell still.

There were no last words. No warnings. No questions.

Lazarus Fierté—as Quinn was quickly coming to realize—was a man of action. He pried the blade from the soon-to-be-dead man's fingers and jabbed it through his eye socket.

The attacker's mouth fell open, a scream attempting to leave his body, but with nowhere to go, it remained silent—trapped as his corpse dropped to the ground.

Lazarus turned and looked at Quinn, squinting his eyes as if trying to see.

"I thought I told you to stay inside." He sounded gruff, not angry or frustrated, but like he had something in this throat. He didn't glance at the bodies strewn around them. Neither did Quinn.

She shrugged. "I didn't listen."

If she thought he would have shown anger at those words, she was wrong. Instead, his gaze turned to the dark shadows clinging to her skin. "How are you doing that?" he asked.

She frowned. "Doing what?"

He waved a hand in her direction, fresh blood coating his fingers. "Cloaking yourself," he said.

Quinn looked down for the first time, noticing the darkness moving across her body. Even she couldn't see much of herself there were so many strands of shadow moving around her.

"I don't…" she began, her voice stopping as she moved her arms and the shadows followed, "… know …" she finished softly.

The first slivers of her own fear whispered through her chest, crawling up her throat. Lazarus took two mighty steps and extended his hand. Quinn looked up at it. Shadows or not, when she reached for him, as their hands clasped, they dispersed, and he hauled her to her feet.

"Are you alright?" he asked, not with the usual concern people held, but something akin to it.

"Yes."

"Good. Get your things. We need to go."

Quinn pulled away and looked at him, and then looked to the men on the ground and finally the empty carriage with doors ajar. "That's it?" she asked. "No explanation about why we were just attacked? *Nothing?*"

Anger burned in her throat, but it was all ice. That freezing calm that took over whenever she got too upset. She stilled. Listless.

Lazarus' gaze shifted to her face, sharpening on her eyes. "Six men, Quinn. That's how many attacked us tonight. When they don't report back, it will be triple that the next time." His voice was cut and dry, and while those embers in his eyes might have flared when he stared at her, Quinn was more clueless than the dead men at her feet.

"Yes, and you still haven't told me *why* they attacked us or who sent them," Quinn replied, mockingly indifferent as Lazarus walked behind her. There was a stuttered gasp and then gurgling of breath before … nothing. Silence.

Quinn turned to see him cleaning his blade on the hem of his tunic. The man she'd stabbed in the chest bled out like a slaughtered animal.

"And I'm not going to until you can prove to me that

you're worthy of any semblance of trust," he said as if they were talking about the weather. Quinn inhaled sharply with indignation, clutching her dagger tighter.

"You're the one who asked for *my* help," she reminded him. "*You* came to *me*, not the other way around. Just who exactly are you, Lazarus?" she asked. She'd nearly killed a man tonight and had assisted him in dispatching the other—saving him—not that she thought it would win her any real favors with him. *Talking to a donkey would yield better results*, she thought.

Lazarus looked at her with obsidian eyes and in utter seriousness said, "Someone you don't want to make an enemy of, Quinn. If you don't get us killed with your dallying, you might find out."

Tired, cranky, with the same crick in her neck and covered in blood, Quinn grabbed her satchel out of the carriage and came to stand before him.

"I'm ready," she announced with a bite. Lazarus glanced over as he adjusted the saddle on one of the carriage horse's back. The black stallion nickered then fell silent when Lazarus put a hand on its side.

"You ride?" he asked briskly.

She shook her head as she bit the inside of her cheek because smarting off would get them nowhere. Like it or not, she was tied to his stubborn ass by contract until she fulfilled her end, or he relieved her of her duty. At this rate, neither would happen since it looked like she might actually be more likely to die working for him.

He sighed, an irritated sound. "The way I see it," he paused, sweeping himself up onto the saddle. Lazarus reached a hand down to her, and she eyed it distastefully. "You don't have much of a choice in this, Quinn. Either ride with me or run behind. I don't care much either way at this point."

Quinn took his hand. If there was one thing she hated more than the situation she'd found herself in, it was running.

Lazarus grinned like he somehow knew it.

Nightmare Shackles

"Nightmares are fueled by reality."
— *Quinn Darkova, former slave, ex-prisoner, and almost-killer*

Her backside hurt. Her body ached. Her head was pounding from sleep deprivation and the mental exhaustion of one bad thing after another with no real break. If she thought riding in the carriage for two whole days was rough, she was— once again—sorely mistaken. A day and a half on the back of a giant beast, with her back pressed against yet another giant beast, and she was ready to stab something—anything, if it meant she could get some decent sleep.

Lazarus had ridden hard after the attack. She wasn't sure if he was attempting to make up for lost time or to outrun the consequences of his actions. There was obviously someone that wanted him dead. Because of that, neither of them had slept.

Quinn let her eyes drift closed as the wind on her face stung her cheeks. But almost immediately after her eyelids slid shut, the horse came to an abrupt stop and her eyes snapped back open.

"What is it?" she demanded, looking around. "What's wrong?"

"Nothing," Lazarus replied. "We're here."

"We're here?" Quinn looked around the country road. They were stopped alongside a tall gray-bricked wall, crusted over with age and spindly dead vines. "I don't see anything."

Lazarus nudged her to get off the horse, and with a grunt she complied. Quinn swung her leg up and over the horse's neck and slid over the side. The impact jarred her, and she stumbled to regain balance. If Lazarus hadn't dismounted behind her and grabbed her about the waist, she would've tumbled onto the dirt road.

"I'm fine," Quinn said sharply, pulling away from him.

"Stop," Lazarus commanded. "Your tunic is snagged on this …" She tried to step away and he tightened his grip on her waist. "The horse will spook if you keep jerking it."

Lazarus ripped the shirt from the buckle on the side of the saddle bag. She gaped down at the now broad hole in her tunic. Before she could say anything, Lazarus grabbed her forearm and began pulling her towards the wall. "Hey!" she hissed, smacking at his bicep. "What about the horse?"

Lazarus looked over to the large black stallion as Quinn shifted on her feet, attempting to relieve the chaffing ache in her thighs. "I'll send someone for it."

Quinn lifted a brow but didn't reply. She wondered what it would be like to have people who would do the most asinine things for you just because you have money and didn't feel like doing it on your own. Chances were, though, she'd never find out. She'd never have the money for that luxury, nor the patience for the life that type of wealth would require, and somehow that suited her just fine.

Lazarus tugged her towards the wall, feeling alongside the dark stone for something. Quinn's yawn was cut short as she jerked her gaze to where his hand had disappeared into a hole in the stone. Lazarus twisted his wrist and then pulled away, stepping back as a section of the wall shifted inward and to the side.

"What in the dark realm …" Quinn whispered in shock as Lazarus hauled her through the opening. Almost immediately, the section that had been removed slid back into place.

Quinn gaped as he led her through an immaculate wooded area. The silence—true silence—tipped her off that this wasn't just some forest. There were no animals, no droppings, and the walking path was not uneven or overgrown. He pulled her through the trees and onto an open lawn where up ahead was a stone manor. Quinn blinked and took it in even as Lazarus pushed her forward, urging her to hurry.

They reached a black staircase leading up onto the wide veranda. "You live here?" Quinn whispered as she continued to gawk. Not a single one of her masters had lived in something so opulent. Her gaze turned back to Lazarus as he moved towards the back entrance. *Just how rich is this man?*

Lazarus and Quinn hadn't set more than two feet inside when a tall, slender woman came around the corner. Her brown hair had early streaks of gray and while she was pretty, there was a harshness to her face that only age could cause.

"My lord," she said, clutching the top of her cloak to cover her nightgown. "We didn't expect you for another day."

"Plans have changed, Lorraine." Lazarus reached back, grasping Quinn's arm once more. He pushed her towards the woman. "This is Quinn. She's my newest vassal. See that she is given new clothes, food, and a room to rest. Is Draeven here?"

Lorraine nodded woodenly, still shocked. Then, with a sense of familiarity and stalwartness, she inhaled and straightened. "Yes, my lord, he's sleeping. As is everyone else. It's the middle of the night. If you just got in, allow me to draw you a bath. You must be weary from your travels."

Lazarus shook his head. "There's no time, Lorraine. I must speak with Draeven. See to Quinn." Lazarus turned to stride away and stopped, turning back, fixing Quinn with a look. "Behave," he ordered. Just one word and then he was gone, disappearing down a long dark hallway, leaving Quinn to glare after him—exhausted and in no mood for his attitude.

Lorraine visibly pulled herself together and turned to the frazzled young woman with bloodshot eyes. "Let's get you cleaned up," Lorraine said. "Follow me."

Quinn trailed after her, staring up at the massive arched ceilings and ornate paintings on the walls, all the way to the carvings in the staircase bannisters. Everything about this manor screamed lavish. Expensive. Excessive, but not unattractive. Lorraine led her through a giant kitchen and up to the second floor.

"Here, this room is free," Lorraine announced, stopping at the end of the hall and turning the knob. "The bathing chamber for servants is at the other end of the hall on the left. Do you have any belongings?"

Quinn patted her satchel, flipping it open to show her the couple of books. "What you see is all I have," she answered, pushing it back against her side.

Lorraine frowned. "Hmmm. Well, I'll take you in and while you're cleaning off, I'll bring you a gown to sleep in."

Quinn shook her head. "Don't bother. I don't wear dresses. Something like what I'm wearing will work fine. I can sleep in a pair of trousers as easily as I can fight in them."

"Fight?" Lorraine looked taken aback for a moment, but she quickly masked it. "I see," she said. "Well, then to the bathing chamber, I suppose."

Quinn nodded and followed her to a separate room at the end of the hall. Inside, there was a large pool of murky water with columns rising alongside it. "The water will be cold," Lorraine warned her. "Lord Fierté usually has fire crystals set in the base of the columns to warm it this time of year, but they haven't yet been replaced."

"A cold bath is better than no bath," Quinn replied as she began removing her dusty clothes. She let them drop on the smooth tiled floor beside her and turned for the stairs leading down into the main tub when she heard Lorraine's low gasp. Quinn stiffened knowing that it was the crisscrossing scars on her back that gave the other woman pause.

Ignoring the audience, Quinn headed for the pool and began her descent into the icy depths. Closing her eyes, she dove forward letting water engulf her completely. Submerged enough to fully clean herself for the first time in years, Quinn kicked off the bottom of the pool and went a few feet out. When the burning in her lungs intensified to an uncomfortable crescendo, she came up for air with a loud gasp. Slicking back her hair, Quinn turned her gaze to

Lorraine, who stared after her—eyes full of curiosity and wariness.

"I'll be back with new clothes and some food."

Quinn nodded and watched the woman back out of the room before she leaned back and stared at the ceiling. She floated there in the murky water for several quiet moments before spotting a wedge of soap forgotten along the side of the pool. Quinn swam towards it, propping both arms against the side as she came to a stop. She grasped the soap between her wet fingers, sniffing the thick, hard bar. It had been a long time since she'd been able to use soap to bathe. Over ten years to be exact. She brought the bar to her nose again and inhaled deeply. It smelled like rosemary and sage.

Lathering it between her fingers, Quinn quickly washed away the dirt from her travels and then washed her hair as well. By the time she was done and had rinsed all of the suds away, only a small bit of the chunk remained. She placed it back on the edge of the pool and glanced behind her at the echo of a door shutting. Lorraine was back—and she held a tray of food in one hand and a bundle of clothes in the other, a clean towel draped over one arm.

"Lord Fierté requests that you eat and rest while you can. You will be leaving again in a few hours."

Quinn highly doubted that. The man didn't request anything of anyone. He demanded, even when he had no right. She chose not to voice any particular opinions as she pushed away from the ledge and swam back to the steps.

Quinn groaned against the stiff aching of her muscles as she trudged up the stairs, water running from her skin in streams, hair thick and unruly as it plastered itself to her back. Lorraine set the tray of food down and handed over the towel. Quinn quickly dried and reached for the clothes, donning the new fabric. The trousers were a bit tight over her hips, but the rest fit relatively well. She wasn't going to complain.

"Where'd you find these on such short notice?" Quinn asked.

"Yan, our groundskeeper, has a teenage son. He kindly lent them to me," Lorraine replied.

Quinn nodded. "Well, Yan's son has my thanks, then."

Lorraine gestured to the tray. "Please eat, and then you may stay in the room I showed you earlier. Someone will wake you when it's time to go."

Quinn debated on forgoing food altogether in favor of more sleep, but she knew she'd need her energy later. Besides, what she saw on the tray had her salivating.

Day old bread, a hunk of cheese, and jams with neatly sliced fruit. Quinn tore into it with little finesse, scarfing down the delicious meal in mere minutes. Lorraine stood by and when Quinn lifted her head, wiping her mouth with the sleeve of her new tunic, she paused, noting the other woman's horrified stare.

"What?" Quinn asked.

"We will have to work on your manners," Lorraine said, blinking. "They're appalling."

Quinn shrugged. "I've hardly eaten in three days."

Lorraine shook her head and reached for the empty tray. "Go rest. You will be moving again soon," she commanded.

Quinn didn't need to be told twice. As Lorraine left the bathing area, Quinn did as well, snatching her satchel up from beside the pool and retracing her steps to the room Lorraine had shown her before. She turned the handle and the door swung open easily, its hinges creaking. In the corner, there was a bed big enough to fit one body—and a small one at that. Quinn didn't care. A bed was a bed. She fell face first into the mattress and was asleep within moments.

Rest, however, was a long way away.

The clanging of chains echoed in the near distance. The soft, constant drip of liquid brought Quinn's consciousness rising to the surface. Opening her eyes, Quinn sat up and froze.

Stone pillars surrounded her. Ice beneath her. A blast of frosty air whispered along her naked spine. Slowly, mechanically, Quinn rose to her feet and turned in a circle taking in the familiar temple. It was a place she hadn't seen in years, not since before she'd been sold.

Soft growls made her frown and without thinking, she

turned. The sight that greeted her lunged into her chest, gripped her cold, black heart and squeezed. Outwardly, Quinn showed no reaction. Her eyes remained transfixed on the girl bound in chains, naked. Blood soaked the girl's fingernails and dripped from her silver hair, now stained red.

The girl tilted her head back. Two small black horns protruded from the top.

Someone—a man—moved forward, laying over the girl and she growled again. The chains rattled and Quinn turned her head. Someone lay dead not far beyond the small light that illuminated the scene. In fact, there were many someone's—all men. All dead.

"Stop." The girl choked out. Her voice was hoarse, raw—shredded from endless screaming. Quinn felt a skitter of something violent ripple through her. A desire, a need to help this girl, though she couldn't figure out why.

The man that hovered above her was pale-skinned and silver-haired. But the girl ... she was different. While her hair was like moonlight, her skin was a rich smoky gray. The man moved against her—but the girl didn't cry, didn't scream.

Quinn was frozen in place, unable to move. She could feel it from where she stood. The harsh frenzy of her fury rising. The man atop her had fear running through him so palpable, so thick, Quinn could practically taste the vileness of it on her tongue, like sweat and mold.

Even for fear, though, something was off.

Something was different.

The chains rattled again, and the man froze. Then he was reeling back—away from the girl. Stumbling. Naked. Bleeding.

Broken. He choked, his lips parting as blood poured from his neck. The girl's mouth was painted red. The color messily smeared over her lips, dripping in thick, sticky streams from her chin onto the skin between her breasts.

The choking man fell dead, but at the very same moment, one of the corpses rose from the shadows and moved forward.

Chains rattled.

"Stop."

She pleaded, but the reanimated corpse did not yield.

He moved forward, positioning himself over her, situating himself between her thighs. She struggled as much as the chains would allow, but it stopped nothing.

Without so much as a response, he entered her.

"Stop."

Quinn felt it then. A new fear—sharper and deeper and more ingrained than any of the corpses, like being bathed in ice and blood. It washed over Quinn, sending her to her knees.

She kept her eyes open and the girl looked up, finally meeting Quinn's stare. Something familiar reached her.

What … who …

"Stop," the girl begged. "Stop."

They did not stop.

They never stopped.

That's what the girl was afraid of.

She was afraid that no matter how many times she killed them, these men would reanimate. They would come for her again and again, forcing themselves between her legs over and over, until sick pleasure found them—only to reanimate moments later.

For each she killed, another took its place.

Never tiring.

Never truly dying.

Never stopping.

When Quinn was shaken awake, she almost punched Lorraine as she stood over her. Startled, the older woman jerked back before Quinn's fist could make contact. Panting, sweating, and blinking furiously into the small room, Quinn tried to catch her breath. Sweat soaked her new tunic, dampening her skin and making the fabric cling to her aching muscles.

"It's time to go," Lorraine said, stepping back, eyeing her warily.

Quinn scrubbed a hand down her face and nodded. Lorraine took another step towards the door and with a last look hurried into the hallway, leaving the door ajar. Quinn swung her legs over the side of the bed and rested her head in her hands.

It took several minutes to realize that black tendrils of fear were twining around her wrists like the girl's shackles, moving and buzzing against her skin as if preparing for a feeding frenzy. Whatever that dream—that nightmare—had been, it had awakened something inside her. Something that would not go back to sleep.

Sweet Torments

"Not all pain was painful, just as not all torture was physical. Sometimes the real torment came wrapped in a package so delectable that its mere presence was sweet agony."
— *Lazarus Fierté, nobleman, master manipulator, definite murderer*

L azarus hadn't slept well in years, but ever since he'd found Quinn, being awake was just as restless. The dark magic that lurked within her called to him, whispering the sweetest, most deadly of promises. The ride to Shallowyn had been its own form of torture, having her so close that he could touch, that he *had* to touch her—and yet so far because he wouldn't do more than that. He refused to, though she fascinated him.

Quinn had her sanity. Mostly.

When emotions ran high, she had slips, much as he did. Hers were less controlled and they occurred more often, but they were not nearly as deadly as his own. At least, for the likes of him they weren't. Not *yet*. He could manage her powers where they currently were. She was still young enough and coming into them that he had time before she reached her ascent into what she would be.

He could see it now as he stared out into the sun sinking below the horizon, the horse under him clomping over the uneven road.

She would be glorious when she reached her full potential, and Lazarus had every intention of being the one to guide her there. He planned to be the one to harness that dark fire he knew grew within her.

If only the growing need inside him would settle. The desire to fuck or to kill was becoming a tad … overwhelming. Taking out the assassins had taken the edge off, but after riding all day and night with his body pressed against her … he shook his head. Lazarus was right back where he started, with a buzzing awareness of her that he couldn't seem to relieve himself of.

The damn girl—useful as she would be—was far too fascinating for her own good.

When people interested him, they either wound up dead or tied to his house for life.

Quinn had no desire to stay on and was inherently

distrustful. She wasn't naïve enough for her loyalty to be bought easily.

His fingers tightened around the reins, and the horse came to an abrupt stop.

"Everything alright?" Draeven asked him.

Lazarus looked to his left-hand man and closest friend as he said, "We should camp."

Draeven nodded once, his sand colored hair turning gray as the light was extinguished from the sky. "Then we camp."

They turned away from the trodden path and led their small entourage into the woods, going just far enough they wouldn't be seen by anyone that might pass them by on the roads. Lazarus dismounted, ignoring the sharp wave of awareness that ran through him when Quinn slid off her horse and groaned loudly.

The sound stirred something in him, and he didn't like it.

"Who is she?" Draeven asked, pulling him from his thoughts.

"No one," Lazarus answered. He pulled his sleeping mat from the saddle. They had been in too much of a hurry when they left Shallowyn to bother with tents. The set up and takedown wouldn't be worth it this time of year anyway. The burden of gear would just slow them down. A few weeks from now, when they were in the Cisean mountains and still heading north they might need more, but not now. Not when Quinn couldn't even ride on her own.

"Alright, Lazarus," Draeven sighed. "Then *what* is she?"

"A vassal," he answered.

"You get a letter from an old man and stay in Dumas a month looking for this girl—who I've never seen before—and in the time you find her, you hear from Claudius and get attacked on the way home." Draeven paused, the doubt he didn't want to show evident. "I don't like it."

"You don't have to like it," Lazarus replied.

"At least tell me why she was so important that you brought her on this trip," Draeven said, tying his own horse to a tree. "Untrained and unprepared," he added, his violet eyes narrowing on Lazarus before flicking back to Quinn for a brief moment.

"She can translate N'skaran," Lazarus said. "I'll need that soon." It wasn't lying. Not really. She could speak it, and with how reclusive the N'skari tribes were, he would have a hard time finding another N'skaran in Norcasta that could do the job he would have her do. It wasn't the actual reason he brought her, though. Not even close.

"Is that all?" Draeven asked, his jaw tense as he returned his gaze to Lazarus.

"What are you getting at?" he replied curtly.

"She can barely ride a horse, and she'll slow us down. Lorraine told me she has scars on her back from lashings, which means she could also be a runaway slave for all we know." Draeven lowered his voice a fraction when Quinn turned and stared very pointedly at the two men as though she knew they were speaking about her. It was eerie, the way she moved unapologetically through the world. Never once had she lowered her eyes in submission to him, as many others would have on instinct. Even now she stared while Lorraine scolded her for it. Quinn gave a muttered dismissal under her breath that only served to frustrate her older companion.

"She's not a slave," Lazarus answered, loud enough for her to hear, before turning for the woods to continue this conversation in private. Draeven followed after, still not letting up.

"Are you sure of it?" his second asked.

"Quite," Lazarus replied. "I had to take her to Driselda to have seventeen brands removed."

"Myori's wrath," Draeven cursed. "Either way, N'skara is one of the last stops, and while they're rare, they aren't so rare you couldn't have found someone by then. So, what is she? Because ever since you got back with her, something has been off with you." He paused, his eyes drifting to the girl behind him. Lazarus was beginning to wonder if he wasn't the only one drawn to her darkness. "Is she what I think she is?"

"And what is that?" Lazarus asked, a darker note filling his tone. He glanced back at Quinn who was no longer watching him and instead began setting up her own sleep roll, purposefully ignoring Lorraine as she tried to explain something.

"Is she like you?" Draeven asked at last. Both men stood there watching the young woman go about her business. Only brief whispers of the darkness inside stirred in the air around her, but it was enough to drive Lazarus insane. A taste of her power, but no more.

"No," he answered. "Not quite."

Draeven blinked, slowly turning towards Lazarus again. "*Not quite?*"

"She's a fear twister."

"Gods help us," Draeven swore. He lowered his head into his hand and took a deep breath. "Now I understand why you're being so guarded about this." He knew that he meant it and that even Draeven knew how rare a find she truly was.

"She's one of the strongest Maji I've ever encountered, and she hasn't even reached her ascent," Lazarus said. "I need to have her tested, of course, and she needs to begin training. I watched her conjure an illusion over all of Dumas and send a quarter of the city into panicked frenzy."

Draeven shook his head, squeezing the bridge of his nose.

"With her trained and by your side, you think the noble houses of Norcasta won't rise against you when Claudius dies," Draeven surmised and Lazarus nodded. "You're not wrong. If she truly is that strong, then you would cement your seat without dissolution ... but there are problems with this plan, Laz—"

"She's signed a contract. I own her for five years," Lazarus interrupted.

"And what about after her time is up?" Draven asked. "What if you train her—and that's assuming that you'll even be able to—how do you know that she won't get addicted to the power and move against you?" His points were logical and valid. Lazarus had already considered them.

"I don't," Lazarus replied. "I have no guarantees she won't flip at the end of it, but if that happens, I'll deal with her when we come to that. Five years is a long time, Draeven. Long enough to earn her loyalty and discern if she's going to be a problem." He hoped so, anyway, not that he would tell Draeven of his doubts. The man was still getting used to the idea. Lazarus needed to take this slowly, with all parties, if he wanted to see the outcome he desired.

Even still, whether Draeven approved or not, he wasn't letting her go. Claudius' words were still as fresh in his mind as that day six years ago when he'd given him a hint into his future. No. Quinn wasn't going anywhere.

"If you train her and she reaches her ascent, you have no guarantees you'll even be able to stop her if she's as powerful as you think she is," Draeven said, lifting his head. There were old ghosts in his eyes. The things they'd done to get where they were hadn't been kind, but Draeven had always held true at every end they met. His place at Lazarus' side—a place where he could change the world for the better—was worth it all. Still, Quinn was a variable Draeven hadn't accounted for.

But Lazarus had. He'd been waiting for the day he'd find her.

Now he had to figure out what exactly he was supposed to do with her.

"I'll bring her to heel, Draeven," Lazarus said through gritted teeth and then with a look back, he added, "I always do."

"For the sake of everyone involved, I hope so," his second muttered so quietly he almost missed it.

Moonlight Inn

"If something is important to someone, figure out why.
Significance is weakness."
— Quinn Darkova, former slave, ex-prisoner, want-to-be-killer,
and reluctant vassal of House Fierté

"As a member of Master Lazarus' household, we uphold his graciousness. We are extensions of his will and—"

Quinn wasn't allowed to kill the woman, that much was clear, but with every attempt at schooling her on the importance of propriety and servitude manners, Quinn thought about it more and more. If ever she got the chance, she'd make this woman the first to go.

Lorraine was too important to Lazarus. She had watched the woman complain to him on many occasions, usually about Quinn's attitude and especially when Quinn talked to and about Lazarus as though he were a living breathing mortal and not some God among them. Her complaints weren't the odd part. The fact that he let her was.

When Lorraine spoke, he seemed to listen—or at least he pretended to. Often times, he would shake his head and just tell her to deal with it, but he never once scolded her for complaining. Not like he did Quinn. Then again, everyone seemed to have a bone to pick with Quinn, or maybe it was the other way around. Not that Quinn would ever admit that. It's not her fault she was forced to go on this blasted journey. They'd been on the road over a week, eating nothing but overcooked fish and berries. She was beginning to get restless, and Lady Fortuna never smiled upon her when she was restless.

Still, she sent a quick prayer to the gods that someone would take pity on her. When she raised her head and spotted rooftops in the distance, Quinn blinked. "Well, that's a first," she muttered to herself, cutting off Lorraine's most recent tirade that she had tuned out several minutes before.

"What is it?" Lorraine asked.

"A town," Quinn said, shifting atop the large beast that had carried them for many days already.

"Hmmm." Lorraine leaned to the side and examined the tops of the buildings in the distance. "It would be good to sleep in a bed for the night," she said absently. "We'll need to gather supplies as well and trade the horses for fresh stock, something to carry us the rest of the way."

Quinn didn't care about any of that—not the bed, the supplies, or the new horses. Getting to a town meant getting off this damn beast and away from Lorraine's constant barrage. She almost—almost—kicked her legs against the horse, hoping to spur it faster, but she quickly held herself in check.

"My lord!" Lorraine called up to Lazarus and the other men that had been on the road with them. "Will we be stopping for the night?"

Lazarus' horse came to a slow stop and he turned as they ambled up alongside it. "We'll stay for two nights," he announced. "The horses will rest. Supplies will be gathered and then we'll set off once again."

"Excellent news," Lorraine said. Quinn resisted the urge to roll her eyes.

Tuning the woman out as she then returned her attention to explaining manners befitting a vassal of Master Lazarus, Quinn examined the buildings and unkempt streets as they arrived on the edges. The buildings were less than pristine, most of them dirty and caked in sludge. The thatch roofs showed no more wear and tear than her sector in Dumas, but

KEL CARPENTER

several of the houses and shops had missing spots of vegetation where they should have been covered.

They didn't stop, but instead headed farther into town. Dominicus lead the way with Lazarus just behind him, and Lorraine and Quinn in front of Draeven who had fallen back to cover the tail end of their group. People watched them from the streets—their eyes following Quinn especially, her coloring an oddity in the sea of tan skin and brown hair. Some children even pointed in awe as their parents dragged them away.

"Hmmm."

"What is it?" Lazarus inquired at Quinn's hum.

"Nothing," she replied. "It just doesn't seem like they get very many visitors here."

Lazarus looked at a young boy who was staring openly at Quinn's long silver hair. Draeven laughed and Quinn turned back to look at him. Shaking his head, the soldier grinned at her. "He can't help it," Draeven said, nodding to the boy whose mother chose that moment to grab him up and march away. "Even boys who have yet to grow into manhood are transfixed by your beauty."

Narrowing her eyes at Draeven, Quinn lips thinned as she said, "If you're looking for amusement, I suggest you look elsewhere."

He put his hands up in mock surrender. "Touchy," he said with a smile still on his lips. "I wasn't making fun of you, I swear."

Quinn turned around and stared ahead, noting that Lazarus was glancing between the two of them with a frown before he finally faced forward as well.

When they reached the Moonlight Inn, Quinn hurried to climb down off the back of the horse. She took one step towards the front door and promptly fell forward, nearly landing face first in the mud.

"*Potes*," she ground out, the N'skaran curse rolling off her tongue as she reached out and caught hold of the horse's bridle to keep her upright. It had the nerve to huff in irritation at her and she sent it a withering glare. Her thighs were rubbed raw, her legs like limp ocean weeds. As she tried to wait to allow her legs to adjust to their new status on the ground, Draeven walked by, tossing his head back with a laugh at her predicament.

She changed her mind. If given the chance, he'd be the first person she'd kill.

As if sensing her inner thoughts, Draeven turned his gaze on her. The bastard had the audacity to grin as he turned and strode through the front door of the inn, his blond hair glinting in the dull afternoon light as the sun began to descend behind the town buildings.

Quinn pushed away from the horse and took several steps towards the inn, intent on murdering him, or at the very least stabbing him, when Lazarus stepped in front of her. She came to a grinding halt before she could crash into his wide chest, and Quinn turned her narrowed gaze upward.

"I would appreciate it if you would not plot the murders of my comrades," he said sharply. "That will be a permanent rule of your contract for the next five years."

Gritting her teeth, Quinn glared at Lazarus. "Fine," she said, moving around him. "But in the future, if you don't want your Lord Sunshine to end up with a dagger in the eye, I suggest you tell him to keep his comments to himself."

"Noted," Lazarus said as she moved to step around him. Quinn could have sworn she saw a twinkle of amusement in his eyes, but she didn't turn back to see. Lazarus was a statue of indescribable complications.

Ones she didn't want to get any more entwined with than she already was.

Stretching her legs as she walked, Quinn stumbled through the creaking door into the inn pausing to look for Lord Sunshine and Madame Manners.

The inside didn't look much better than the rest of the town. A worn looking staircase led up to the second and third floors, nicked and chipped from years of use. The furniture in the front room had a layer of dust like it hadn't been used in quite some time. The skinny old man that came to greet them resembled a living skeleton with sunken eyes and bony fingers as he took their money and directed them to the stairs where they'd find their rooms.

"I'm sorry we don't have anyone to look after your horses, sir." The old man's voice shook as he relayed the information to Lazarus. "We don't get many visitors in Ishvat, but the stables out back will be able to hold them overnight for your stay."

"Not a problem, we won't be here for long," he said as he took the keys. Lazarus nodded towards the front door and Dominicus and Draeven nodded back as they followed his silent command and went back for the horses.

"You'll be bunking with Lorraine," Lazarus said, handing Lorraine the key along with a pouch of coins that he'd pulled from beneath his cloak. "Take her with you to get supplies. We'll be in the stables until you return."

Lorraine nodded. "Of course, my—Lazarus."

Quinn glanced sideways, catching the look Lazarus gave the old innkeeper, who seemed to be more busy humming to himself than paying attention to Lorraine's slipup. He motioned with two fingers for them to step outside, and Quinn and Lorraine followed.

"We'll need food rations for another week, and—" Lazarus pulled a slip of yellowed parchment from his pocket and handed it over. "See if you can find this," he finished, meeting the other woman's eyes meaningfully.

Lorraine nodded and slipped the parchment into the folds of her dress before Quinn could get a glimpse of what was written.

"And, Lorraine"—Lazarus reached for Quinn and dragged her closer, pushing her at the other woman—"keep this one out of trouble."

Midnight Misdeeds

"Gambling is a poor man's vice and a smart woman's web."
— Quinn Darkova, former slave, unofficial prisoner, want-to-be-killer,
and vassal of House Fierté

The room smelled stale, like the hay in the beds had been left to sit for far too long, and the wooded floors damp and in need of fresh air. Quinn wrinkled her nose against the distasteful odor, but Lorraine didn't seem to mind as she bustled in with the remainder of their purchases that hadn't been stored in the horse's saddles. Quinn took in the room, a single small bed shoved up to the wall near the lone window and she headed for it.

When she landed face down into the straw

mattress, she coughed, turning on her side to watch Lorraine ready herself for bed.

Dinner had been a block of cheese and cured rabbit around a cracked table that was missing a leg, followed by hushed talk that Quinn wasn't permitted to hear so Lorraine excused them both. Back in Dumas, she would be getting ready for her act right now, but ever since she'd signed that contract with Lazarus every day had been consumed by riding and short, restless sleep, along with the occasional daydream about stabbing someone. Quinn was tired, but not physically. She was tired of being watched and controlled every moment since she signed the next five years of her life over. Not that she had a better choice after the stunt in the marketplace. She'd been kicking herself for that slip in sanity every damned day. Still, she was beginning to recognize Lorraine's nightly routine by now and knew the others would be retiring soon as well.

Turning onto her back, Quinn fitted her hands behind her head, linking her fingers to prop herself up as she stared at the wood ceiling thoughtfully.

"Aren't you going to get ready?" Lorraine asked as she unpinned her hair and began to braid it down the side.

"Hmmm," Quinn said in a dismissive response.

Lorraine opened her mouth to tout another lecture, likely on her manners, but there was an abrupt knock at the door that Quinn made no move to answer. Dressed in her night shift with her hair undone, Lorraine cracked the door to peer out. She took a quick step back and pulled the door open the rest of the way. Lazarus stood there, his large frame eating up most of the entryway. Quinn sat up.

"Do you still have that parchment I gave you?" he asked, directing his question to Lorraine without sparing her a glance.

"Yes, sorry, my lord." Lorraine turned away and rifled through her cloak, finding the yellowed paper and handing it over. "I wasn't able to find what you needed."

Lazarus shook his head. "I didn't think you'd be able to in this small of a town, but I wanted to be sure."

Quinn listened intently, her eyes sliding down to Lazarus' pocket just as he turned his dark gaze on her. She slowly raised her head and met his eyes.

"I expect you to stay in tonight," he said sharply.

Quinn shrugged.

"I mean it," he snapped. "Do not leave this inn."

Quinn flopped back down on the straw mattress and waved at him. "Got it," she replied. Lazarus kept his eyes on her for several moments before he sighed and thanked Lorraine one last time before leaving.

"Your manners are atrocious," Lorraine said as she crawled into bed beside Quinn. It wasn't long before she drifted off and Quinn was left to stare at the ceiling in peace.

An hour or so later, the sound of raucous laughter from the alley below pulled her from her inner musings. Quinn sat up and silently slid off the bed and onto her feet, padding toward the window. She looked down and tracked the movements of three figures as they made their way toward the main road.

They were probably nothing more than small town drunkards, Quinn surmised. But that didn't really matter. She was pretty sure that those men could lead her somewhere entertaining, or at the very least, somewhere that didn't smell of mildew and away from a place where every move was being watched.

Quinn glanced back at Lorraine, making sure she was still asleep. There was no way she could walk out the front door without Lazarus knowing. There was too much risk of someone seeing her. She'd have to climb out the window—and quickly, if she wanted to follow the men in the road. She slid her fingers under the bottom of the window and edged it up. Every squeak and groan from the frame had her snapping her gaze back to Lorraine, but through it all, the other woman snored softly. The first makings of a smile curled around the corners of her mouth as Quinn turned and slid her feet out first before working the rest of her body through the small opening.

Her muscles strained as she held herself to the side of the inn with one hand on the window sill. Licking her bottom lip, Quinn balanced herself on the thin wooden border as she reached up and closed it shut behind her. Then, with both hands latched onto the window's edge, Quinn swung her legs and released her grip, landing hard on a pile of hay just a few feet to the right.

Grinning at her ingenuity, she got up and dusted herself off before striding toward the street. The men walking along it had no idea they were being followed. As far as they were concerned, it was shadows and dirt. That's all.

For Quinn, it was a breath of freedom. Fear might be her drug of choice, but it was freedom that chased the nightmares away. A dream she reached for, through the invisible bars that others could not see. An illusion for the night, but not forever.

It would have to be enough.

She followed them through the quiet town, not even needing to pretend otherwise when they never thought to turn or glance around them. They strode forward like bumbling idiots, high on spirits and low on wits. They didn't look because they were confident, self-assured. They didn't know to look closer at the shadows or to listen for the things that go bump in the night. That made her life easier tonight, because they didn't notice as she followed them into a slight tavern on the outskirts of town.

The wooden frame rattled behind her as the door swung shut and the scents of smoke and sweat filled her nostrils. She earned a few narrowed glances as she strode past the bar and into the low candlelit room where men were being entertained one way or another.

The three that led her here had just taken their seats at a table in the corner where an older man was enjoying the company of a whore and another much younger man enjoyed his bottle of spirits. Quinn sauntered over, plastering a wicked little grin on her face as she plopped down into the final empty seat. The table fell to a hush as all eyes turned on her, and then not so subtly, to the dealer.

A sober man with a clean-cut beard and plain tunic looked her over. "You play?" he asked, shuffling the worn deck of cards between dexterous fingers. Quinn leaned forward, tapping the tips of her nails lightly on the weathered roundtable.

"Depends on the game," she replied in kind, noting the shortened clip of his words. Lazarus still wouldn't tell her where they were going, but north was apparent. If the creeping cold hadn't told her, the accents in this town would have. She'd heard them before. Not these specific men, but others like them. Cruel masters and fragmented memories. She tilted her head, giving nothing away as he said, "Rikkers."

"I play."

He cut the deck and continued shuffling. "Have anything to bet?"

His eyebrow arched as he squinted, examining her person. Quinn sighed with exasperation and from her pocket pulled a faded leather pouch, full of glass pebbles shaped almost exactly like coins. She tossed the coin purse onto the center of the table, and leaned back in her chair, crossing her arms over her chest. "Will that do?" She lifted both eyebrows, keeping her expression neutral so they couldn't see the condescension in her expression.

The dealer looked at the bag of what he thought was coins for a moment, considering checking, and then nodded. "That'll do." Quinn released a breath.

Then the game began.

Eight cards were laid in front of each of them, face down. Quinn swiped her hand across the table, scooping hers up. The old man pulled a card from the stack and the harlot started giggling. He whispered something in her ear that made the girl blush and Quinn rolled her eyes. He placed a card from his hand on the table face up, and then the bottle drinker went.

He couldn't have been much older than Quinn, but his bloodshot eyes and raspy cough said otherwise. His lank hair fell unkempt across his forehead as he leaned forward and pulled a card, and then discarded another in the pile. It was her turn.

Quinn actually had a fairly decent hand to start with, given how Lady Luck had smiled on her when she begged to be off the road, she wasn't sure if it would be pushing it or not to pull from the pile. One of the two discarded cards was one she needed, but to pick it up this early might give too much away. Leaning forward she pulled from the facedown pile and prayed once more that her luck hadn't run out.

The corner of the card barely turned upward when knew she picked right. Her face entirely stoic, she tossed a throwaway card in the face up pile and turned to the man next to her as the game continued on.

Within two rounds she'd already figured out two of the three to her left held nothing as did the man to her right. The third, the one with ash colored-hair and a hooked nose, he had potential. The only one she couldn't get a read on was the old man with the half-naked woman on his lap. The woman let out a mewling sound and began grinding against him and the old bastard grinned at the other men around the table, his teeth yellowed, some missing. The three drunkards hooted with laughter, leering at the woman that Quinn was fairly certain was either faking it or had taken something to encourage the way she was acting. Either way, it disgusted her.

The next round came and went, and Quinn was still missing two cards but knew the game wouldn't make it two more times around the table. She drummed her fingernails on the wood surface, the corners of her lips turning up just slightly. The men took notice.

The tension slowly ratcheted up as each person took their turn and the dealer looked to her to make her move. Two cards down and only one to draw. She pulled the one she needed from the face up pile and tossed one of the spares aside. With nothing more than a flick of her eyes, the eighth card changed and with it, so did her smile.

The hook-nosed drunk let out a curse when she presented her hand.

"That's game," the dealer nodded.

Quinn swept her arm out to gather her winnings. She stored most of it in her pockets, including the glass pieces, leaving just enough bronze coins with a single silver on the table to play another game.

This time she played with a smirk, growing bolder and bolder with every hand. Another four games down and her pockets filled with silver and bronze. She sensed tempers rising and rose to take leave. They'd gathered quite the crowd around their table the last two games, and Quinn had to push through the stench of body odor and liquor as she made her way for the door.

Men jostled her, their hands brushing over the thin fabric of her tunic—a bit too much for her liking. Behind her, the scuffing of chairs being dragged across the sticky wooden floor gave Quinn the urgency to ignore it for the moment as she pushed through the last of the crowd and through the battered door out into the cool open night.

Taking a long draw of the clean air, Quinn started for the main road that would lead her back to the

Moonlight Inn. What she was going to do to get back inside when she got there … that was an open question. Climbing back up wouldn't be an option and going through the lobby would just attract attention, not to mention piss off Lorraine who would just run her mouth to Lazarus. Quinn gnawed on her bottom lip as she looked at the night sky wondering if tonight would just bring more of those terrible dreams when she returned or if she'd finally get some peace.

She could sleep in the stables for a few hours and pretend she had gotten up early to look after the horses, she thought. It wasn't foolproof, but it was something.

The tavern door smacked against the wooden frame drawing Quinn's attention. She didn't need to glance behind her to know who had followed. The real question was how she felt like handling them.

Her tongue lightly trailed over the edge of her teeth as she swiped her thumb across her bottom lip. They'd each had multiple drinks tonight, and that was after stumbling into the tavern—who knew what else they'd taken before they'd arrived. It wouldn't be unreasonable to think they might pass out in a ditch on the side of the road. *No*, Quinn thought, *not unreasonable at all*. Quinn slipped her hand under the edge of her tunic, pulling the dagger from its sheath.

She slowed a little, purposefully pretending to look down the dark alley—and not at them—before turning onto the narrowed street. She paused, rolling her eyes when sloppy footsteps came barreling down the alley behind her.

She turned around, facing the three that thought to follow her. A light breeze blew down through the streets, whipping her hair behind her. They didn't notice the dark tendrils forming at her fingertips. Not when it was only moonlight and shadow.

"Hello, boys," Quinn purred. Her voice husky and filled with a lovely hint of a dark promise. They slowed to a stop before her, the one on the far-right squinting into the night, confused. They'd expected her to run or beg. They expected screaming. They expected fear.

These children had absolutely no clue who or what they were dealing with.

"How'd you do it?" Hook-nose asked, cruelty and dark intention lined his expression. He wasn't here for a friendly chat. Quinn smiled spitefully. She wasn't either.

"I don't know what you're talking about," she lied, and what a great liar she was. That last hand had only had half the cards it needed when she grew impatient and crafted an illusion to change the cards they saw. Maybe she should have let them win once. Not much that she could do about that now. They'd followed her, not the other way around. In her mind, that meant her hands were washed. Her sins absolved before they even got started.

She'd wandered out into the night hoping for

something to entertain her, craving that brief taste of freedom. Trouble found her as it always did, and deep down Quinn knew this was what she really sought. This was what the restless magic that writhed in her veins was searching for.

"You're lying," he said, taking a step forward. His eyes traveled up and down the length of her body. "You know what we do to liars here?" He licked his lips and Quinn's stomach turned. Not with fear, but disgust. Her lip curled back.

"We should teach ya somethin' better to do with that pretty mouth of yours," the third one said. "Somethin' much better than tellin' lies." He was the shortest, but broad-chested. Quinn narrowed her eyes on them as the two took a step forward.

Her heart hammered in her chest—slow, steady— but the sound of blood pounding filled her ears. Fear and excitement swirled through her, sliding through her veins. It was both a poison and a cure in that potent combination. She didn't feel fear like others did—but instead absorbed theirs and used it, manipulated it, to make her stronger.

In her, fear was something darker, something *other*. She felt no desire to run or flee or beg or cry. Instead, she felt powerful. Invincible. Drunken bastards thought to corner her in an alley, and not a single one of them had even an inkling that it was her who set this trap. That they were merely prey—buzzing gnats falling into the spider's web. Even when she grinned, they didn't seem to comprehend their precarious situation.

"I can do a great many wicked things with this mouth," Quinn agreed. She took a step forward and moonlight bathed her face. "None of which you will find out tonight."

The one on the right was the only one that had the decent sense to shudder at the playful excitement in her voice. The only one that had the presence of mind to take a step back.

"Grab her, Beck," the hook-nosed bastard snapped through gritted teeth. "I wanna see what she's hiding under that tunic of hers." Beck moved and Quinn parried, swinging her elbow towards his face.

There was a crunch as cartilage cracked under the sharp pressure of her arm. Beck cried out, a hand going to his face. Blood poured between his fingers as he stumbled back. Quinn tsked at him with an irritated scowl. "Pathetic." Moving forward, she knocked his hand aside and she went to punch him again, but he quickly backed up, nearly falling in his haste to avoid her blow.

Blood and snot dripped from the mushed pulp in the center of his face. Tears reflected the light of the moon as he let out a blubbered, "you bitch!"

Quinn paused, tapping a finger to the corner of her mouth, a cold, cruel look filling her gaze as she said, "I'm not the one that thought it would be a smart idea to corner a woman in an alley and try to rape her. You're the one that started this, *Becky*."

His eyes widened and he bellowed a roar of outrage before he ran at her. The rage consumed him, but that wasn't all. Quinn could still sense the fear within him, just waiting for her to reach out and grab onto. Not yet, she decided, as she sidestepped his attempt and stuck her foot out in a quick movement. Whether or not he saw and tried to stop, it was too late. He barreled forward, his boot catching against hers as his anger dissipated for a fraction of a second —shock taking its place as he fell.

Thunk.

His head whipped back and came forward, colliding with the compact dirt. Beck moaned but didn't move to get back up. Quinn turned and pointed her knife at the other two.

"Who's next?" Her smile was all teeth.

Hook-nose stepped up just as the other stepped back. Quinn turned her sights on him and grinned.

"Lars, I don't think we should do this," the one on the right murmured. His fear was practically palpable. She inhaled it like a fresh breath of air.

"Stop being such a coward, Finn, and help me deal with her." Lars came for her, unaware of the hulking shadow that appeared at the end of the alley. Sensing who it was, Quinn's lips thinned and she bit the inside of her cheek.

She'd hoped to deal with this—have a little fun—

without *him* ever the wiser. She had, in fact, hoped that he wouldn't even have known she was gone. It appeared that neither of her hopes were going to be realized. As Lazarus stepped into the alley, a wave of icy anger from a wayward wind hit her face. His nearly midnight eyes were far darker than the vast expanse of the night sky, no stars to light the abyss that created them. There was a darkness there in his gaze, so primal and cruel that Quinn shuddered.

To say he was displeased was an understatement.

He stared at her over the hook-nosed bastard's shoulder as fingers pressed into her arms and her back hit the hard brick of a wall. Quinn hissed as a hand closed around the wrist holding her knife and the other wrapped around her throat. Lazarus simply stood there and watched across the alley while the ash-haired man—Lars—tried to pry the knife from her numb fingers. His breath blew across her face as he spoke, but Quinn wasn't listening. In fact, she wasn't paying him any attention at all.

She stared at Lazarus, waiting, watching him just as he watched her. Both of them urging the other to move with nothing but their gaze. He shook his head once and Quinn sighed.

He had no intention of saving her. She had gotten herself in this and he was going to make her get herself out, and then ream her for it. She didn't mind dealing with the rabble, but she didn't want to if it meant facing the music afterwards.

Quinn gritted her teeth and turned her chin just slightly as the hand at her throat squeezed. Something hard started grinding into her lower stomach, pushing her tunic up with its fervor. Still, Quinn looked at Lazarus. Curiously waiting, trying to piece together what the slight flutter in her chest meant as his eyes hardened into obsidian gems. His hands clenched and she wondered if he realized it. This reaction he had to seeing someone abuse her—touch her.

It intrigued her far more than she wanted to admit. The hand at her throat slipped away, reaching for her trousers, and still Quinn watched him. Waited. Her lips parted as teeth bit into the crook of her neck where it met her shoulder. Sweaty fingers touched the skin of her belly and that was where Quinn drew the line. She had enough experience with skeevs to know that their inability to use magic made them too bold when they never knew what they were facing. She didn't need the knife in hand to take care of him as she let it fall to the ground and let the darkness rise.

Black wisps slithered through her veins, sliding off her skin like black vapor. The man touching her didn't notice. He was far too concerned with pleasures of the flesh that he felt was his right to take, consent or no. He didn't know that the very last thing you should do when you corner a fear twister was touch them.

He licked her skin and then froze. His muscles locked as fear overloaded his system. Terrible, enthralling, paralyzing fear. It seeped into his skin, pushing through muscle and tendon and bone, until every bit of his body was locked into whatever he saw. His eyes widened and Quinn turned her head back, noting the wide unseeing gaze that looked through her. She smiled. Tendrils wrapped around his arms, stretching up his neck and chest, thick and fat and restraining. The wisps circled his throat. He wheezed once and Quinn maneuvered her free hand between their bodies, pushing his chest. Like a living statue, he gave no resistance and simply fell backwards into the filthy alleyway.

His lips moved, muttering gibberish as Quinn readjusted her tunic. He trembled, slowly wrapping his arms around himself, completely lost in his own mind as Quinn took a step over him.

The last man, the only one of the three that wanted to leave, turned to run away from her. Quinn shook her head. *Stupid boy. You should have run when you had the chance.* He hit Lazarus square in the chest, but the man who held her contract didn't move an inch. Finn bounced off him, and while she couldn't see his face, she could sense his fear intensify as the boy looked up at the man he hadn't seen until it was too late. Lazarus' hand shot out, his scarred fingers wrapping around the boy's neck, holding him upright. Only a moment passed before his eyes flashed, never leaving Quinn for a single second as he tossed the other man aside. Finn hit the wall and slumped over, completely limp. Not dead, but unconscious.

Silence sat between them, spanning the distance and filling the void where words went unsaid.

Quinn let out an exasperated sigh and the slight sound seemed to stir something in him. Lazarus snapped, hands shaking with barely suppressed rage as he strode forward. Quinn didn't back away as he stopped before her. She made no move to stop him as he leaned forward, and with more gentleness than she expected, tugged the collar of her tunic aside. Her lips parted, but he wasn't looking at her now. He was staring at the teeth marks that undoubtedly were beginning to bruise on her skin. His fingers brushed over them, gentle but calloused.

"You stupid, stupid girl," he whispered. She tilted her head and his hand fell away. Her eyes flicked downward just as a shadow seemed to slither and disappear beneath the cuff of his sleeve.

Quinn frowned, slowly looking back up into his depthless eyes.

"You said you're not a fear twister," Quinn stated. Not a question … and yet, it was.

"I'm not."

Quinn crossed her arms over her chest and raised one eyebrow. "Then what are you?"

He gave her a hard look and leaned in close. "Like calls to like, Quinn. For now, that's all you need to know." His breath blew across her face, and she inhaled sharply. Wood burning over an open fire. Smoke and ash. He tasted of warmth, but not comfort or kindness. It was the kind of blistering heat that could set even the coldest of women aflame.

"And if that's not enough?" she asked, hardly more than a whisper.

This close she could see the scar that ran down the left side of his face, stretching from eyebrow to cheek. Without thinking, she lifted her hand reaching to—

"You don't get to decide what's enough here, Quinn," Lazarus said. "You're my vassal. For the next five years, *I own you.* If you want me to trust you with things, maybe you should learn to stay in your room like I told you to."

Quinn blinked and stepped away. Shaking her head, she shifted to step past him, her shoulder slamming into his upper arm as she stared out into the empty streets and beyond.

"I'm your *vassal*," she spat, striding past. Her back to all of them as she turned onto the main road that led back to the Moonlight Inn. "Not your slave, Lazarus. Or have you forgotten the details of the contract we signed?" She didn't wait for his reply, or even care if he had one. She strode off, not caring if he followed.

Own me? She scoffed, and the darkness inside twisted. *Stupid, arrogant man. No one will own me. Never again.*

"I gave you one command. Stay in your room. And what do you do—"

"I go for a walk because I'm tired of being watched night and day," she snarled. The sky turned black, truly black, as every star in existence winked out and a canopy of darkness spread above them. Quinn clenched and unclenched her hands, because somehow, some way she knew that it was her. She was doing this.

The void descended, creeping from the sky into the horizon as Quinn's temper spiraled. A black wind swept through the sleeping town, and while not a hair on her face moved, the dreaded chill it brought with it was enough to give Lazarus pause.

"Wait."

Her footsteps came to a halt, and she turned her head to the side just a fraction as warm fingers wrapped around the sleeve of her forearm. "Quinn, wait." The void paused in its creeping, waiting to hear what he had to say the same as she did, both of them withholding judgement.

"You don't treat Lorraine this way, and she's a vassal. You don't treat Draeven this way, or Dominicus. Just me. Why is that?" Quinn asked.

"Because you go for a walk and I find you in an alley, cornered by three men—"

"I handled them," she interjected.

"I know," he answered. She paused and frowned. His acceptance was the last thing she expected after the rant about owning her. "You get cornered, Quinn, and leave a string of bodies in your wake."

"So, it's my fault that they wanted to rape me?" she asked, her temper rising once more.

"That's not what I said," Lazarus replied with a hint of ire. "Although, I'm not so stupid to think that they just *happened* upon you. You have a way of finding trouble, and on this trip that is the last thing we need. That's why I asked you to stay in your room."

Quinn snorted and the void started to slowly disintegrate.

"If that's what you call asking, I'd hate to see what you consider an order."

Lazarus didn't find her as funny. "I'm not trying to strip you of your freedom, but I need you to follow my commands and understand that there is a reason for everything I ask."

"I'm not a blind follower," she said, spinning around to look at him as the stars slowly popped back into existence. "You told me you wanted me because I'm a fear twister. You said you'd help me learn how to control it. All you've done thus far is drag me across Norcasta and stick me with Lorraine—and if I have to hear lessons on my 'manners' one more time—"

"I'll speak with Lorraine," he said calmly. There was a twitch in his cheek that was either annoyance or amusement. She couldn't quite tell.

"I want my own horse," she continued, and Lazarus only sighed.

"You can barely ride as it is," he said, lifting a brow.

"I don't care," she shrugged. "I'm tired of hearing her voice. Lord Sunshine makes me want to stab him. Repeatedly. And I'm fairly certain Dominicus is afraid of me, which would make for an uncomfortable ride for both of us. Either give me a horse or put me on yours, but I'm not riding with the rest of them any further." He watched her, a pregnant pause lingering before answering.

"*If* I do this, what do I get?"

Her eyebrows drew together. That wasn't the reply she'd been expecting. "What do you want?"

"I want you to listen to me. When I ask you to stay somewhere, you stay. When I tell you to help Lorraine with something, you help." Quinn wrinkled her nose. "You stop fighting me about this arrangement, and I can make it a lot more pleasurable."

"That's a lot to ask for a horse and some peace and quiet," Quinn pointed out. "You need to sweeten the deal."

"What else do you want?" he asked, staying remarkably patient though she could tell that thread was fraying.

"Information." His jaw ticked, and this time she knew it was because she was pushing her luck, but in that brief pause he hadn't said no and so she pushed. "I have no idea what I'm doing here, Lazarus. You pulled me from my home and brought me on this trip, not because me or anyone else wanted it, but you. Why?"

Lazarus ran a hand down his face, his eyelids falling closed as he pinched the bridge of his nose between his thumb and forefinger, inhaling deeply. Quinn waited as he weighed what to tell her.

"It's complicated," he began, and she let out a frustrated huff, starting to turn away as his fingers tightened around the arm she forgot he held. "Don't walk off. Let me finish." The chastisement had her biting her tongue, but she stood there, turned back, and listened. "There are a lot of pieces still in motion right now, and you're only one of them. A great number of very small slipups could put us all in jeopardy, which is why I'm careful not to tell anyone the full extent of what we're doing here. Not Lorraine. Not Draeven. Not Dominicus. No one, Quinn."

"They at least know something—"

"They know bits and pieces, but it's far less than you believe. The difference is that Lorraine, Draeven, and Dominicus trust me. They know there is a reason for what we are doing, even if they don't see it yet. You don't have that same trust for me ... yet," he paused, then added, "nor I for you."

Well, she thought, *he isn't wrong.*

"Then what do we do? You don't trust me, and I don't trust you." His fingers slipped from her arm and cold filled the empty space instantly. She hadn't even realized warmth had settled in before it was gone.

"We give it time," he answered. "We learn how to work together, how to ... *trust* one another."

"That's not enough——"

"We've been over this." His voice was midnight and shadow, and something … else. Where Quinn became the apathetic cold to the world, Lazarus burned with a savageness that could not be contained. At the core of it, he was right that they were no different, but in the way the darkness showed—they were far from the same. "I have an idea that might help this situation we've found ourselves in."

"Oh?" she asked, biting her cheek to stop herself from being so drawn into his terrible, consuming gaze.

"Once a week, you get to ask me a question and I'll answer it."

"Truthfully?" She raised her chin, tightening her arms around herself as a very real wind swept down the streets, stirring the dirt and dust.

"Truthfully, *but*——" His eyes flashed with something she couldn't place. "I get to ask you a question as well, and you have to answer it."

Quinn pressed her lips together because Gods be damned, he had her.

"Alright, I'll bite." She nodded. "But this is part of our contract now, so you can't go back on it in a week after I've done my part."

Mirth danced on his face as the slightest hint of a grin settled. "It's part of our contract now," he agreed. "Along with you not stabbing or otherwise harming my other vassals," he paused, waiting for her to agree. "Right?"

"Mhmm," she hummed.

Something settled in the air with both parties' agreements, the contract changed. She couldn't see it because it wasn't tangible, but she could feel it through the emblazoned signature scrawled across her skin.

The tables were turning. Her cards were changing.

But as they turned and walked the rest of the way back to the Moonlight Inn in silence, Quinn couldn't stop thinking about what she'd seen in the alley that night.

Like calls to like, he'd said. But what exactly does that mean?

She wasn't sure, but a week from now she was going to find out.

Field of Vision

"There is strength in the darkness, if you are strong enough to take it."
— *Quinn Darkova, former slave, hopeful-murderess, somewhat willing vassal of House Fierté*

Quinn stared straight ahead, arms crossed and chin bobbing with the steady clomp of hooves. Strong masculine arms brushed against hers as Lazarus guided the horse, temperamental creature that it was. Days had passed, and still every time she came near it the damned thing snorted in derision. It was only the man that sat behind her, holding the reins, that even convinced it to not put up a fight every time Quinn mounted. Not long ago he'd told her that she could ride or run. Some days she wondered if running was the lesser of the evils, and then she took a look down or up the hills and kept her grumbles to herself.

What she really wanted was her own steed.

"You did say that riding with me would be a concession," Lazarus said as if reading her mind. She continued to ignore his subtle attempts at talking. When she wanted to be chatty, he was silent, but now that she preferred the quiet over having to hear Lorraine and Draeven, he wanted to chat. She couldn't understand it. The man made no sense.

"I'm on the horse, aren't I?"

She couldn't see him, but she felt that subtle shake of his head.

"Through no effort of your own," he remarked lightly.

"It's not my fault this beast hates me," she harrumphed. "Besides, I would have preferred a horse of my own."

Lazarus shook his head. "You can hardly ride," he sighed.

"I would have managed." *Maybe*.

It was becoming increasingly clear that horses weren't fond of her in general. While Bastian, Lazarus' steed, was the most opposed, the other three also kept their distance from her. She wondered if it was her magic. If she was so far gone that she couldn't tell that it was leaking out, but if that were the case there was no way Lorraine or Draeven would act as they did.

Halfway through the last few days, she began to wonder if demanding to ride with Lazarus had been a mistake, but every time she thought about being put back with Lady Manners or Lord Sunshine, she immediately recalled those nights alongside Lorraine and being forced to listen as she 'educated' her on the correct way to sit in a saddle with *Master Lazarus*. Quinn shook her head. She was learning to handle small doses being near that woman, but longer than a few hours and she might happily commit murder.

A few more hours passed, and the sun set beyond the horizon. Lazarus directed his horse off of the road and through the tree line with Draeven, Dominicus, and Lorraine following silently behind. They stopped at a clearing in the woods and Lazarus swung a leg back, sliding down the saddle and off the horse, leaving Quinn to get down on her own.

Grumbling to herself and shooting a glare at his retreating back, she swung her leg over and moved to dismount with as much pride as she could muster and held onto it even when the balls of her feet struck slippery ground. Her legs locked, threatening to send her sliding in the mud.

"*Potes*," she muttered under her breath, casting a wary glance at the party.

Draeven and Dominicus gave her strange looks and Lorraine only shook her head, probably determining by her tone that she had said something 'vulgar.' She would be correct in this case, not that Quinn volunteered that information.

"Lorraine, Dominicus—set up camp. Quinn—" Lazarus turned just as she righted herself. Bastian snorted, clicking his teeth and startling her. She growled, grasping the saddle in a death grip. Lazarus lifted an eyebrow. "You and Draeven come with me."

He turned on his heel, leaving her to follow him into the woods.

Muttering under her breath, Quinn huffed. "Yes, *your highness.*"

Draeven fell into line beside her. "You're not far off," he said with a chuckle.

"What?" Quinn eyed the other man warily.

Draeven shook his fair head. "You'll find out soon enough."

Quinn sighed in frustration, but didn't reply as they followed behind Lazarus, moving farther into the forest and away from the campsite. She was beginning to wonder if the man was planning on walking them right off a cliff when he stopped and turned.

"We're going to train," he announced.

Draeven moved to the side and mumbled something she couldn't hear. Confused, Quinn turned on him. "What are you doing?" she asked.

Draeven turned and relieved himself of his sword and light armor, sliding it all off with graceful movements. "I'm watching."

2222

222222222

"Aren't you—"

"Draeven will observe," Lazarus said, cutting her off.

Quinn scowled at him, but turned to face him, nonetheless. "Alright, then. What do you want me to do?"

"Defend yourself." He paused as her whole body tensed. "Using only your magic."

"What?" she spluttered. "Defend myself from wh"—Quinn barely had time to react as Lazarus came at her with a blow to the chest. She hit the ground hard. Her spine shook as it collided with the forest floor, knocking the wind from her lungs. She tasted copper in her mouth as she rose back to her feet, more than a little irked. Quinn spat a wad of saliva tinged with blood and didn't hesitate to call her magic.

It was never far from the surface. Not these days.

The darkness came to her like an old friend, onyx tendrils slithering out from under her skin. It curled around her wrists and played along her shoulders, weaving through her hair.

Crystalline eyes focused on Lazarus with an uncanny stillness.

"Do not let your emotions control you," Lazarus said as he stepped aside and began circling her. She followed his movements, wondering if he would give her an opening or a warning—an attacker's tell. Or perhaps he would drop another hint, a sign that she could unravel, something to tell her what he actually was.

His eyes wandered to the bite mark on her shoulder. Or really, where it should have been, but wasn't. She'd woken the morning after to smooth, unblemished skin and knew deep down that its absence should have worried her more than it did because there was no way this man before her was a healer. And yet he had healed her. Somehow.

It made her wonder what else he could do; what other games he could play.

"Control the darkness, Quinn. Use the fear, not the other way around."

"I know that," Quinn snapped.

"Do you?" Lazarus raised an eyebrow and nodded upward. Quinn tilted her head back, her eyes widening as she noticed the tops of the trees had all been bent backwards—bent, but not broken. Their spindly limbs stretched up and outward, avoiding the ebony darkness encroaching on their base, coming from her.

Draeven's jaw slipped, falling ajar for a brief second as he whispered, "Gods above."

Quinn swallowed hard, hating this feeling—this undeniable, terrible, awful feeling—like she was being put on show. Something to gawk at. *A thing*. It was different from the amphitheater where she performed, because there she was Mirior—the faceless ghost from the in-between. But here, she was Quinn. Her attention swayed when it shouldn't have, and he struck again, sending her flying backwards. Quinn's back hit the large trunk of a tree and when another blow came immediately afterwards, from something she couldn't see, couldn't stand a hope of predicting—she flung her hands up. Wisps of fear shot from her fingertips, weaving together like tangible threads. They wound tighter and tighter, forming a wall between the two of them.

She climbed to her feet, a steady thumping in her chest building. Something passed through his gaze as he stopped short of slamming into the barrier she didn't think he could even see. "Clever, but even if you have an enemy in front of you, you should always be aware of your other surroundings," he stated as something slammed into her from the side. Draeven grinned at her as she coughed in surprise. He rolled to the side and sprung to his feet.

Quinn released a grunt of outrage as Draeven ambled back to where he had been sprawled before. "I thought you said you were just watching!"

The blond behemoth shrugged, but it was Lazarus who answered. "Draeven *is* watching," he said. "He's watching for when you let your guard down. Now…" Lazarus crossed his arms behind his back and clasped his wrist in one hand, "use that magic. Wield it as you just did—stretch it out. Can you feel it?"

"Feel what?" she ground out, cracking her neck as she clambered back to her feet. Her muscles would need hot stones when this was over, not that she would get it. She could only imagine how vexed Lorraine would be if she boiled stones in the same pot in which dinner was made.

"Everything." She shot him a look of incredulity, and he elaborated. "Every Maji is different, but there is one thing we all share. The ability to feel those around us. Draeven can find others through their rage. You can find them through their fear. All creatures have a snippet of magic inside of them—usually unusable, often so small that even the most powerful of magic seekers cannot sense it—but you can, I can, and Draeven can. You just have to look. You won't be able to sense what kind, but you will be able to sense the minor presence of such, like listening for a pulse."

Quinn frowned as the wall she had woven fell away. She closed her eyes and put her hands up, fingers spread as she called to the power inside, letting it flow through her, invading her every sense—heightened by the cut off of sight. The tendrils separated into tiny threads, not tangible to the others, but there. Her brow pinched as Draeven and Lazarus waited to see how her magic would manifest this time.

The wisps dropped to the ground, multiplying in a network of crisscrossing strings. They crept over the wet leaves, reaching upwards into the trees, spanning the awning gaps from branch to branch. Slowly, they moved, unguided by Quinn and simply flowing through her as they encircled the entire clearing. Draeven cursed and Quinn's eyes snapped open.

Her breath caught in her chest as Draeven jumped, trying to outmaneuver her web of fear. She hadn't thought they could see it, much like the wall, but as he hooked a hand around a low hanging branch to pull himself up and away, she began to wonder.

"You can see this?" she asked.

"We can," Lazarus nodded. Sweat beaded her brow.

"No one has before," she said softly. Her eyes not sure which way to look as the netting thickened with smoky black threads. "What does it mean?"

"The manifestation of your power is visible to us —all Maji can see magic. That is not strange," Lazarus said, slowly lifting a hand to the strings. "The interesting part is the form yours has chosen to take…" he murmured, though he didn't seem to realize it. "You have quite a lot of it."

"I'll say," Draeven chimed in, his face tipped back as he examined the strands just beneath his left boot.

Lazarus took a tentative step forward.

Quinn sucked in a breath. "I can *feel* you." The strands didn't stretch or strain as he moved through them, but she felt it as if they did. He changed direction and the strands thrummed with power where he brushed past them, coming to stand behind her.

"Good," he said quietly, whispering in her ear. She

shivered and the strands began to unravel. "Keep it steady," he commanded.

She stiffened as the hairs on the back of her neck rose where his warm breath touched. The network snapped back into place. He waited a beat and when the strands stabilized once more, Lazarus began to direct her. He had her raise the web, eliciting a yelp from Draeven as the man shot him a reproachful look and climbed higher into the tree to avoid the tendrils of dark fear. She didn't think they'd do anything to him, but the reaction was amusing enough that she liked feeling them slowly creep toward him and his surge of anxiety that pulsed outward.

Quinn laughed softly under her breath and Lazarus gave her a swift command to lower it into the ground where the strands disappeared completely.

"Draeven," Lazarus said quietly. "Come here."

Draeven pursed his lips, no longer looking as thrilled to be commanded about, but dropped down from his perch, nonetheless. He landed on a branch halfway up the tree and continued swinging down until he was standing on the squishy forest floor.

Quinn gasped, drawing Lazarus' attention. "Feel him still?" he asked. Quinn paused, and that pulse of anxiety flickered. She nodded. "Good." Then he looked back to Draeven. "Walk around," he commanded.

Draeven began to walk, circling the area, only pausing to check if she could tell. "Faster," Lazarus said when that became too easy. Draeven sprinted from one side to the next.

"It's harder to feel where he is when he's moving," Quinn admitted.

"That's okay," Lazarus said. "I want you to practice this as much as possible. It's called a field of vision. All Maji can create one. Soon you'll be able to do it without thinking, and when you're well-practiced, you may not even have to use the physical manifestation."

Her hands dropped away as she tried to keep the field up using only her mind—the wisps began to seep back up from the ground and Draeven jumped back as one slithered over his foot, starting to wind its way up his leg. Quinn lifted an eyebrow and directed the thread to follow him. He shook it off and stomped on it, but the thread merely squirmed from under his foot and slithered away before dispersing.

"That's your first lesson," Lazarus said. She stiffened as she let the web unravel entirely and stopped teasing Draeven. "You control the power, not the other way around. The more you practice, the easier it will become."

Quinn nodded, but still didn't turn to meet his dark eyes. "What else can I do?" she asked.

Lazarus didn't respond right away, but she noticed when Draeven looked over her head, nodded, and grabbed his things and headed back to camp. Then, with creeping stillness, Lazarus leaned in close. She could feel the heat of him at her back as he turned his head and spoke in a low, quiet voice that sent shivers crawling up her spine. "You can destroy the world," he said. "But only if you learn to control it."

She gulped, her heart thudding against her breast. "And if I don't?"

"You already know the answer to that."

She thought about his words and then asked, "Is that what you want to do?"

He chuckled darkly, but there was no amusement in the sound. "No," he answered. "I don't want to destroy the world."

She grew more curious, more daring. "What do you want to do, then?"

His breath whispered against her temple. "Remake it."

Quinn whirled around, but he was gone. The only remainder of his presence was the small rustling of leaves and the smell of burning wood tickling her nostrils.

After a moment of staring through the trees as the last of the sun's rays disappeared from the small sliver of sky above her head, she started back towards camp —marching with her head down and her thoughts muddled.

"There you are." Lorraine's voice dragged her from her inner thoughts as she arrived back at the campsite to see that Dominicus and Lorraine had everything set up. Draeven was laid back with a bowl of something in his hands as he talked quietly with Dominicus. But Lazarus was nowhere to be seen. Draeven caught her looking his way and silently shook his head. "Dinner is ready."

"Thanks," Quinn said absently as Lorraine led her over to a spot by the fire and handed her a bowl of whatever was cooking in the pot.

Quinn sat, letting the bowl warm her palms for several moments before she started eating. The bowl was filled with meaty stew—Dominicus must have caught something. While a bit bland, Quinn didn't complain—she had gone far too many times without eating much at all to turn down perfectly good food.

As the moon rose higher in the night sky, the fire started to die down. Lorraine took their bowls and began cleaning while Quinn waited for Lazarus to return. When Dominicus turned in for the night, grunting as he rolled himself in his blankets, Quinn gave up and turned towards Draeven and Lorraine.

She bit her lip, wondering if she should voice her thoughts. She wasn't sure if they could be trusted, but then she wasn't sure what harm it would do if Lazarus knew she was asking about him. He probably already expected it.

Lorraine—surprisingly—was the one to draw it out of her. "If you think any harder on whatever is going on in that mind of yours, girl, you're likely to give yourself head pains."

Quinn sighed and scooted closer so that her side

was facing the fire as she turned and looked at the other woman. "What do you suggest, then?"

Lorraine shrugged as she worked. "Ask what you want to ask."

"No promises on the answers," Draeven said.

Quinn shot him a look and he winked at her, earning one of her signature scowls. "How can I trust you won't go running off to Lazarus?"

Lorraine stopped what she was doing and turned to Quinn with an exasperated sigh. "That's *Master* Lazarus," she snapped. "How many times must I—"

"You don't know," Draeven interrupted in answer. Quinn glanced his way. Once he had her attention, he shrugged and leaned back, watching her curiously. "But we don't tell Lazarus everything. That would just piss him off if we went running to him about every little detail."

"This is about him," Quinn said.

He shrugged again. "And? What do you want to know?"

"Why do you follow him?"

There was a brief moment of silence. Neither of them appeared shocked by her question, however. Lorraine was the first to answer.

"Master Lazarus has been good to me," she said simply.

"How so?" Quinn asked.

"He brought me into his household when he

didn't have to. Paid off my debts. He's putting my boy through school."

"So, he's bought your loyalty, then," Quinn deadpanned.

Lorraine's eyes flashed with something akin to anger. Draeven didn't say anything, but his shoulders stiffened slightly.

"Money bought my services," Lorraine said quietly. "I work for him for compensation, but he did not have to do everything that he has for me. He didn't have to help my family or give us asylum."

"Asylum?" Quinn frowned. "What——"

"We all have our secrets," Lorraine interrupted. "Your curiosity does not entitle you to answers, just as we aren't entitled to yours."

She was right. Quinn nodded her understanding as Draeven spoke up.

"Lazarus is a complicated lord," he said, securing her attention once more.

"How long have you been with him?" she asked as Lorraine moved away.

Draeven blew out a breath, leaning back and staring up at the tree tops. "That's a good question. I'd like to say forever, but I know that at one point in my life there was a time when I didn't know him. It's just been so long now that I can't recall it."

"How did you meet?" Quinn prompted.

Draeven laughed. "I was dancing with Mazzulah when Lazarus found me," he said, his eyes carrying him away to a far-off place that Quinn couldn't see. "He yanked me up by my bootstraps and pulled me away from the hangman's noose. He handed me a sword, and with it, a purpose. I never knew how much I needed it until later," he paused. "I still follow him because he still gives me that. That's what keeps us going when times are not well."

"Purpose?" Quinn repeated, frowning in confusion.

Draeven nodded. "He's not a good man, I know that. But he's not evil, either. Lazarus is my friend and my lord. He is the wielder, and I his weapon."

"You follow him to let him use you?"

"Everyone uses someone, Quinn," he said, his eyes slowly refocusing as he tipped his head back down and looked at her across the fire. "I follow him because I trust him. Lorraine follows him because she trusts him. He has proven himself to be a leader worth following. Not to you. Not yet."

When Quinn expected him to go on, he merely stood up and patted her shoulder, eliciting a jerk from her as she leaned away. He sighed. "Go to sleep, Quinn. We have a long ride into the mountains tomorrow," Draeven said as he ambled away, heading for his own mound of blankets.

Quinn sat there, staring into the heart of the fire as the rest of them fell into slumber.

The birds were silent. The night creatures of the forest were quiet. And finally, Quinn gave up on waiting for Lazarus to return from wherever he had disappeared to. She crawled beneath her own blankets alongside Lorraine and stared upward as she willed her mind to shut off. But it wouldn't. It continued to circle that one word—trust.

Trust Lazarus. Trust him and follow him. How could she when she didn't even know who he was or what he was capable of? As Quinn finally felt herself slipping into oblivion, she wished she could use that field of vision of hers to see inside Lazarus—to know if he was someone deserving of her trust.

The Hand that Feeds

"Darkness is far more powerful than light, and far more destructive if not controlled."
— *Lazarus Fierté, nobleman, murderer, dark Maji, and keeper of secrets*

H e woke before day break, lulled from his sleep by the sweet torment that was *her*. She slept on the opposite end of the fire as him, the absolute farthest place away. Yet the scent of her still called to him, even in his sleep.

Lazarus sat up, his actions silent as he rose to his feet and began to move through the camp, to the forest beyond in a vain hope of escaping her, of outrunning what he knew in his blood was beginning to become an obsession. A raw need. A dangerous desire.

He ran a hand down his face, wiping the sleep from his eyes as he inhaled a fresh breath of air. Even here, her magic tinged the air. It whispered of sweet promises, delicious dreams and so many things wicked. Today was going to be another rough one, riding so close to her, all while keeping the distance that they both needed him to—not that she realized it yet.

For as much as she saw, in this, she was completely oblivious.

The branches shifted behind him as his left-hand's not-so-silent footsteps followed. "Having trouble sleeping?" Draeven asked quietly.

"Always," came his reply. And he did. The whispers were usually restless when he was away from home, but never like this. Now they were stirred into an outright frenzy, and the cause was a silver-haired woman with far too much mystery under her flesh.

"This is worse than normal," Draeven remarked, approaching his left side.

"Do you have a point?" Lazarus asked, blunter than he usually was.

The other man shook his head and sighed in exasperation. "It's the girl, isn't it?" Lazarus didn't respond immediately; he didn't need to. Draeven sighed again and nodded into the hazy gray. "It's the girl."

"She's different," Lazarus said after a heavy pause.

"She's deranged," Draeven replied distastefully. "Or if she's not, then she soon will be. They always are." Lazarus shook his head.

"No," he said, looking to the canopy of trees, replaying the web of fear she'd created in his mind all over again. "It's more than that. She's like me."

"She's a dark Maji—"

"It's more than that," Lazarus repeated, harder this time. His left-hand only stood there and waited for him to continue. "I've met other dark Maji, Draeven. Ones that are sane. I'm telling you, there is something about her that calls to me."

The blond-haired man seemed to weigh his words. "Have you considered that it's because she's the darkest you've met? There's only one magic that is naturally darker than a fear twister. Maybe she calls to you because she is the closest you have found both in sheer power and absence of light."

He had considered it. He'd considered it many times. Had gone so far as to assume that's what it was. That answer didn't explain all things, though—only the surface questions brimming in his mind.

"I don't wish to consume her," he said so softly that Draeven almost missed it. The answering look told him both too much and too little.

"I don't think you can," Draeven responded. "She's highly untrained, but the things she can already do…" He shook his head. "I think it would destroy you both if you even attempted something as dangerous as that. It would be like trying to control a storm. A wicked, impossible storm."

Lazarus nodded because he suspected as much as well. Never in his time had he come across one he didn't think he could take, but that was no longer the case.

"Her magic would drive me to the brink of insanity. Even if I wanted to, I won't," Lazarus said, thinking again of that web. He hadn't lied when he said Maji could see other's magic, but he hadn't told the full truth either. Most magic was completely invisible to the eye, unless wielding it at dangerous levels.

Quinn's very footprints were like blackened soot. The darkness she kept inside her bled out into the tangible world, because even now, before her ascent, the sheer power she was holding in wasn't meant to be contained. It was meant to be set free, but the liberation of something that untamable would cause too much damage.

He didn't think that Draeven or other Maji could see it quite that clearly yet, but if she continued at this rate it wouldn't be long.

"She doesn't see it, but one day she will be a force that the world will come to fear," Draeven replied, pulling him from his reverie. "My question remains for you, Lazarus, about what you will do then. If you cannot consume her, will you kill her?"

"I don't think it will come to that," he replied stiffly. Draeven laughed, a quiet mocking sound.

"Every ruler in this land is going to want her once they see what she can do—and you," Draeven kept his voice down but the inflection of urgency was there. "You are bringing her right to them."

"We're not going to any of the countries that might sway her loyalty," Lazarus replied, quite sure of himself.

"You don't currently have her loyalty to sway," Draeven answered testily. Lazarus shot him a look, one that shared the worries he wouldn't speak of. "I think you know that."

"The contract she and I have would not allow her disobedience to me."

Draeven snorted, a sound of derision.

"The Cisean people are too old-fashioned and won't endear themselves to her, and it will make it easier to gain her trust before we reach Ilvas," Lazarus replied dismissively.

"You hope," Draeven said, not backing down. "Thorne has a soft spot for pretty things and wild girls, both of which are qualities she possesses."

"I'm not concerned about Thorne," Lazarus retorted.

"Then what are you concerned about?" Draeven asked. The violet of his eyes flashed a shade more indigo as a streak of rage ran through him. For all his pleasantries and easy-going nature, Lazarus' left-hand was still as much bound to his brand of magic as he and Quinn were.

Lazarus didn't know how to answer. Not when he couldn't put what he was contemplating into words. Not when he didn't understand it himself.

"Nothing," he said eventually. "Nothing that has to do with the plan."

Draeven snorted. "Come now, Laz, even I don't buy that. Like it or not, this girl is part of the plan now. You made sure of it." The sun began to peek over the horizon, the dingy gray of an early fog turning blue. "And just as I watch you, I'll keep an eye on her too. Not that it should be too hard with how much she complains."

A ghost of a smile graced Lazarus' lips as they watched the sunrise together.

"Thank you, Draeven."

"Always, my friend." He turned to leave, patting Lazarus on the shoulder. "When you're ready to talk about it, I'll be here."

Lazarus stood there for another few moments before returning to camp. All were up except for Quinn. As usual, she was passed out stone-cold, a sheen of sweat dampening her skin as she slept fitfully. He wondered then if it wasn't just him that had been sleeping so poorly in the other's presence. Or perhaps she always slept that way. It was difficult to tell.

When they finished packing, Lorraine finally shook her awake, quick to move out of the way as

Quinn bolted upright, her fists at the ready. It was the same routine for over a week now, and as the woman climbed to her feet, still in a haze, Lazarus looked to his left-hand.

Draeven was too kind to be the right.

But Quinn … she wore cruelty like a crown.

Yes, he thought to himself. *When the time comes, she will be my right.*

It was just a matter of getting them there without her killing anyone she wasn't supposed to, which some days, was harder than it sounded.

A Bird's Feather

"Always take heed of dark dreams, for they are windows into places you have already gone but have no wish to return to."
— *Quinn Darkova, former slave, fear twister, and vassal of House Fierté*

With her eyes closed and the feel of Bastian's jerking footsteps beneath her, Quinn sent out a quick pulse of invisible power. The male body behind her stiffened. Apparently, it wasn't nearly as invisible as she'd hoped, but Lazarus didn't say anything. She could sense the horses and only two of their riders—Quinn frowned and glanced behind her. Perhaps Lorraine was too far back. Of the other two, she was able to discern that Dominicus had very little power and little fear, but the other one...

Quinn opened her eyes and glanced to Draeven as he turned to the weapons master just in front of them and said something too quiet for her to catch. She watched him silently, examining the way he sat in his saddle. Draeven was a tall man—not quite as tall as Lazarus—and not nearly as imposing. Perhaps it was because he was lighter, both in looks and disposition. Perhaps it was the way he seemed to blend with those around him, where like her, Lazarus stood apart. Different. Where Lazarus was a shadow man, Draeven walked in the light of day. While a pompous ass at times, she sensed a core of honor, one that Lazarus didn't possess. She wondered how they had come to be close, despite their obvious differences in every sense.

When Lazarus' steed whinnied at something, she jerked her gaze and her thoughts back to the present. Lazarus steered the horse up a narrower path into the foothills of the Cisean mountains. Quinn tipped her head back and stared up at the dark trees, the tops nearly black.

"Be on guard," Lazarus called ahead as Draeven moved to the forefront.

Lorraine fell in line just behind Dominicus and Lazarus took up the rear. Seconds crawled into minutes, minutes crawled into hours. Quinn adjusted in her seat as the feel of hard leather on her backside began to send jolting pains up her spine as every shift

of the horse's weight had her bouncing hard enough
to bruise.

They rode on—up into the mountains where the
soft buzzing noises of wildlife fell away. Sheer rock
and barren trees leaned over steep ravines. One
wrong step would send them hurtling down. Quinn
looked out over the edge as they climbed higher, but it
didn't make her heart beat any faster, nor did her
palms sweat. She simply stared into the abyss as tiny
pebbles fell from the rim. The sounds of them
bouncing off the rockface echoing up the gorge.

Too soon they were back on a wider path with
nothing but threadbare trees and miles of compact
dirt. Quinn eyed the path warily, growing bored until
the slight hum of other's fear pulled at her senses. She
blinked and eyed the three in front of her, finding
their apprehension both amusing and pleasantly
sweet. There was nothing up here, but they were
worried. She glanced down at the large hands holding
the reins. The three in front of her were worried.
Lazarus was unaffected.

"Do you hear that?" Dominicus asked, breaking
the silence. His gruff voice was low, a rumble of
thunder in his chest.

All eyes turned to him. "Hear what?" Lorraine
asked, confused.

"*Nothing*," he replied, his shoulders tight. "There's
no sound at all."

Ahead, Draeven slowed his mount and glanced

back. His gaze met Lazarus' for a brief moment as they all came to a slow stop along the path. Something passed between the men—an understanding of sorts.

"Let's stop and make camp before the day is completely gone," Draeven announced. Lazarus nodded towards a section where the trees split off slightly—just enough for the horses to pass through single file.

Unsheathing the sword anchored at his hip, Draeven drove it through the branches of the trees, marking a decidedly easier path for the rest of them as they moved into the gloom of the forest. The nature of this wood, however, was much different than the one they had slept in the night before. The air was dry, and the trees were barren. There was no hint of moisture or squish of soft dirt and decaying leaves. Only the occasional snap of a dried-out twig.

The absolute silence that Dominicus had pointed out was beginning to annoy her as they dismounted and began readying the camp. Silence meant broken bodies and deadly secrets. It was where the predators lurked, and where the stifling rules of religious propriety she'd been raised in hid the true evils of the world. Quinn herself had mastered the art of silence. The fact that the wood had as well made her take pause.

It wasn't natural, much like her. The flapping of wings and howl of the wind and rustling of the leaves

—that would have been normal. But this absence … this void … something was off.

Here, the sounds of their feet moving over dried leaves, Lorraine's quiet actions, Dominicus brushing the horses, and the sing of metal on metal as Draeven sheathed his sword—all seemed obscenely loud, like a beacon to whatever lurked in obscurity.

Those sounds slowly began to descend back into silence as they bedded down for the night, the sun falling away to make room for the rising moon. Unlike the day before, there was no practice, no jovial teasing from Draeven, no talking. They ate a bland vegetable stew and then crawled into their makeshift beds, all without any words between them. As if the sound of nothingness that rang in her ears was so loud it impressed itself upon them.

Quinn fell into a fitful sleep alongside Lorraine. Every breath, every snore, every shift that rubbed the material wrong—half startled her even as she slumbered.

Soft rain splattered across her face, drawing her eyes open. A droplet hit her cheek and slid down into her hairline. Another hit her chin. And another, her chest. It poured down on her like a purification ritual, washing away her thoughts, her sins.

Slowly, Quinn sat up, her mind in a thick fog. Her movements felt stilted—as if her limbs were tied to strings and those strings were being manipulated by someone else. She got to her feet on shaking knees, feeling weak and confused. That confu-

sion, instead of dispersing as she continued to get her bearings, only encroached more.

One look around had Quinn pausing. There were no horses. No people. This was no longer the clearing Quinn had fallen asleep in, though she was still in the same dark woods. She shuddered, reaching out, her fingers brushed against the heavy clouds of fog as she fanned the denseness of it away and stepped deeper into the forest.

There was a tether here, tugging her into the dark. The shadows closed around her—welcoming her into their arms. The trees fell away from her peripheral as Quinn's gaze fixed on what was in front of her, an opening cloaked in black ivy. She reached out to swipe the ivy aside. It dropped away, falling to the forest floor to reveal a door. She turned the knob and stepped forward as it swung open.

The soles of her feet touched something soft and slippery. Small granules stuck to them as she took a slow step forward. Quinn glanced down, only then noticing her boots had been removed. She couldn't remember taking them off. Then again, this wasn't the real world—this was the world of dreams—of nightmares—and the laws here followed no man's dictations. Not even hers.

The sand slid to the side with every step she took, but still Quinn strode forward, climbing the dune in front of her, leaving the forest behind. Hands out, Quinn latched onto rocks protruding up and out of the mound of sand and scaled upward.

Finally, there was a break in the silence—a sharp squawking. It was just over the top of the hill. Gritting her teeth, she *put a bare foot on one of the jutting rocks and used it to push her body the last little bit it needed to reach the uppermost point. Quinn's light head crested over the edge and her breath caught in her chest as the rest of this strange land came into view.*

Miles and miles of sand drifted off in every direction—swept away in some places to reveal dried ground with spider web cracks that raced away from each other, spreading out like the black veins of the plague. The sight was as strange as it was devastating. There was no vegetation, no forest, no life.

That noise sounded again, closer than before. Quinn's head turned until she caught sight of the only living thing in the vicinity. Pitch black wings fluttered as the bird attempted to take off, lifting several feet from the ground, only to come crashing back down with that terrified and frustrated scream of pain. Unsure of what exactly the creature was, Quinn clambered up and over the sand dune and slid down, narrowly avoiding the rocks peeking out from underneath the grainy sand.

She landed on the other side and slowly made her way over to where the bird flopped uselessly against the dry and cracked ground. As she neared, it began to flap its wings harder—terror widening its dark eyes as it attempted to flee. Fear, she sighed. It always came back to that. Any other time she might have turned around and left the animal to fend for itself since it didn't want her help, but something kept her bound in the path she had taken. Her legs moved without permission.

A flash of color caught her off guard and as Quinn bent low over the trembling, outraged creature, she noticed a streak of silver in its feathers. A single strand of mercury among the sea of obsidian black. She reached out and brushed a finger over the feather, earning a shriek from the animal as it squirmed away.

"I'm not going to hurt you," Quinn snapped with irritation. The bird froze and regarded her with disbelieving, but intelligent eyes. Quinn blinked. "Can you understand me?"

The bird tilted its small head by way of answer. Quinn couldn't determine if it had responded or if she imagined it.

Cupping her hands under the animal, Quinn nudged it into her palms and lifted it up to her chest. Trembling, it let out an undignified cry that she ignored as she searched the animal's feathers and limbs for whatever kept it from flying.

When nothing could be found, Quinn huffed and put the bird back down. "There's nothing wrong with you," she said.

Flapping its wings, the bird tried to take flight once again but couldn't. One wing sat stiffly, hardly moving as if it were heavier than the other, and the bird fell in an awkward heap at her feet.

Hands on her hips, Quinn stared down with pursed lips. What is wrong with it? *she wondered. Its wings were unbroken. Its legs were fine. When its head lifted, though, she noticed it tilt in one direction. Quinn squatted down, and it seemed less inclined to squawk indignantly this time. Instead it remained still as she lifted its wings and spanned them out, touching them with gentle probing fingers.*

She focused on the silver-white feather—the pretty spot of color in the otherwise ink-colored down was warm, but the rest of the animal was cold. Quinn didn't pause to think what that might mean, or why that single silver feather was different. She reached out, locking two fingers around the base of it and pulled.

At first, the feather resisted its removal, but with a second hard yank it came free. The bird let loose an ear-splitting scream and launched into the sky. Quinn stared down at the silver feather in her fist as it circled above her head, free to ride the winds at last. The feather was so much heavier than it should be, but nothing other than its weight gave her the impression that it was anything more than what it resembled.

With another loud shriek that drew Quinn's attention, the bird shot upward several dozen feet and exploded. Gasping, Quinn fell to her backside and gaped as a creature rose out of that plume of feathers that danced on the breeze. The thing that came forth from the animal's skin was immense. Its wings spread across the dull sky—darkening everything in sight for a mere blink of a moment. Black smoke rose from its outstretched limbs as the bird's beak opened and lifted upward in a silent cry to the wind.

Then, with a sharp turn of its head, the bird's eyes locked on Quinn. They were no longer as black as the pitch of its wings. Instead, they were crimson—the color of freshly spilled blood. The creature—not a bird, but an animal from beyond— tucked its smoking feathers close and fell... no, Quinn realized, it's diving.

Quinn scrambled backwards, rising to her feet a split second before the ground beneath her disappeared, crumbling beneath her bare soles as the black force she had freed swept under her, lifting her to the wind. Those terrifying red eyes peeked back as Quinn's hands clung to its form, wisps of darkness rising between her fingers.

The animal seemed to be trying to tell her something, though she couldn't understand what and would never know because in the next instant, the creature pivoted dumping her into the vast opening below. Quinn fell down, into the abyss of nothing, panting and clutching the only thing she could. The silver feather.

"Wake up." Quinn was jerked away from her fall by the sound of a low familiar voice hovering over her. She tensed, ready to throw Draeven across the clearing for coming so close, but he merely leaned in and whispered, "I wouldn't do that."

Indignation rose in her, trailed by a chilling calm as once more the silence of the forest drew her attention. It wasn't a total quiet, because something was off. Something was *here*. Draeven's eyes weren't on her and Quinn turned her gaze to the side.

"They're here," he whispered, rising to his feet. His hand went to the hilt of his sword just as Dominicus rose from his bed, moving to wake Lorraine from her sleep before he stepped in front of her.

"Get ready," Draeven commanded as dark figures began to step out of the forest, large and imposing.

Something fell from Quinn's grasp as she reached for the dagger under her cloak. When she looked down, a spot of silver flashed in her vision, surprising her. A single feather, as silver as the hair on her head.

Into the Mountains

"If you turn your back on those who would stab it, you deserve sweet death—for you were too gullible in life."
— Quinn Darkova, former slave, fear twister, vassal of House Fierté

A low hum of voices rose into the air, chanting in an intelligible language that Quinn had never heard before as the dark figures circled them. Magic thickened the air as they came out of the trees, gliding into the early morning fog. Draeven shifted, turning his back to her as he raised his sword. Quinn rose to her feet, the brief flash of silver—the feather—now gone as she reacted to the danger in their midst.

"Who are they?" she asked, lifting her voice so that it carried over their chanting. She turned, her back touching Draeven's as they both took in their enemy and found themselves far outnumbered. The figures were sturdy, masculine bodies, every one of them built to be the size of monsters. They were either at Lazarus' height or taller, Quinn noted.

Thick furs lined their chiseled chests and legs. Each of them wore what appeared to be a mask—*no, those aren't masks.* They wore skulls with the jaws unhinged, and the pelts of dead animals trailing behind them as cloaks.

"The Ciseans," Draeven said as the largest of the group lifted a horn to his lips and blew. A great echoing battle call sounded, and men fell into formation, the first circle around them going to their knees and extending their halberds as one. The next circle of men stepped up behind them, and the third row stood slightly behind, waiting for their command.

The man with the horn lowered it from his lips, letting the sound ring in the empty air. His eyes shone a pale green through the wolf's skull adorning his head. When the note stretched out so long it blended in with the silence of the woods, he spoke.

"*Eum chaka riek faerr mar,*" he called out.

"Um…" Quinn glanced back over her shoulder at Draeven. "What did he say?"

"Don't know," Draeven muttered, cursing himself. "I don't speak Cisean."

Quinn groaned. "Please tell me someone does, because wolf boy over there looks like he might be hungry, and I am not excited about being someone's dinner." As soon as she said it, a second voice called out. One from beyond the clearing, at the edge of the trees. The mountain men turned as one, toward the voice Quinn knew.

"*Hayr chaka vurd kaeverkn!*"

They parted before him, each ring of men peeling back to make a gap just large enough for him to come forward and stand before the man in the wolf pelt. Phrases were exchanged back and forth between the two while Quinn and the others stood by, tensely waiting for a verdict. Lorraine had risen and was tucked halfway behind Dominicus as the other man held his sword at the ready, waiting for the moment things would turn sour. *If* they turned sour.

Lazarus spoke, relaying information about their group. A short pause followed and then the man spoke in a deep baritone. "Come with us."

The men kneeling rose to their feet and lifted their weapons, stepping back to allow Lorraine, Dominicus, and Draeven to pack. Quinn lifted an eyebrow at Lazarus, not lowering her knife even as the others stowed their own.

"Put it away," he murmured to her, warm fingers wrapping around her wrist to force her to lower the blade. Her arm stayed locked, the metal still pointed at the men with the halberds, even if they had stopped pointing them her way.

"And get stabbed in the back?" she asked, incredulity leaking into her voice. "No, thank you."

"Quinn——" Lazarus started with a growl. His midnight eyes flashed with something heated that she couldn't place before the man in the wolf pelt stepped forward.

"Little she-wolf," he interrupted. Quinn tilted her chin and turned her crystalline eyes on him, letting him see the darkness that she often tried to hide. His pale green eyes held more warmth than she expected for someone who seemed ready to kill them only moments ago. "You protect pack fiercely," he said, nodding with respect and approval before turning and speaking to the other Cisean warriors.

Quinn looked pointedly at Lazarus and a muscle in his jaw twitched. She smirked to herself, lowering her knife to her side, but not stowing it. "What happened to you behaving?" Lazarus asked, just as Draeven walked up.

"They have halberds and wear the skulls from beasts larger than I. Going anywhere with them unarmed is asking to be murdered, and I'd deserve it were I naïve enough to do it," Quinn replied, turning on her heel to take a headcount of the possible assailants.

Lazarus may be willing to lower his weapon, but I won't be swayed so easily. Behind her, she heard them whispering. Draeven's voice raised slightly as he said, "She's going to get us all killed."

Quinn drifted farther, ignoring them as she came to a stop beside Bastian. The horse snarled and moved closer to the wild men just to be away from her. Quinn wrapped her free hand in his reins and pulled him up short, the early start and adrenaline running through her system shortening her already explosive temper.

She heard Lazarus' reply as she forced his steed to submit to her. "Possibly."

She frowned to herself while hooking the toe of her boot in the stirrup. If the last two weeks had taught her anything, it was how to mount a horse, and she did. Knife in one hand and reins in the other, she grabbed the lip of the saddle and hoisted herself up and onto the great beast. It reared back once, and Quinn dug her heel in its side, clicking her tongue between her teeth.

Bastian, for as much as he might hate her, yielded.

Quinn turned a fraction to look at Lazarus. To see the shadow of a grin on his face, even as he tried to hide it from them.

"Come," the man in the wolf pelt said again. Quinn didn't break eye contact with Lazarus as he strode forward and mounted behind her. The heat of his body was like a wildfire contained in flesh, even beneath his trimmed tunic and trousers. She wondered briefly what it might be like to coax that fire out. To see what darkness he was hiding…

Bastian shifted with unease as the men with

halberds began to move, pulling Quinn from her thoughts of the body behind her.

They delved deeper into the woods, off the trodden path, leaving her no choice but to follow.

Chin held high and knife gripped tightly, Quinn held the reins with one hand and led them into the forest, not knowing if they would come back out.

THEY RODE THROUGH THE MORNING, TILL THE SUN was high in the sky, before the mountain men slowed to a crawl. Trickling water sounded in the distance, growing to a dull roar as they turned the corner of the rock face they walked along.

A spray of white water rained down between two large boulders, hitting the flat stone beneath it and flowing out into a gentle stream that ran down the mountain and through the dead trees. One by one the warriors stepped through the waterfall and didn't come back out.

"What are they doing?" she asked as the man with the horn approached them. Hours later, she still held her knife in her sweaty palm and the man took notice. His pale eyes gleaming with something foreign that she didn't understand.

"You come," he said, gesturing for them to get down. Lazarus moved first, sliding from the horse and stepping towards the waterfall. The man with the wolf pelt waited, offering her his hand. She ignored it and swung her leg over, loosening her hold on the reins as she fell two feet and landed on the hard ground. It was just as jarring as all her dismounts had been, but she didn't feel as if she'd topple sideways at any moment. Guiding Bastian with one hand and holding tight to her weapon with the other, she followed after Lazarus who looked irritated that the Cisean warrior had offered her assistance.

One corner of her mouth turned upward as she swaggered forward and came to a stop beside him. Lazarus' eyes swept from her to the other man, the one who watched her without wariness or fear.

"Go there," he said, pointing to the waterfall.

Lazarus grabbed her wrist holding the knife and pulled her forward with him to the edge where the ground turned soft and a slight mist of crisp water splattered her face. She leaned forward, squinting into the darkness behind the falling water.

The hand at her wrist jerked as Lazarus stepped through the onslaught, pulling her with him. Quinn let out a yelp at the sudden cold, glaring at him as he continued leading her forward, trudging deeper into the cave they'd found themselves in.

"You could have warned me," she snapped, pulling at her wrist. Lazarus stopped, turning to tower over her.

"You saw them go through just as I had," he replied. She pursed her lips.

"And dragging me around like a savage?" she asked, her voice rising an octave, causing the two warriors in front of her to turn.

"If you consider this to be *dragging*, keep playing games with the boy behind us and find out what happens," he answered, the words fixed with a slight growl. Quinn narrowed her eyes, her lips parting as the spluttering curse behind them signaled Draeven's arrival.

Lazarus dropped her wrist and motioned for her to go first.

Quinn muttered an N'skaran curse under her breath and strode deeper into the cave. *No ... this is not a cave.* She looked up the cavern walls that would be too dark to see if it were truly a cave, following it down farther to the very end where two of the masked men stood. Waiting.

Light poured in from behind them. *We're in a tunnel...*

They stepped to the side as she approached, and her knife came up. A warning of what she'd do if they tried anything, but they simply stood there as she stepped out into the light of day.

The breath she'd been holding finally exhaled out of her lungs as she took in the nettles on the forest floor that came from the most towering of trees. They stood tall, so tall she had to crane her neck back to even see the tops. The green leaves and bursts of color were jarring.

Her jaw dropped as she stared up at the dwellings that sat in the trees.

She'd heard stories of the Cisean mountains. Stories of savage men who brutalized any and all they came across. Whispered words of what one might find were they to enter these mountains without the tribe's consent.

She didn't expect to find such beauty inside of the mountains. She took note of her surroundings as sunlight spilled through the breaks in the leaves, shining down on her. Laughter snapped her to attention as two boys and a young girl came climbing down the rope ladders she hadn't noticed and proceeded to run through the forest barefoot without a care in the world.

That was until a woman leaned over the railing, high above. Her red hair spilled over her shoulders, framing a lovely face that was flush with exasperation as she called out in a foreign tongue. The children came to a stop and looked over at Quinn.

Two seconds was all it took and they bolted through the trees, out of sight.

"Come," said the voice behind her. The pale-eyed warrior made no move to touch her as he fell into step at her side. Another presence, one of darkness and burning fires came up on her other side. She didn't need to look to know who was there.

"She-wolf has name?" the man asked. Quinn

smiled to herself, and just because it would piss Lazarus off, she gave it.

"My name is Quinn. What's yours?"

"Vaughn," he answered with a nod, his full lips coming up to smile back at her. Even with the skull of a wolf on his head, she found it charming. Enough to stow her dagger as they walked through the winding path of the forest floor.

They came to a stop beneath a tree that had a base as wide as she was tall. "We go up," Vaughn said.

"What about the horses?" she asked, wariness in her reply. He smiled and it was almost boyish.

"Borsht and Hakt take care."

"Alright," she replied, dropping the reins. Lifting her knife to her teeth, she bit down on the edge and reached for the rope. No matter how nice Vaughn might seem, she wasn't taking chances with whatever waited at the top of this ladder.

Ignoring Lorraine's muttered displeasure of her manners, Quinn started climbing and didn't stop till her hands gripped the edge of a wooden floorboard. She curled her fingers around, hauling herself over the edge. Her leg came up and as soon as her boot found purchase, she rose to her feet.

Two eyes—as red as raksasa demons—looked back.

She pulled the dagger from her teeth.

"Who are you?" she asked, striding forward into

the large room. Warriors stood at either side of what she could only call a throne. A sapphire rug covered most of the wood past the door she'd entered through. A woman dressed in furs was sprawled across the lap of the man sitting on the throne, without a worry or care.

Quinn wrinkled her nose in distaste, focusing on the brawn of a man with long orangish-red hair and a beard woven in braids. He wore furs like the group that surrounded them, but his mask—if it could even be called that—was not that of any ordinary creature.

It was the skull of a dragon, and he didn't wear it on his head, but mounted it on his wall. The man clicked his tongue and said, "I am Thorne, leader of the tribes that guard the Cisean mountains." He patted the girl's thigh and she slipped off his lap, not offended in the slightest. She slid to the floor and walked across the room out of the only open door Quinn could see, and onto the deck that overlooked where they'd just come from. He rose to his feet and came to stand before her, a full two heads taller with fists as large as her face. "Who are you?" he asked.

Quinn opened her mouth to reply when another voice cut her short.

"This is Quinn," Lazarus said by way of greeting. "She's a member of my house."

He didn't say more than that as the red-eyed man watched him.

Apparently, he didn't need to.

"Lazarus Fierté," the man said in a booming

voice. "My old friend." He smiled as Lazarus strode forward, stepping in front of Quinn so the King could clap him on the back.

Two things became startlingly clear to her in that moment.

The first—whoever Thorne was—he was the reason they were there.

And the second—by the look in their eyes—Thorne and his other warriors had taken a keen interest in her. One that Lazarus was obviously not alright with, if his gritted teeth and tense shoulders were any indication. Judging by the gleam in Thorne's eyes when he looked at Quinn, the Cisean man saw it too.

Though he attempted to disguise it with his distance as he took a step back from Quinn, Lazarus was fooling no one. Least of all himself.

Necessary Friendships

"There are no true friends, only great allies and even greater enemies."
— *Quinn Darkova, former slave, fear twister, vassal of House Fierté*

"Leave us."

Whether it was in deference to his guests or simply because he felt like it, the Cisean leader, Thorne, abandoned the use of his language completely and slid into a heavily accented Norcastan tongue as he returned to his seat.

The warriors nodded in unison and exited the room quietly and efficiently. "Not you, Vaughn." The pale-eyed warrior paused on the threshold and looked back. "Take Joachim with you and please allow my friend's vassals to assist in preparing a place for them to stay."

Vaughn cast a glance at Quinn as he nodded, but it wasn't Quinn that moved when Thorne turned an expectant eye on Lazarus. "Lorraine. Dominicus," Lazarus said. "Follow him."

They nodded, trailing after Vaughn as he finally left what had become clearer to Quinn was the Cisean leader's throne room. A heavy silence lingered around them. Draeven kept his gaze sharp and trained forward on the large man. Red eyes slid over Quinn. She didn't flinch away but met them head on which seemed to amuse Thorne a great deal.

"You've brought me some interesting entertainment, Lazarus." Thorne turned his demonic ethereal gaze to Lazarus as he spoke. "We didn't expect you for several weeks. You had my men in an uproar."

"Our plans had to change," Lazarus replied stiffly. "I apologize for the inconvenience—"

Thorne waved his hand, cutting Lazarus off. "Please, my friend. I am not like your aristocratic kin. No apologies necessary." A smirk stretched his lips. "However, had you not been recognized by Vaughn, things may have turned very bad for you. You are lucky."

"I will be sure to give him my thanks," Lazarus replied. Quinn didn't believe he would, not for a second.

Thorne nodded, shifting in his seat as he perused

Draeven and then Quinn. "I recognize your left-hand, but the girl is new."

"As I said before"—Lazarus leveled Thorne with a look—"she is a member of my household."

Thorne nodded. "Yes, you did say that, but what kind of member I am wondering." His smirk turned roguish. "Has the great dark heir been tamed?"

If it were possible, Lazarus stiffened even further. Quinn frowned as she observed them, curiosity tickling the fringes of her mind. But instead of the abrupt or rude comment she expected from Lazarus, he took a deep breath, the tension in his shoulders releasing all in one go, and with it the tension in the room fizzled out as well.

"A cad as always, Thorne. She is a new vassal. Nothing more."

Quinn lifted an eyebrow but said nothing.

Thorne nodded, the grin still on his face as he turned towards Quinn. "And does this new vassal speak at all?"

"I speak well enough," Quinn said, "when I have something to say."

Lazarus shot her a look that she ignored in favor of focusing on the man before her. Thorne rose from his seat once again and moved forward. "You are an interesting one, aren't you? And you are obviously not from Norcasta." He reached for a lock of her hair, his fingers just a mere breadth away from a long silver strand when a dark, tanned hand locked around his wrist.

Quinn blinked, turning her gaze away from Thorne and up to Lazarus as he invaded her space. "My vassal does not like to be touched, Thorne."

On the other side of Lazarus, Draeven's mouth hung open for a brief moment before he snapped it shut and controlled his features once more. "Protective, hmmm?" Thorne didn't seem offended as he tugged his hand away from Lazarus' grip.

"It's not me he's protecting, sir," Quinn said pointedly with a small smile.

"Oh?" Thorne looked her over curiously. "You think he means to protect me?" Behind the Cisean leader's back, Draeven's eyes widened as he shook his head rapidly at Quinn.

"Well, he doesn't mean me."

Thorne blinked, the smirk dropping from his lips before he burst into laughter. Lazarus glared at her with a silent promise of a later scolding. Quinn didn't care. She'd rather get it from him than Lady Manners any day.

"If that's the case, then you'll have to watch out, my friend. Your vassal—Quinn, was it?" He turned his eerie red eyes back on her and she nodded. "Quinn is a very beautiful woman and you know how my warriors feel around beautiful women."

"Oh?" Quinn stepped forward, once again ignoring Lazarus even as, this time, he put his hand on her arm, intent on holding her back. "And how do they feel about beautiful women?" she asked.

Thorne laughed again. "They are just as protective over their women as your master seems to be of you, little one. Because I can assure you that he is not necessarily thinking with his larger mind and therefore, he cannot be thinking about me."

Quinn grit her teeth at his arrogance and shrugged off Lazarus' hand. "I can protect myself."

Thorne's laughter faded as he examined her—noting the way she held herself, apart and separate from the men, but still close enough as though she were an equal. She did not mind stepping in front of them or alongside them. With a sharp look to Lazarus, Thorne nodded at her. "I can see why you are so vigilant," he said.

"Quinn is of no concern to your men, Thorne. She is merely a vassal on a mission with me. If you are so inclined, I would like to start our treaty discussions."

Quinn glanced back at Draeven, confused, but the blond giant merely shook his head and nodded for her to take a step back. Although she bristled at being commanded, Quinn recognized that her being silent and not the point of interest made it easier to catalogue their interactions. She took a step back and let Lazarus approach Thorne.

Quinn's brows drew down low as Lazarus leaned forward and spoke to Thorne in a tone just low enough that she couldn't make it out. Thorne's head didn't move, holding still for a brief moment before he began to nod. "Of course, my friend, we can talk about that in more detail at the feast tonight."

Lazarus shook his head. "I'd like to discuss it now, if possible."

Thorne looked to Quinn and Draeven. Without turning, Lazarus spoke to them. "Draeven, take Quinn and join the others. I will be with you shortly."

"But—"

"Go, Quinn," Lazarus cut her off.

Draeven didn't waste any time. He had Quinn by the arm and was dragging her out of the treehouse hut before she could think of anything further to say to get him to allow her to stay.

"You have a death wish, don't you?" Draeven asked with exasperation.

"Of course not," Quinn answered seriously.

They strode along the pathways, over the bridges that had been strung up between the homes built into the sides of the large oaks. Several men, sans animal skulls, walked by. It didn't escape Draeven's notice that many stopped along the way and allowed Quinn to walk through, all the while giving him analyzing looks.

He snorted.

"What is it?" Quinn asked.

Draeven shook his head. "Lazarus has his work cut out for him, that's all."

Bargain's Struck

"In times of desperation, sacrifices must be made to ensure that the worst does not come to pass."
— *Lazarus Fierté, nobleman, dark Maji, collector of men*

Thorne watched as Quinn went with Lazarus' left-hand. "She's a wild one, that woman," he said as soon as they were out of earshot. "Her aura is rather untamed." Lazarus shot him a look and Thorne shrugged with nonchalance. "I'm just warning you now, my friend. I'd watch that one very closely if I were you. She's obviously unaware of the Cisean customs, especially for women. She might well be taken from you before you realize it."

"For all her faults, I doubt that Quinn is someone who goes back on her word and even if she wanted to forsake me, she has sworn a blood contract with me. Still, I will take your counsel into consideration," Lazarus said, careful to keep his words neutral and not let on how much the very idea of that got under his skin.

Thorne gestured towards an open doorway to the side of the small throne room. "Come, I'm sure you're thirsty after your long travels. Let us get a drink and then talk."

Lazarus nodded, following behind the Cisean leader as they strode into a separate portion of the treetop hut—a tiny room with a table and two chairs. His wife, Siva, entered, still dressed in her furs. Her long blonde hair spilled over her ample breasts, held up by a fur covering the Cisean's considered clothing. Lazarus said nothing as Thorne smiled warmly. "Get us a few ales, my love, would you?" She nodded, casting a curious glance at Lazarus before disappearing again.

Thorne groaned as he settled into his chair. "Alright, speak," he said. "What is it that you wished to see me about."

Lazarus sat back, steepling his fingers as he said, "Claudius is not well."

"Yes, and his blood heirs are sniveling children despite their age, with little to no knowledge of what it takes to lead a people," Thorne replied as Siva came back with two large mugs of amber liquid. She set them down on the table and leaned over to press a quick kiss to the Cisean leader's lips. She said something quietly in their native tongue and Thorne shot Lazarus a quick glance before nodding.

Lazarus lifted a brow as Siva left, and Thorne grinned around the rim of his mug. "Caught that, did you?" he asked, taking a long drink. "Seems it's already started."

"I will handle Quinn," Lazarus said through gritted teeth. "Do not worry."

"Oh, I'm not worried," Thorne said, his chest rumbling with barely suppressed laughter. "But it's even obvious to Siva that my warriors are very interested in your girl."

"Quinn and I hold a contract, regardless of who or what may interest her." Lazarus took a hefty breath, stopping himself from continuing before leveling the other man with a dark glare. "The matter at hand," he said, drawing them back on track.

Thorne sobered. "Yes, about your king. Proceed."

"Claudius is naming me as Norcasta's heir."

"That is what the people are telling me these days. What do his blood heirs think?"

"They're reasonably unhappy." Lazarus' expression didn't change as he relayed this information, which only seemed to amuse Thorne even more as he downed another gulp of his ale.

"Reasonably?" Thorne shook his head. "You only say that because it's exactly what you expected."

"Men like Claudius' blood heirs are predictable," Lazarus agreed.

"Aren't they, though?" Thorne leaned farther back in his seat. "But that still doesn't explain why you came here? And why so early?"

"I was attacked about a half a day's ride from Shallowyn two weeks ago."

"Oh?" Thorne's eyes settled and focused on Lazarus. "Did you leave anyone alive?"

Lazarus shook his head and looked away, glancing to the open doorway. "No."

"Hmmmm. Then you don't know for sure who sent them," Thorne deduced.

"I have my suspicions," Lazarus replied, "but it confirms something else."

Thorne nodded. "Your ascension to the throne will not be a simple and easy process."

"No." Lazarus moved his mug away and leaned forward. "I need friends at my back."

Thorne laughed again, but this time it was hollow. "You collect many things, Lazarus, but friends are not amongst them."

Lazarus stilled but didn't take his eyes away from Thorne. "No, but you do."

"That is very true." Thorne paused for a moment before draining his mug completely and then slamming it down on the table, dropping his voice as he propped his forearms on the rough table top. "And I'd be an idiot to not ally myself with the greatest dark Maji of our generation, wouldn't I?"

Lazarus stiffened, moving his arms back. "I wouldn't call myself that."

Mostly because he wasn't sure if a certain woman was actually the holder of that title.

"No?" Thorne tilted his head, his gaze fixated and serious. "Either way, I accept your offer of friendship. One cannot exist in this world without friends, not if you want to keep living. Whether you recognize that your vassals see you as their friend or not, that is what they see. They are loyal not to a future king, but to a friend and that is far more powerful than any skeev born into privilege could hope to attain."

Lazarus remained silent for several seconds. His head lifted, his dark eyes meeting Thorne's gaze. "Claudius' children are not without magic," he said quietly. "They still have the blood of a Maji running in their veins. They have an affinity."

Thorne scoffed, turning away. He reached for Lazarus' untouched mug and lifted it to his lips for a long pull. "I have met the bastards Claudius calls children. I have seen their auras. They are practically non-Maji, they are so weak."

"They will have many followers," Lazarus said.

"Non-Maji like them, I predict." Thorne looked down into the swirling amber liquid in the mug in his hand, watching as the bubbles circled the center.

Lazarus watched him for a moment. "Do you understand what I am asking of you, Thorne?"

With a sigh, the Cisean leader returned the mug to the table. "We will sign a treaty between our countries *before* you ascend," he replied. "When you become the next king of Norcasta, I will announce my alliance and support of your rule. That should help to quell the royal brats."

Lazarus shook his head. "No, Thorne. I am not asking that you ally yourself with Norcasta." Thorne frowned in confusion, his features smoothing when it finally occurred to him what Lazarus was really getting at.

"What is it that you're asking, my friend?" he questioned slowly.

"I am asking you to ally yourself with *me*. Should I rule Norcasta, your alliance entails the country, but otherwise—should things go ... badly—you will support me, as your friend."

Thorne scrubbed a hand down his face. "You do not ask for much, do you?" he said, sarcasm apparent. "You are strong, Lazarus. I give you that, but what else will my people get? I cannot offer you this level of *friendship* for free."

Lazarus grinned, a shock of teeth that looked more like a predator's warning than true amusement. "I would not ask anything of you for free, Thorne."

Thorne, as if unable to help himself, sat back. A weaker man might have fled. Lazarus had to admire his own choice in ally. The Cisean leader would be a great enemy for any man and therefore, a formidable friend for him to have in the near future.

"What are you offering?" Thorne asked, suddenly sounding far more tired.

"My own loyalty to your people, Thorne. I will take care of them as if they were my own. That, in itself, is a great price. Should you require aid—I come. Should the winters be rough—I will send provisions. Should you need *almost* anything to make this friendship agreeable—I will supply it."

Thorne scratched his chin and shook his head. "Gods, I hope you become king, Lazarus. Or else my people would think I was weak in agreeing to something like this so readily." Nevertheless, Thorne held his hand out and Lazarus reached across the table and took it in his own.

"Your people will realize that I am a far greater ally than an enemy," Lazarus said.

Thorne grimaced as they shook hands. "I don't doubt that."

"I will swear my fealty to you and you to me," Lazarus confirmed. "We will not be enemies, but … friends." His grin dropped as his lips curled back in discomfort.

Lazarus did not have friends. Not really. He had Draeven who was like a brother to him. His left-hand. His greatest ally. He had other vassals, servants and staff, but not friends. Then again, this was more than a friendship. It was an alliance. One that might save him his empire when the time came.

Thorne's booming laughter echoed in the small room once more. "You look as though you've eaten a bad choice of meat, my friend. Do not worry, I will not ask you to repeat it so much."

Lazarus pulled his hand away. "You may shout it from the rooftops if you prefer," he said. "It does not matter to me what you call our alliance so long as you keep your end of the bargain."

Thorne stood up from the table and Lazarus followed. "The Cisean people are a proud race. We always keep our promises."

Lazarus nodded and as they crossed the threshold heading through the hut back to the throne room, he spoke once more. "There is something else."

Thorne looked back over his shoulder. "Oh?"

"I have another purpose for coming so early," Lazarus said. "I need use of your springs."

"Is it for the girl?" Thorne asked.

"Yes." Lazarus kept his expression impassive as they entered the throne room. A warrior stood just outside the main doorway. Lazarus eyed him speculatively, but if he intended to trust Thorne with his country, he needed to learn to trust the man's intuition about his own people.

"If possible, I would like to request the use of a stone."

Thorne turned and settled back onto his heavy

throne, their conversation having come full circle. "I will require answers for something like that," he finally said.

Lazarus narrowed his eyes on the Cisean leader. "What are your questions?"

"The girl," Thorne stated. "What is she? What is her power?"

"She is a dark Maji," Lazarus said simply.

Thorne frowned, not pleased by his way of answering. "I am not stupid, Lazarus. Any Cisean can tell that her magic is dark. The power leaks off of her person, nearly blinding in its strength. I am asking *what* her abilities are. If you cannot give me this, I cannot give you a stone."

Lazarus grit his teeth, his mind working. In the pocket of his trousers, the paper he had given Lorraine crinkled against the fabric. He reached inside and pulled it out. "I require a specific stone." Lazarus strode forward and handed the paper to Thorne.

Unfolding the yellowed parchment with lowered brows, Thorne read the inscription. His eyes darted back up. "A Servalis stone? She must indeed be powerful if you need that."

"Do you have one?" Lazarus didn't let his gaze stray, but kept the other man locked.

Thorne nodded. "I do."

"If you give it to me, I will tell you what she is."

"Are my people at risk being near her, Lazarus?"

Lazarus finally turned his head, looking back at the warrior. "She is under my control. We have a contract," he reminded him.

Thorne scrutinized Lazarus' stance for a moment before exhaling with a heavy breath. "I'm not sure I would say that," he muttered. "But, she, at least, is easier to read than you. I will give you the stone for an answer. She is similar in power to you. Rare, I assume." Thorne narrowed his eyes, and Lazarus could see it then that he was wondering—if only for a brief moment—if she was the same as him.

No, he thought. *And thank the gods for that.*

Lazarus met Thorne's red-eyed stare. "Quinn is rare," he nodded. "She is a shadow in every man's mind. A nightmare—a thought that follows you into old age—always present, always there, hanging in the periphery of your consciousness." Thorne sat forward, curiosity urging him closer as Lazarus dropped his voice. In the barest of whispers, he told him. "She is a fear twister."

Feast of Fools

"Uncontrolled emotions are the bane of a survivor. They show weakness. They show desire."
— *Quinn Darkova, former slave, fear twister, and vassal of House Fierté*

"Gods above, I could live here," Quinn groaned, settling into the warm water. Her back hit the rocky edge as she lounged, resting her head on the ledge.

"We're here for business," Lorraine remarked, a subtle rebuke but not an outright one. Given this was the first hot bath she'd had in years, Quinn didn't particularly care. Even Lady Manners' griping couldn't ruin this for her.

"Whoever said you couldn't mix business with

pleasure?" Quinn asked, lowering herself deeper into the water and ducking under before Lorraine could reply. She ran her hands through her hair, massaging her scalp, while the scalding water nipped at her skin. Blissful.

A slender arm wrapped around her waist, pulling her up.

Her head broke water and she coughed a little, looking every which way for why Lorraine was spluttering in dismay. "Are you alright?" she asked, touching Quinn's head and turning it side to side. She pulled her to the ledge again, and Quinn let her.

"I'm fine," Quinn frowned. There was no one here, only them. Not even the Cisean women would enter the hot springs as long as Quinn and Lorraine were using them. So she didn't know what had the woman so concerned. "Lorraine?" she prompted, the older woman's incessant fingers poking and prodding.

"You were under for several minutes. I thought you might have hit your head…" Her voice trailed off, suddenly unsure. Quinn's lips parted, before the beginnings of a chuckle came that turned into an all-out roar. She was breathing hard and clutching her side when the laughter finally passed. Wiping her eyes, Quinn looked up at Lorraine who was not nearly as amused.

"I'm from N'skara," Quinn said by way of answer. When Lorraine still didn't get it, she continued. "We are raised on the water, Lorraine. Children are taught to hold their breath for minutes at a time from a young age."

"Oh." The older woman blinked, her lips parting. She glanced down at Quinn and then to her own naked body, as if the proximity had just occurred to her. She crossed her arms over her breasts and stepped back. The water swished to the side, echoing in the low cavern.

"It's alright," Quinn nodded. She grasped the edge of the hot spring and hauled herself out, basking in the warm steam of the spring, naked as the day she was born. "You didn't know." She reached up and pulled her hair to the side, wringing out the water.

"You're very forward with your body," Lorraine said, moving the conversation to safer waters instead of prying into her past.

"Modesty is for the privileged. When you're a slave, not even your body is your own anymore. Clothes are gifts, not rights." Her lips pinched together as memories welled up. Ones she still was not ready to think about, or to face. "My skin is a roadmap of where I have been and what I have done to survive. I won't be ashamed of it."

Lorraine regarded her differently in that moment. Not condemning or with exasperation, as she often did, but as if she saw Quinn in a new, changed light. A kinder one than the young N'skari woman would paint herself in.

A cough at the mouth of the cave drew their

attention. Quinn got to her feet and looked over as the woman from earlier—the one who laid splayed across Thorne's lap—stood by herself. She shivered when Quinn gazed at her with her cold eyes.

"My husband thought you might like warmer clothes," she called out, her Norcastan tongue far less broken than that of the warriors they'd encountered, but not so good as the man who ruled like a king. "They are gifts of friendship," she added.

Quinn watched her take a few steps in and lay the bundles of fur on a dry patch of the cavern floor. She looked at Quinn, admiring her form for a moment before smiling and walking away.

Quinn took a step towards the pile when Lorraine asked, "What are you doing?"

She hooked her thumb towards the pile. "Taking a look at our 'gifts'." Lorraine eyed the pile from the warm water of the spring while Quinn padded over, lifting up the scraps of fur. One was a slim looking top made of leather straps and scraps of fur that would cover her breasts but not her stomach or arms. Lorraine made a sound of dismay behind her which meant she wouldn't be wearing it.

Quinn fitted it to her breasts, slipping the line of trim over her head and hooking the second behind her back with the clever metal clasp they put on it. She leaned over, humming in content at the way her breasts stayed secure to her chest and warm while she could still move. Digging through the pile, she found undergarments, a second top, and two pairs of trousers lined with fur. Dressing quickly, she pulled on the smaller pair of pants, shucking her legs through the ankles. The fit was a bit tight, resulting in pants that fell just below her navel and were glued to her backside. She squatted down, stretching the material so she could move more easily.

"Master Lazarus will not approve," Lorraine said from the spring as she shook her head. Her thin lips pressed together in distaste, and Quinn only smiled as she reached down for one of the cloaks and clasped it around her shoulders.

"*Master* Lazarus," Quinn started, exaggerating his title to the point of mockery, "is the reason we're here and I don't know about you, but I don't want to wear the same clothes I've been wearing for the last week. Besides, it would be rude to not accept 'gifts of friendship'." She smiled and it was a vicious, wicked grin that it had Lorraine giving her a deadpanned glare to showcase her lack of amusement. "What would the people think?" she asked, unable to hide the glee in her voice to use Lorraine's own words from these last two weeks against her.

"Some days I wonder what he sees in you," Lorraine muttered as she lifted herself out of the spring. Despite her older age and temperament, she still had the body of a younger woman. Her skin was firm, healthy, and relatively unmarred from the malice of the world.

"Power," Quinn answered her simply. Lorraine paused. "Dark, terrible, savage power. That's what he sees." The other woman did well to try and hide her shudder, but Quinn felt that slight quivering of fear. It slid over Quinn's skin like a lover's kiss, begging for more. Lorraine wrung out her long brown hair and dressed in the second set of gifted clothing. Her shorter stature made the pants looser and they actually came up to the top fur covering instead of leaving a few inches of skin on display. She took the second cloak and pulled it tight, gathering up their dirty clothes before turning to Quinn, ready to leave.

It was only then that she responded. "That's not all he sees."

Quinn frowned and opened her mouth to ask her what she meant by that, but Lorraine was already walking. They stopped at the edge of the cave to put their boots back on before continuing onward, up the shallow hill where Draeven waited.

"Finally, you're—" He turned and froze, his eyes widening. "What are you wearing?" he asked, keeping his voice down so the two Cisean guards that stood a few feet away would not hear.

"Clothes," Quinn answered tartly. "That the Cisean's were nice enough to give us. You should be glad I'm not naked."

Lorraine choked on a cough beside her as Draeven ran a hand down his face, muttering to himself about *gods, let it be fast*. "You know what? We don't have time for this. We are late to the feast and they've started without us. If Lazarus has a problem, he can take it up with Thorne … or *you*." He stepped aside and motioned for them to move it.

"He better not take it up with me," Quinn protested as she led the way down the hill and onto the winding path of large oak trees.

"Oh, may the gods be merciful," Draeven muttered, redirecting her when she reached for the rope ladder of the tree hut they were staying in.

"What? Where are we——"

"I've just said. They're holding a feast in our honor, Quinn. Come on." He prodded her in the back, and she snapped. Quinn turned, bringing her fist up at the same moment and punched him square in the jaw.

"Ow!"

"Stop prodding me, bastard," she growled. The two Cisean warriors stepped up beside her, glaring at Draeven.

"She-wolf no like you touch," the one on the left said. Draeven rubbed his jaw, opening and closing his mouth.

"Quinn, can you explain to them I wasn't trying to hurt you?" Draeven asked, eyeing them warily.

"I most certainly will not," Quinn replied, turning on her heel. He reached out to stop her and the same one that had spoken stepped in front of her, while the other came up on her side to escort her forward.

They stayed like that, one walking beside her and one behind her as they led Quinn to the feast while Draeven and Lorraine trailed behind.

"She has a point, you know," Quinn heard Lorraine tell Draeven. "You shouldn't have prodded her like cattle. She's part of this house now."

Draeven's reply was lost in the noise as they approached a set of wooden steps that led up into a tree hut far larger than the others. Two guards stood on either side of the railing, halberds at their sides and pelts around their shoulders. They nodded to Quinn as she climbed the stairs to the very top. Where there should have been a door, only three walls and a thatch roof stood. The place for the door had been left open so that those seated could look out over the forest behind her.

Five long tables were filled to the brim with exotic fruits and stews and roasted meats. Most of the places at the tables were full, only a handful of seats had been saved at the center—the largest—where both the Cisean leader and Lazarus sat. The woman from earlier who had brought them clothes sat on Thorne's lap, ripping juicy meat from the cooked leg of a bird and feeding it to him with her fingers. She wasn't the only one, Quinn realized. Most women didn't have seats of their own, but instead lounged on the laps of their men, not a child in sight.

Thorne sat at the head of the table, with Lazarus on his right and the pale-eyed warrior, Vaughn, to his left. Beside Lazarus, the seats had been taken, the one closest occupied by a stunning beauty with hair the color of rubies. Quinn narrowed her eyes at the slight hand that touched his arm.

Quinn took a step forward, toward that side of the table and paused. A flash of anger ran through her as her stomach hardened, as though someone had poured cement down her throat and let it settle. Heat ran to her head. The rush making her woozy with power. It was that trickle of darkness that started to swirl around her and the creeping tendrils of a web being spun that made her pause.

She wavered on the edge as Lazarus looked up. His dark stare sliding from the beauty at his side to the tendrils of fear snaking along the table, straight to Quinn as she reached up and unclasped the cloak. It slid from her shoulders and she caught it with one hand before it hit the floor.

And his dark, midnight gaze … it burned.

The smallest of smiles sat on her lips as she pivoted and walked up the other side of the table. Vaughn jumped to his feet and pulled out the chair beside him. "She-wolf Quinn, sit by me," he said very seriously.

"Alright," she said, taking the open seat. Vaughn settled in on her left as Draeven took his seat on her right. No one helped him, though one of the warriors who'd escorted her did pull the chair out for Lorraine.

"I'm glad to see you joining us, Quinn," Thorne

said. His booming voice drew her attention, his red eyes unsettling. Quinn reached out, snatching the giant leg off the bird in the center of the table and grabbing a handful of crimson berries she hoped weren't poisoned.

"I'm a vassal of his Lord Fierté," she said. "Where else would I be? Hm?" She lifted a delicate silver brow before digging into the meat. She groaned with how deliciously juicy it was, not like the slave's portions she'd eaten most of this last decade that kept her painfully thin. They'd smoked the meat to bring out its natural flavors, seasoning it to perfection. Quinn took another large bite, then another—only stopping when she'd demolished the entire thing and picked the bone clean. She licked the juices from her fingers and paused, feeling eyes on her. Lorraine cleared her throat but remained passively scolding instead of vocally berating her.

"She-wolf Quinn has good appetite," Vaughn said, nodding in appreciation. She didn't miss the way his eyes trailed from her slick fingers to her mouth.

"You have no idea," Draeven quipped. Quinn turned to glare at him.

"*Black baac*," she cursed and rolled her eyes at his insinuations.

"Have you *seen* how much you eat?" he asked, his fork hitting his tray with a clang.

"Do you have to be such an ass?" she growled.

"Do *you*?" he shot back, picking at his own piece

of meat. Quinn narrowed her eyes, sending an inky dark tendril slithering up from her skin and down her arm toward him.

Draeven's eyes widened a fraction before he jumped up, hitting his chair so hard it slid back into the one three feet behind him.

"Quinn," Lazarus snapped. She froze, redirected the tendrils back to her, lifting her right hand where it wrapped around her. Comforting. Consoling. "What did we talk about?" he asked, a not-so-subtle reminder that she was supposed to be on her best behavior.

She turned, and her crystalline eyes were ice cold as she regarded him.

Or, more specifically, regarded the pale hand caressing his forearm.

She didn't understand why the sight of it bothered her. She knew that wasn't quite right … she understood. She just didn't like what it meant. Lazarus never let anyone touch him, not of their own accord. Not Draeven. Not Lorraine. Not even her.

Oh, he could touch and push and pull all he wanted, but kept his distance when it suited him. He stayed as far away from her as he could, at every possible chance, but here—*now*—he let this girl who was nothing … who was *no one*, touch him.

She knew there was a word for this slicing sensation through her chest and the heat that pounded in her blood, like he was there, even now, touching her without her permission.

But she didn't want it. She didn't want to feel it. She didn't want to give him any more than he already took.

And so, she shut it down. Closed it out and turned to the cold.

That was one embrace that she would always welcome, along with the clarity it bought her.

A hand reached to touch her, and she moved. Reacting on instinct, her upper half twisted, and her fingers came up, gripping the wrist of the offender in a vice.

Fear bloomed, like the most pleasant of flowers, its black tendrils stroking her senses.

She tilted her head and inhaled deeply.

Ahhh. This. This is what I need to take the edge away…

"She-wolf Quinn?" a voice asked, soft, gentle, and completely masculine. It didn't share that darkness with her that she wanted—needed. But it would do. For now, it would do.

She blinked. "Yes, Vaughn?"

"You okay?" he asked, and the expression in his eyes was nothing short of heartwarming. She didn't want to be warm though. She didn't want to feel this night, because then that emotion would sneak back up on her and into her heart. It would rip through all those barriers she kept, because she cared for nothing and no one but herself.

She didn't want that, but what she did want … her gaze strayed to that pale hand, still curled around

Lazarus' forearm. She followed that thick bicep up, along his taut chest, to the hard set of his jaw, and finally to those eyes. They might have blistered her if she hadn't cut herself off and slinked deeper into the cold.

As it was, she simply smiled. "Yes, I'm just fine."

Demons & Doorways

"Darkness is a dreadful gift ... and a sweet curse."
— *Lazarus Fierté, nobleman and dark Maji*

Lazarus clenched his teeth so hard that had he been less aware of it, they might have cracked. She'd gone cold, right before his eyes, colder than she'd ever been with him. He didn't like it—the way her magic pervaded the air and darkened the veins beneath her skin. It slithered up and down her arms like an animal protecting its master, ruthless in its quest to serve.

She wasn't fooling anyone, certainly not him, when she loosened her grip around the boy's wrist. She'd struck so sudden that the table went silent, though she likely hadn't noticed. Lazarus said her name twice, and still, she didn't respond. No, she responded to *him*. The boy that Thorne was enjoying putting in her path at every turn. The red-haired bastard leaned in, speaking low enough only Lazarus would hear.

"Just a vassal, eh?" He tilted his chin, giving Lazarus a pointed look before smiling to Quinn. She still had that look in her eyes, like a feral creature ready to strike. But she released Vaughn and patted his hand like nothing happened, and the table breathed easier for it. Never mind the terrible power she summoned without a thought and dissipated it just as easily.

"She and I have a contract," he reminded Thorne through gritted teeth. He suspected what caused the outburst when her gaze hovered on the pale hand that touched him and for the first time in a long, long time, Lazarus felt something almost like … unease.

A restless anxiety stirred in him when her cold calculated gaze had settled on the hand touching him. It was the same reason he went back to the alley the night she was attacked in Ishvat. No one knew—not Lorraine, not Draeven, and certainly not Quinn— that he ripped the boy who had touched her into little, tiny pieces, scattering his entrails with a dark satisfaction coiling in his gut. No one realized how dark, how deep his fascination—his obsession—with her was beginning to run. Except maybe Quinn herself.

None of them had realized why he had been in a hurry to get out of that town come morning. They'd all just been content, especially Quinn, with leaving.

But now ... he looked down and followed the trail to the beautiful woman on his arm.

Would Quinn do the same? he wondered, and he worried. This wasn't good. This wasn't how it was supposed to go. Claudius said she would make him the greatest empire this world had ever seen ... *or destroy him.* He'd heard the second half of the warning, all those moons ago, and it still hadn't stopped his search for her. It never occurred to him why she would give or take to begin with, only that she would.

"And where does she fall with this contract when you become king?" Thorne mused, just a fraction too loud. He saw it the moment the words registered. She'd been leaning into the boy, Vaughn, listening to whatever he told her when she froze and slowly lifted her cold eyes to his.

"King?" she asked, looking between them.

"Of Norcasta," Thorne nodded. For someone who was supposed to be his *friend,* he was doing a great job at dividing his vassal from him.

"King of Norcasta," she murmured, nodding to herself. "I suppose it all makes sense now."

Thorne leaned back, looking between the two of them. "He hadn't told you?"

Her answer was clipped and curt, and above all, cold. "No."

"I see," Thorne said slowly, facing Lazarus once more. "I assumed your vassals already knew of your intentions. My apologies if I've overstepped." Lazarus bit into a boysenberry, the usual tartness followed by sweet, lacking as he tasted nothing but ash.

"Oh, he tells me nothing," Quinn said. She took the goblet in front of her, not even looking at its contents as she downed it in one go. Lazarus grimaced as her face screwed shut.

"She-wolf Quinn?" Vaughn asked.

"Oh, for the love of—" Draeven muttered, finally taking his seat again.

"Water," she rasped. The boy, Vaughn, slid the plain cup on the other side of her plate towards her. Quinn sniffed it distrustfully before tasting a sip. Soon she emptied its contents and slapped it down on the table. "Thank the gods," she groaned, her eyes falling closed.

"What is it?" Lazarus asked, pulling away from the red-haired woman at his side.

"I don't drink spirits," she replied, her voice like ice. It chilled him to the core that she spoke to him like that and yet spoke nicely with the boy.

He gritted his teeth.

"Why not?" Draeven asked.

"You're not entitled to answers," she replied. "None of you are. Except maybe Vaughn." She patted his hand again, letting it linger, and Lazarus clenched his jaw. Her eyes fell closed once again and Thorne shot a quizzical glance between them.

The beat of drums filled the night as torches were lit, and the celebrations moved to the deck over-looking the forest below. Men lifted women, carrying them toward the drums, and the females laughed and smiled all the way. *How easy it must be to have one of those women*, Lazarus thought. *How boring.*

"… dance?" Lazarus turned his head, catching the tail end of conversation between Vaughn and Quinn.

"I don't dance," Quinn said, though there was a slight smile to her lips.

"You dance," the boy said, smiling at her like she was a warm fire in the dead of winter. But he didn't know. He didn't see her as she truly was.

Quinn wasn't sunshine and flowers. She was moonlight and shadows. Blood and bone. The edge of a knife, so beautiful and yet so sharp it would cut should you touch it without knowing how to handle its edge.

"I don't know how to dance like they do," she said, pointing to the couples that bounced and leapt and hollered into the night. "The way I was taught to dance is different."

Lazarus' lips twitched and his eyes narrowed a fraction as he caught those words. *Taught to dance … who would teach a slave?* Unless she wasn't always one. It occurred to him then how much he was learning about her tonight, these pieces of her that she was giving away to Vaughn so flippantly but wouldn't dare let Lazarus touch.

It infuriated him. Almost as much as when the boy leaned into her and said, "You show me?"

Quinn gave him a lazy smile that said the bastard had worn her down. "Alright, I'll show you."

Wood scratched against wood as they scooted their chairs back. Vaughn got to his feet first, holding out a hand. Quinn took it in hers, and even though she wore a smile on her face, Lazarus saw straight through it, to the ice around her heart. He could see it in her eyes, the way she danced with Mazzulah, the god of the dark realm. They moved to the deck, well within sight still, and the Cisean people moved to make room. The drums changed, going deeper, harder than they had before. A bass rooting itself in the air and pulling them along for the ride.

Her shoulders stiffened for a brief second, and then she pulled back craning her neck in an elegant but harsh sort of pose as she lifted her left-hand and circled him. He repeated the motion although far sloppier than her precise and even graceful movements.

"You said you could control her," Thorne said lightly, leaning forward to take a sip of his ale. "But from where I'm sitting, it looks like the other way around, my friend."

"We're still working out the dynamics of our

arrangement, Thorne," he said dismissively. He should have known that Thorne would not leave well enough alone.

"She's young, probably untrained, given the level of power she's channeling without even trying. How did you find such a treasure, Lazarus?" he asked, twirling the goblet of ale.

"I didn't." And he was telling the truth. Technically. "She found me."

Thorne paused, took another swig and hummed. "All the more curious that fate would draw you two together. She's taken a liking to my warrior, though."

Yes, she had, and Lazarus resented it.

"He's a boy."

"He's a man and one of the finest warriors we have. If it weren't for the darkness in her, I'd say they would make a fine match."

Lazarus' grip tightened around his own ale when her body began moving. Her hips swished, and the damned furs she wore hid nothing, not from his eyes or any others. She moved with a lethal grace, compared to the bumbling of the boy trying to keep up with her.

The dance she chose was not one he knew, but it was a formal affair. That much was clear.

She was drawing on her roots, he realized. This was something she'd learned if not in N'skara, then from its people.

"She is an unfitting match because she is a dark

Maji—one that doesn't just accept the darkness. She embraces it ... it becomes her." Lazarus took a swig of the ale and then proceeded to drain the goblet. Tonight, the dark whispers were worse than usual, and he turned to his vices to chase them away.

"Fortunately for you, Lazarus," Thorne said, tossing a few berries in his mouth while he openly watched Quinn, "that is the case. Quinn's a beautiful woman with a lot of fire. She would do well here in the mountains where she would be free." Lazarus tensed. "But I think her heart would always yearn for another, one that could understand her. To hold such power, and so dark ..." Thorne shook his head. "It is a gift, but also a curse."

Lazarus downed another goblet of ale, but the more he drank the louder the whispers became. He eased back into the wooden chair, watching the tantalizing twists and turns of her body. He wondered if she noticed the way they watched her.

Knowing her, she probably did and reveled in every second.

The very thought infuriated him. He pushed the chair away and got to his feet, ignoring the whispers as best he could as they followed him, prodding at his mind and his soul for a weak point. They became louder and louder, chasing him from where he stood, until he wasn't sure if it was the whispers at all, but rather a voice that was very real.

He came to a stop and his mind cleared.

When the sounds died out he was looking down at Quinn. The music still beat, but she wasn't moving. The others danced around them, pretending not to notice. Not to see. But not her.

No, she simply smiled, and it was wicked.

Playing with Fire

"Playing with fire doesn't mean you'll get burned. Those that understand the flame understand that it cannot help what it is— and take heed."
— *Quinn Darkova, former slave, vassal of House Fierté, fear twister*

L azarus stood from the table with such a sharpness that it drew several eyes. He had barreled towards her from the long wooden structure, moving fast yet stumbling, only to come to a stop and stare like a drunken fool. At her. After all the lies and tricks, she wasn't in the mood. Not even a little bit.

"Do you need something, *Master* Fierté? Or should I call you Prince"—she said scathingly—"since you're to be a king?" The titles fell from her mouth one after another without regard. He hadn't given her any thought when he lied, she saw it fit to return the favor.

"Quinn, this isn't the place—"

"You're right, it's not. I'm enjoying a dance right now, making friends, playing nice, *behaving*—just as you wanted me to." She turned to resume dancing with Vaughn, ignoring Lazarus entirely. She should have known that wouldn't do. Lazarus was not a man that took to being ignored well.

Calloused fingers grabbed her wrist, pulling her to a stop. Vaughn stood a few feet to the side, frowning between the two of them but not daring to interfere.

The breath hissed between Quinn's teeth. The spirits she'd consumed writhing as they wreaked havoc through her completely intolerant system. Strands of fear rose up as she called them to her and shot them down her arm to where Lazarus held firm.

He loved pushing and pulling her as he pleased. Maybe it was time for *him* to see why fear twisters earned their name.

The inky tendrils crept from her bare skin to his, coasting up his hand, wrist, and forearm before wrapping tightly. Where he should have shuddered and bucked, dropping to his knees before her as an empty vessel … he stood.

Slowly, Quinn turned to look at the man who somehow withstood her.

Murky, depthless eyes stared back. She kept pumping fear into him, watching as his own bodily response only marginally changed. Far less responsive than any man, woman, or child had ever been. He shifted on his feet, his eyes brandishing unshed darkness.

"You don't get to walk away from me," Lazarus growled. Quinn's eyebrows came up as she slowly turned her front fully to face him once more. There was something in his expression. Something she'd only seen the makings of once before.

A savageness that enraptured her. A heat that scorched her soul.

Quinn didn't want it. She didn't want to see or to feel any of it—any of him. But if he was so bent on setting her aflame, maybe she should just strike the match and watch it all burn.

Her hand came up lighting fast, and she could have sworn that thunder boomed when she swung. A crack split the air and the music died out.

Lazarus' face didn't twitch, not as the flush of a red handprint bloomed on his tanned flesh. "*Scortum*," she snapped in N'skaran. "Oh, my apologies, *my Prince*, I forgot that you don't speak that language. Allow me to translate. You're being a prick."

"And you're playing with fire," he growled as he stepped around her and began hauling her through the crowd. "A fire you don't know how to control." Some of the men let out a laugh and the women squealed in delight just before the music began again. The melody no longer lulled her into a false sense of calm, but instead trailed behind as they turned into the brutal wind that whipped through the trees. He pulled her along the high wooden walkways, either not noticing or not caring how the wood planks swayed beneath him. They came upon a tree hut far removed from the party where the noises were a world away. He flung open the heavy wooden door and hauled her through.

A taupe colored wooden table with two sturdy chairs sat to one side of the room. On it, a candle was already burning, giving off faint traces of light. A narrow hallway to their left led to a small bedroom.

Lazarus paused in the doorway and quit dragging her.

Not that Quinn stopped fighting.

"Let go of me, you pompous ass—"

"Why were you upset tonight?" he asked in a tone so silky and smooth that she paused. The reason she was fighting temporarily forgotten. She'd expected anger, and perhaps, some yelling. But this … she narrowed her eyes, not trusting it.

"Why were *you*?" she replied.

They stared at each other, neither willing to talk; neither willing to yield.

"You made a fool out of me." He grimaced as soon as the words came out. Looking to the ceiling and running a hand down his face, he pinched the bridge of his nose. "Fawning over that boy … wearing those clothes—"

"I didn't do anything more than speak to him, and Lorraine is wearing the same thing," Quinn interrupted, lifting a silver eyebrow. "And if you want to talk about embarrassing, let's talk about why *you* never told me you're next in line to become king. Hmm? Shall we?"

"It's not that simple, Quinn." He dropped her wrist and turned away.

"Oh, it's not?" she snapped, unrelenting. "You didn't *lie* to me about your intentions?" She circled him even as he turned away from her.

"I never lied to you. You signed a contract to be part of my house for five years, whether it's the house of a noblemen or king matters not," he said, turning for the hallway.

"So, you can just walk away when it suits you, but I do it because you're making a fool of yourself and, suddenly, I'm playing with fire?" she growled, following after him. "*Black Baac.*"

"You're driving me insane," he groaned, striding into the bedroom. She didn't hesitate to follow him in.

"You're already there," she shot back, stopping at the foot of his bed.

He rounded on her and the expression on his face made her halt. His eyes were unfocused. Hazy. She squinted, slowly inching forward.

"You have no idea," he murmured, the words barely audible in the silent air between them, his hands bunched into fists at his sides. Quinn blinked.

"What are you talking about?" His constant changing was giving her a headache—or was that the spirits talking? It was hard to tell when the colors swished together and shone so bright it hurt. The fear in her veins wrestled against the small modicum of control she held, wanting to come out and play again. To test him. To *taste* him.

"Your magic," he breathed, inhaling deeply. There was a spark of something in his gaze that she didn't want to put a name to. She wanted to go back to the cold, safe space, to where the world didn't sway as much as it did. "You used it on me. You tried to hurt me, and I fear…"

Quinn tilted her head up, her expression puzzled and heart pounding.

"What do you fear?" she asked so softly that she wasn't sure if he had heard her.

But then he answered, his words low, quiet, and so full of dark promise that they set her nerves on edge. "That I'll lose control."

Her lips parted, because it was the most straight-forward he'd ever been. There were still so many things unsaid, and so many secrets that she didn't know which dark corner to prod. Come the morning they might both regret this night. Regret the things that were said and the way they'd acted. But here and now, in the moment…

"You stupid, stupid man." She leaned into and when he didn't back away, a thought came into her mind. Just a little wicked. She stretched up on her toes. Her breath fanned the shell of his ear, and she felt the shudder that ran through him. They'd ridden together day after day for weeks, pressed against each other, but this was different.

Tonight, there was violence and dark magic riding them both.

She whispered, "You already have."

Her lips skimmed his cheek as she moved further south, skating down his jaw ... only briefly—not even a second—pressing to his hard mouth before she pulled away. She inhaled the scent of spirits and smoke and flame. Underneath it all was something that called to her. That drew her in, pulling her close.

He said that like calls to like.

She was only beginning to understand as she turned for the door.

"Wait," he commanded, more clarity in his voice than he'd had only moments before.

"You're drunk, Lazarus. Go to bed," she said, not turning to face him.

"It's been a week, Quinn. You owe me an answer," he said, surprising her. She'd expected poor attempts at seduction, but instead he asked her for answers—knowing her head was not all there this night and that in the quiet darkness of his room she might not dismiss.

Clever bastard, she thought to herself.

"And my question?" she asked.

"You already asked it," was his reply. She thought for a second, and then nodded. *Clever bastard, indeed.* She would need to be more careful with the silver-tongued demon that held her leash.

"So, I did." She paused. "What's your question, Lazarus?"

She thought of all the things he might ask. The answers he might try to pry from her and wondered if the contract would demand it. If her only choices would be to lay it bare before him or die in silence. Her nails curled into her palms as she bit her cheek.

But Lazarus was anything if not unpredictable.

"Why don't you drink spirits?" Such a simple question.

Such a vulnerable answer.

Quinn glanced over her shoulder to where he stood at the edge of the bed, right where she'd left him. "I already have enough demons of my own. I know better than to open the door for more."

And then she walked away into the brutal chill of the night, knowing deep down it wouldn't comfort her as it once had. There were some things not even the harshest of winters and winds could bury.

Dreams and Nightmares

"Fears can never be washed away. They will always find you, no matter how strong you are. If you escape them during the day, then they will find you in the night."
— *Quinn Darkova, former slave, vassal of House Fierté, fear twister*

L eaves crunched under her boots as Quinn strode away from Lazarus' tree hut and toward her own. The drums from the feast beat in the distance as she curled and uncurled her fingers letting the fear wisps dance across her skin. The events of the night played over and over in her mind as she reached out to grasp the rope ladder and began climbing.

The frigid mountain air rattled her ascent, but there was something more lingering. Another magic, not hers, not *his*, but something other. Something subtle. It settled in the air around her like a stranger from afar, curious and watching, but not actively touching. She shook her head, trying to clear it from her mind and the ladder swayed. Biting the inside of her cheek she kept moving, her stiff fingers rigid when she finally grasped the wooden floor. She hauled herself over the ledge and laid there for a moment, enjoying the reprieve from the wind and the night and … other things. Things she didn't want to think of, at least for tonight.

Quinn pulled herself up into a sitting position and sighed deeply, her longing gaze shifting from the bed to the floor where she currently sat. She contemplated shedding her fur clothing but decided against it as she rose to her feet and stumbled into bed.

Her eyes fell shut as the wind howled and the branches wavered, scratching against the side of the hut. She rolled to her side in frustration, letting out a huff as she tried to settle enough for sleep to take her.

King, her mind whispered, *Lazarus Fierté, future king of Norcasta*. She'd been shocked when she heard it, but the more she thought, the more she wasn't sure what to think. Working for a nobleman and working for a king were certainly different, but not *that* much. However, kissing a nobleman and kissing a king … those were very different things.

And even more to the matter was what Lazarus wanted her for to begin with. He still hadn't said much, but she was beginning to wonder, beginning to see. He wanted her trained but cooperating. He wanted her to harness her power, but not to use it on *him*.

There was only one reason he'd want that, and deep down she knew it.

Just as she knew she wasn't all that opposed to it. *Not really*.

Quinn's thoughts trailed off as her mind finally grew fuzzy. In the distance, she heard voices— Lorraine's and Dominicus' as they entered the hut. Exhaustion kept her rooted to her bed, back turned and eyes closed. She was just on the precipice of sleep when she felt a cool hand touch her forehead. She froze but sensed no ill intent. The hand moved and her breathing evened out again.

"She's asleep," Lorraine whispered softly.

A second set of footsteps paused farther away. "Are you okay here?" Dominicus asked.

"With Quinn?" Lorraine asked. "Yes, of course. She might be brash, but she'd never hurt me unless she felt threatened. For all her talk she's still just a child."

"She's a woman, Lorraine," Dominicus corrected her, "and though she may be several years younger than you, I would not relegate her to a child. She is many things, but innocent is not one of them."

Quinn's lips pressed together. She kept her eyes

closed as she listened intently, waiting for Lorraine's reply.

"People are complicated, Dom," she said, her voice soft and understanding. "Quinn is no less so. She may be a young woman, but in many ways, she has the emotional maturity of a child—one that has been forced to endure and survive horrible things."

"You're not her mother," Dominicus said.

"No, I'm not," Lorraine agreed. "But I've been tasked with watching over her, nonetheless. We all have. I'm not striving to take the place of her mother —the gods know I'm not suitable, but—"

"Your son loves you, 'Raine." Heavy footsteps moved closer to where Lorraine's voice sounded. The other woman gasped, and Quinn's body tightened. She clenched her fists, ready to jump up from her pallet, but the soft sigh that followed let her know Lorraine was in no pain.

"I know he does."

"Then stop trying to mother Quinn. Stop trying to teach her manners. Just let her be."

Lorraine's soft chuckle soothed something deep inside Quinn. The tiny kernel of something dark putting her at peace. "That I can't do," Lorraine said. "I think she could benefit from some manners."

Dominicus scoffed quietly. "If you think you'll teach her—as resistant as she is—to be a lady, you are more insane than Lazarus is for bringing her along."

"The gods have a plan for everyone, Dominicus—

you, me, Lazarus, and even her. I may never teach her to act like a lady, but I can show her that I care by trying." Quinn felt those kind brown eyes settle on her back, just before a hand did—brushing her hair away from her face the way her mother never had. "I teach her because I see a future for her at Lazarus' side—one where she could make use of these lessons. I didn't understand why he brought her with us in the beginning, but … I'm starting to." Those gentle fingers barely touched her as they dusted the stray strands of hair. "There's a change coming. A new age approaching—and I for one am happy to be on this side of it."

"A change is coming?" Dominicus asked.

"You don't sense it?" Lorraine said softly. "King Claudius is on his deathbed and when—not if—but when he dies, Lazarus will be king. I can feel it in my bones. The tide of relative complacency that we have been riding will shift, and he'll need us. They both will."

Dominicus huffed out a breath, the sound deeper than anything Lorraine could emit. "If she doesn't kill us before then."

"She won't." Lorraine sounded so sure, it made Quinn uneasy that she didn't feel that same assurance in herself.

"If you say so, 'Raine." Dominicus sighed. Heavy footsteps moved away from her, from Lorraine, as Dominicus returned to the trap door.

"I'll see you in the morning. Bring the girl. Vaughn asked us if she could train with them and Lazarus gave his consent."

"So long as you or Draeven are there watching her, I gather?" Lorraine replied, a note of terseness in her voice.

"Of course," Dominicus said curtly. "Wouldn't want her to get the idea of staying in Cisea and marrying one of the mountain men. Gods help us, how Lazarus might respond because this all might be for nothing if she did."

Lorraine's muffled laughter confused Quinn even further. *Marry?* She wasn't the type. They had nothing to worry about.

"Goodnight, Dom."

Quinn listened to the soft sounds of Dominicus' retreat down the ladder and Lorraine getting ready for bed. She wanted to sit up and say something. She had so many questions, but at the same time, she had no clue how to put them into words. The longer she laid there contemplating her thoughts and confusion, the blearier her mind became. Quinn didn't even realize when oblivion opened its sweet arms and welcomed her into the fold of dreams and nightmares until it was too late.

She stood on the surface of an ocean, but it was hard and stable. Under her feet—wrathful churning waves were caged in the deep blue sea. Quinn blinked down at the cyclones beneath her before lifting her head to the sky and nearly cursing. Once again, she'd landed in some faraway place she'd never seen before.

Dark gray clouds moved overhead, and before her a floating staircase was the only thing that existed in the wide expanse. Left with little other choice, Quinn strode towards it and hooked one hand around the half stone wall using it as a railing. The stone steps curved around, circling up into the dark gray above where the temperature should have dropped, but felt neither warm nor cold. Still, wind lifted her hair and blew it back from her face as lightning flashed in the clouds—close, but not enough to touch her.

Black vines crawled through the cracks in the stone, slowly creeping after her as she walked by. She paused and they stopped as well, waiting for her next move. Quinn glanced over her shoulder and decided that they weren't a threat—just curious as they trailed after her. She resumed climbing, circling the baseless tower of steps until she came to an open archway in the center of a field of clouds.

A figure in the distance caught her eye. A man of shadow backlit by such incandescent light that it never occurred to her that she should be cautious. She didn't consider the impossibility of walking over clouds as she stumbled forward. The possibility of falling to the hard surface of water below never crossed her mind as she sprinted, closing the distance.

Lazarus stood tense, his muscled back and shoulders tight as long spindly shadows crawled over his skin, the ends curling back around to sink large razored teeth into his taut flesh. He didn't grunt or groan or moan, and he certainly didn't scream or cry. He didn't fight as they took their pound of flesh, biting him again and again. Blood ran in rivulets down his bare chest. He held his head in his hands as if he couldn't stop them even if he wanted.

Quinn froze a few paces away as she took in the markings that covered almost every inch of his skin from the neck down to the waistband of his trousers. The feeding frenzy of darkness that encircled him didn't pause as he jerked his head up and their eyes met—crystalline to charcoal.

Lazarus panted, the blood from his open wounds flowing freely with no sign of stopping. Quinn blinked, looking between him and the gashes on his body. She didn't understand why he just sat there and took it; why he didn't try to stop it. She took a small step forward, and he took one back.

"What are you doing here?" His voice was gruffer than usual, filled with pain and an edge of panic. Quinn studied him, not speaking as her gaze dropped to the blood pouring from his chest, shoulders, and abs. Those tendrils of darkness were savage and unforgiving.

"What did you do to deserve this…" She trailed off as she lifted a hand, fingers itching to touch his bloodied skin. There were shadows there—moving beneath the skin just as the murky tendrils came out of it. The darkness seemed so alive within him, but something about it made her pause. Made her think. She knew the shadowy magic that clung to him, but it was not the same as hers. Simply like.

Like calls to like, *he'd said. Then again, this was only a dream … or was it?*

Quinn reached for him again, feeling more emboldened than when she was awake. She reached for one of the inky tendrils.

"Don't," Lazarus warned roughly as she took a step towards him.

"Why are you bleeding?" she asked.

A coil of dark energy slipped away from him, inching down and away—almost inquisitively as it pursued Quinn. She lifted her hand and beckoned it forward, locking it in her grasp when it came close enough. Lazarus' eyes widened for a brief second and he jerked himself back even as she held onto the creature that had been feeding off him. The thing—whatever it was—didn't detach itself from Lazarus as he moved away, but instead, twisted around her fingers. Quinn's eyebrows furrowed as the little sliver of darkness rubbed between her fingers, curling in her palm as though it were a curious animal that relished in the feel of her hand against its own nonexistent flesh.

"What is this?" she asked, lifting her eyes to meet Lazarus' once more.

A stygian gaze returned her stare. "Let go," he demanded—he trembled. She'd never seen Lazarus like this, so troubled. So ... vulnerable.

Quinn opened her fingers and let the thing fall from her grasp. It slunk away and back under Lazarus' flesh, disappearing from view. She wondered what it was that it could feel so similar to her own power and yet she knew it wasn't the same.

"Lazarus," she said softly, an unspoken question.

He looked away as he answered. "It appears that I'm not as immune to you as I'd thought I would be."

"What do you mean?" she asked.

He sighed, turning his face back to her. "Fear, Quinn."

"*This is what you fear?*" she concluded, moving closer, and this time he didn't move away—though he did stiffen. "*This is your nightmare?*"

Lazarus glared down at her, and this was the first time she felt that he was truly well and angry with her. Not just frustrated or irritated as he often was, but defensive ... like an animal backed into a corner. His own fear of vulnerability made him cold. Cruel. But Quinn knew a thing or two about cruelty and wasn't dissuaded when he said, "You need to leave."

"*Why?*" she asked. "*It's only a dream, after all.*"

Quinn gasped and she could feel herself slipping. The clouds darkened and lightning flashed through them. Her bare toes sank, and she reached for him. Her fingers closing around his arm, keeping herself steady as the dream took another turn.

"*No!*" she snapped—at him or it, she wasn't certain—but lightning flashed again. The seas below became wild and vicious as the cyclones broke free of their watery prison.

Lazarus jolted at her touch and she realized something in that brief flash of a second.

That he was warm. His proximity burning.

His already charcoal eyes darkened even further as he leaned forward and growled, "You do not *command me, Quinn. I am your master.*"

"*Not here, you're not,*" she shot back, clinging to him. "*Here, you're just like me. Lost and wandering. Conflicted. Confined.*" Her fingers curled as she dug her nails in hard enough to break skin.

"*You think you understand me, little she-wolf?*" *Lazarus'*

237

question was spoken in a dangerous tone, drawing Quinn back to her circumstances.

He rose to his full height, his hand snaking out, wicked fast, as he wrapped it around her free hand and yanked her closer—pulling her into his chest until her breasts pressed against him.

"Like calls to like," she whispered. Something heavy and foreign raced through her veins, straight to the heated place between her thighs. Lazarus inhaled deeply, and she could swear that he knew it—the way her body responded to him.

"You still have no idea," he said, his voice low and burning.

He released her almost as abruptly as he had grabbed her, sudden enough that her grip on his forearm had loosened and when her hands dropped away, bloody fingerprints smeared against his skin. Lazarus scowled, his gaze dropping to her chest where his blood had smudged onto her crisp cotton shirt.

"Are you sure about that?" she asked in a challenge.

He didn't stop as she stared at him—her cerulean eyes haunting. "Wake up now, Quinn, and do not make me regret this."

She blinked, a slight pucker forming between her brows. "Regret what?" she began to ask, but almost as soon as the question escaped from between her lips, the clouds beneath her feet gave way and she fell.

Lightning struck. The world dispersed. The water whirlpools. The clouds. The staircase.

All of it vanished and left her falling back into nothingness.

Quinn woke with a start, her hands coming up to defend herself.

There was blood on her fingertips. She stared, waiting for it to fade like it never happened, just like the dream, but it never did. Sitting on her cot, the light of the early morning creeping through, a weight settled on her chest.

And deep down she knew it then ... these weren't dreams or nightmares.

They were *real*.

The Servalis Stone

"If something survives long enough to be considered ancient, it undoubtedly has a secret that let it become that way."
— *Lazarus Fïerté, dark Maji, heir to Norcasta, royally pissed*

A cool breeze drifted over his heated skin. Lazarus felt the flame of his burning rage far too close to the surface today as the voices he usually kept at bay crawled through him restlessly. Their incorporeal bodies burrowed beneath his flesh, searching for the dark power that evaded them. They'd only gotten a taste of it last night and were feral in their search for *her.*

Quinn's essence still lingered in his mind from her walk through his dream—his continued nightmare.

Lazarus had lost himself in the voices last night; in those demons that he never showed anyone, and in the depths of his sleep they came upon him with a vengeance in which they were owed but would never truly have. They ate at him from the inside out, just as he had once eaten them … and then she appeared. In a blaze of dark glory her silver head walked straight into his nightmares without caution or abandon. She disrupted their meal, striding up to him without a clue as to what she'd walked in on and they saw her, sensed her darkness, and went to her.

But unlike him, the man whom they raged at, they *wanted* her. Almost as much as his own magic did.

He'd have convinced himself it were a dream, if not for the bloody fingerprints on his arm when he woke. There was no other explanation for it. No other reason the voices would be so reckless in pursuit of her. She'd come to him at his darkest and he'd let her fall.

They were both better off for it.

Lazarus brushed off the calling of the voices and strode quickly through Cisea. It was calm in the mid-morning, people striding to and from their next assignments. The Cisean people were as hardworking as they were paranoid of outsiders. Eyes followed him everywhere he went, if it wasn't the guards that Thorne had trailing him far enough back so he wouldn't see, it was the women and children keeping tabs on his whereabouts and reporting to their men. They watched him because he was an outsider and a man, despite being a *friend*. He was also the one who held the leash of a certain young dark Maji that had half the warriors entranced. Draeven had already had to turn away three men who came forward with gifts of courtship. Not that Quinn knew. He liked it better that way.

Lazarus headed towards Thorne's hut with steady, sure strides. The people watched him, some more curious than others. He heard the whispers of children asking their mothers about his aura, of noting how it looked like a certain woman from his party. They knew what he was, but not what he was truly capable of if pushed. Only one even suspected and that was, perhaps, why Lazarus respected the man so much.

Thorne stood holding several sheaves of parchment as he spoke with two nearly identical red-haired warriors in hushed voices when Lazarus entered his throne room after climbing up the rope ladder. Red eyes glanced up, and Thorne nodded in his direction before he handed the papers back to his warriors and told them to leave.

"Something I should be concerned with?" Lazarus asked, nodding back to the exit the two warriors had taken.

Thorne shook his head. "No. Just some reports from our outer scouts. Likely nothing important, but

our men are always vigilant. It's how we've maintained our hold on the mountains."

Lazarus jerked his chin down in acknowledge-
ment. "I came to speak with you about the spring."

"I assumed as much." Thorne turned towards his
seat. In another room, under another man, the throne
might have appeared ostentatious, but Thorne made
it work. It suited him well, not the other way around.

"I will need the Servalis stone before I take Quinn
up there. I was hoping to leave this afternoon."

Thorne frowned and looked over Lazarus, noting
the dark circles under his eyes. "Shouldn't you rest a
bit first?" he asked. "You've been on the road for quite
a while, my friend. Another night's sleep won't hurt
either of you. The ceremony will be difficult on her
body if her power is as strong as I expect it to be."

Lazarus shook his head, turning his chin as he
moved closer to Thorne's seated position. "We don't
have the time. I doubt those following us have inexperienced riders. It is also unlikely that they would take
the same breaks as we have."

Thorne considered that for a moment, his brows
drawing down low over his eyes as he scanned
Lazarus' face. Finally, he closed his eyes with a sigh
and gestured for Lazarus to follow him as he rose
from his throne. "The process will begin as soon as
she enters the water," Thorne began as he led him out
on a deck overlooking the whole of Cisea.

Lazarus looked down, watching its people as they

milled about. In the hundreds of years since these people had entered and conquered the mountains, their technology hadn't grown, but their knowledge had. The Cisean people knew more about Maji and their abilities more than anyone else in the vast lands of the continent—except perhaps the N'skari.

"When you enter the cavern, you must do so when the sun falls over the horizon. Leviathan will preside only when Leviticus has descended into sleep."

"Under the God of the Moon and Shadows." Lazarus nodded. "I can do that."

Thorne's hands wrapped around the railing of the deck, his eyes far away as he continued. "There will be light, of course. Have her strip down. No clothes are to enter the water, as they are impure."

"That will not be a problem." Lazarus forced the thought of a naked Quinn from his mind. The time for it to drive him into insanity was not now. Not when the whispers liked that idea so very much.

"Hand her the Servalis stone and have her enter the waters *alone*. She will need to climb to the highest point of the pool where Leviathan's eye may see her."

"Where the moon can see her?" Lazarus moved closer to the other man, turning and resting his lower back against the railing that appeared weak at a moment's glance, but seemed to handle Thorne's grip quite well.

Thorne nodded. "There is an opening at the top

of the cavern's ceiling for him to observe. Once she is in the spring, the water will activate the stone's magic. It will drain her of her own magic completely and then return it to her. This is how it measures all that she is and what she will be." Lazarus nodded. "But be warned, she will be weak when she leaves. Try to get her back here as quickly as possible. She will need to sleep for a while to recover."

Lazarus darted a glance at the man before shifting his eyes away. "How long is a while?"

Thorne's lips quirked and he released a dry chuckle. "A day or so. It all depends. Why? Nervous, are we?" Lazarus grunted a nonresponse. He wasn't keen to waste time getting there, particularly if Quinn was going to need rest after. Some things were unavoidable.

Thorne shook his head and his expression sobered once again. "How will I be able to determine the strength of her abilities?" Lazarus asked. "She hasn't yet hit her ascension. I expect it will be soon. She shows signs of overcharge and manifesting more rapidly."

Thorne's frown deepened. "It should have happened by now, Lazarus." Dark hair slid against a tan cheek as Lazarus turned his face towards the giant of a man. Their gazes connected and locked. "What aren't you telling me, my friend?"

Lazarus' lips pressed together before he took a breath, parting them as he imparted a sliver of

Quinn's past she would not be happy he was sharing, though he knew she'd refuse to feel embarrassed about it. No, that was not like her. She was far too honest, too abrupt—and so very unapologetic for it.

"Quinn was a slave of the Norcastan state for several years. A decade or more, I cannot be sure," he replied. "I think it might have impeded her ascension."

Thorne sucked in a breath and scowled. "I do not approve of the slave trade, much less the trading of females, Lazarus."

Lazarus nodded. "I know. Nor do I. She is no longer one, obviously. She is under my employment of her own volition. I assure you."

Red eyes narrowed for a moment, his thick brows furrowed in disapproval. Lazarus said nothing more as he waited for the Cisean leader to respond.

Finally, Thorne nodded and answered his question. "Several things will happen at once that should help you. First, if the water darkens or begins to churn on its own, it means her power is above average. I have no doubts this will happen, but actual strength is often measured by the stone."

"How?" Lazarus prompted.

"The Servalis stone is clear. When the water darkens the stone will absorb it. The darker the stone, the stronger the Maji," Thorne explained. Lazarus nodded. He'd heard rumors of it but wasn't sure *how* exactly it worked.

"Anything else?" he asked, already drained and the process hadn't even begun.

Thorne turned his gaze away, once again looking out to his kin and countrymen. "There will be pain."

Lazarus frowned. "Explain," he commanded.

Thorne shot him a dark look, but Lazarus did not back down. He stared back, daring Thorne to test him. Thorne's lips curled, and he turned fully to face the other man.

"It is clear that your *vassal*"—he lifted a brow as he spoke the last word before continuing—"is more than an average Maji. First, she is dark. Second, she is a fear twister. Regardless of the spring, she's survived into adulthood and still hasn't reached the ascension. That's unprecedented and should give you great pause in handling her."

The judgement in his expression had Lazarus gritting his teeth, but he refused to respond to Thorne's quips about how he was with her. "Her aura leads me to believe she is second to none that reside in this village when it comes to power—even I. Despite what she is, that isn't why she would feel pain. It's because of the sheer amount of magic she holds inside of her. When the stone leeches her of her power, it will be crippling. She will feel as though she is dying, as if all her life force is being sucked right out of her. In a few instances..." Thorne's words trailed away as his eyes grew unfocused and his throat tightened.

"In a few instances, in the distant past," he

continued after a moment, "there have been recordings of the stone and the ceremony actually doing so. But if you are careful, that shouldn't be the case. However, the stronger a Maji is, the more reliant they are on their magic. They often don't realize it until the ascension, but the stone has a similar effect. Just as the ascension kills half of those that undergo it, not all Maji make it through the waters. Both of these drain the holder of their magic entirely, and only those who are strong enough to survive see it returned. The more powerful the Maji that enters the water, the more pain they will feel when it is gone."

Lazarus turned his face away from Thorne, frowning as he considered his options. He did not want to cause her pain, but the Cisean spring was one of the easiest ways to do this, and at the moment, the most accessible way of getting what he wanted. She had handled the removal of her brands rather easily, though. Perhaps, it would not be so bad.

And if she could survive this, he would have no doubts about her surviving the ascension.

"Alright," Lazarus said finally. "Thank you for this. We will leave this afternoon. I came to retrieve the stone, and then I'll inform my second of my departure."

Thorne turned, leading Lazarus back into the tree hut. He moved to the entrance of a small room and held his arm out, stopping Lazarus from entering. "Wait here," he ordered, disappearing inside. Lazarus waited patiently and when Thorne returned, he held a heavy leather satchel.

"The stone is inside," he said. "But before I hand it over, I desire one more thing."

Lazarus narrowed his eyes and waited.

"When you leave, I insist you take Vaughn with you. He will lead you out of the mountains and act as an emissary of the Cisean people in your future court."

"If you want him as a symbol of our alliance, I can assure you it is not necessary," Lazarus replied.

A gleam of Thorne's normal humor passed across the Cisean's face. "Afraid he may take the girl from you?"

Lazarus scowled. "That is not the case." Because he'd kill Vaughn before it came to that. Not that he said as much.

Thorne shook his head. "Whether it is or not, I will insist this time, my friend. I have no doubt that in a few months' time you will be on the throne or well on your way, and I would like this friendship to be one that others see. It will keep certain parties out of the mountains, just as it will give the royal brats pause. You see? I will only give you this stone if you agree to these terms." Lazarus stifled a growl. He did not like being commanded, ordered, or backed into a corner. But he knew there was little choice in the matter now. The boy would be a distraction for sure, but his presence was irrelevant.

Lazarus nodded. "I can accept these terms." Thorne waited another moment before he nodded back and handed the satchel over. Lazarus took it and turned to leave, pausing only when Thorne's hand closed over his arm.

"There is one more thing. I would ask that you keep your use of the spring between us, my friend." Thorne posed the request politely, but the glint in his eye let Lazarus know that it was no request at all. "As the elected leader of my people, I have certain permissions. As my friend, my ally, I can give you certain allowances, but Lazarus, make no mistake—this spring is sacred to the Cisean people. We have been guardians of these mountains since before the ancient times and some might not take kindly to my allowance of you using it for this purpose."

"I can do that."

"And whatever you do, *do not* enter the water with her," Thorne said, his voice dropping. "If you get into the water, the stone will take from you as well. The two times it has happened, no one made it out alive."

"Noted." Lazarus turned and grasped the other man's hand in a firm, masculine manner. The movement, the willing closeness, startled Thorne. "I will do my best to ensure we return, and your secret—it stays between us."

Thorne stayed a moment, assessing the truth in Lazarus' eyes. Whatever he saw there must have assuaged his concerns, for he sighed, nodded, and then stepped back, allowing Lazarus to leave the hut.

Lazarus tucked the leather pouch Thorne had given him into his cloak without looking inside. Quinn would be on the female training grounds at this time. He headed that way. No doubt, Draeven would be somewhere close by. His second-in-command—his left-hand—had taken to watching the girl, his curiosity mounting on the distrust he first felt towards her. Lazarus knew Draeven was concerned about Quinn, worried, and therefore, he never let her out of his sight.

Sure enough, as soon as Lazarus stepped out of a line of trees and onto the training grounds, he saw the flash of silver hair just before Siva took her down. Not far from their sparring session, Draeven stood by with arms crossed and eyes focused. Lazarus headed straight for him, noting with a scowl that the boy was not far—his eyes glued to Quinn as she spoke with Siva from her prone position on the ground.

Draeven must have sensed his presence and turned to greet him just as Quinn jerked her arm out and sent Siva flying. He waited as the two women spoke some more in low tones difficult to hear over the grunting and clashing of weapons nearby. Once it was obvious they were done, Draeven raised his voice and called for her.

Ice blue eyes turned on him, stabbing deep into his gut and curling around the vile organ in his chest that kept him alive. Her frozen fingers closed over the vessel of lifeblood and squeezed. She had no clue. Absolutely none. But Lazarus wanted to see that darkness in her eyes come to life, he wanted it to fester and multiply. And when it did, he would forge her into the greatest weapon the world had ever known.

A Warrior's Staff

"Weapons come in many forms, the greatest being our minds."
— *Quinn Darkova, vassal of House Fierté, fear twister*

Sweat poured into her eyes as Quinn maintained her stance, circling Draeven as he circled her. His violet eyes were sharp, analyzing as he clenched his jaw and then swung. Quinn sidestepped out of the way and went down on one knee, bringing her own blade up to halt the assaulting weapon. Draeven's eyes widened as he jerked it back and away. She knew he wasn't expecting her to be any good at this. Men always loved to overlook her, forgetting not only what she was, but in this case, where she came from.

Quinn jerked her foot out and Draeven stumbled

before righting himself. She popped to her feet and resumed circling.

"She-wolf is strong," Vaughn commented from the sidelines as he spoke to Dominicus. Dominicus grunted, though it was neither an affirmation nor a negation of the fact that he was right.

"That was smart," Draeven complimented her. "Getting physically closer to throw off your opponent."

Quinn lifted an eyebrow and sighed. "Yes, I know," she said in a mocking tone. "That's why I did it." She thrust her sword out and Draeven blocked it with one arm while the other shot out and gripped Quinn's neck as her body came too close to his.

Quinn's eyes widened and she dropped one hand from her sword to grab onto Draeven's wrist as he lifted her slightly up on her toes. He smirked. "Don't get too arrogant."

She was going to make him eat dirt for that.

Quinn narrowed her eyes, sinking her nails into his hand as she unleashed a long tendril of fear. The thing hardened and slithered up Draeven's hand from where he held her. Cursing, he dropped her and stumbled back. Quinn pivoted, swinging her sword and aimed for his neck. Before her blade could meet flesh, Draeven jerked his own up. Metal clashed on metal, the clang echoing over the training grounds.

Draeven grunted as he pulled back and swung again, throwing so much weight behind it that all

Quinn could do to keep her hand from bending backwards was let go. Her blade fell from her grasp, landing on the carefully brushed soil as she stepped sideways and Draeven fell. Landing face first where she wanted him.

He rolled sideways and glared at her as he spat out a glob of dirt. "You could have beheaded me," he said as he climbed to his feet.

Quinn shrugged as she leaned down and picked up her sword. "It's training. If someone comes at you with a sword, they're not going to stop." She turned away and started towards the end of the field.

"Yeah, well, be more careful next time," he called back.

Quinn pursed her lips and looked over her shoulder. "You might want to get over your fear of slithery animals," she retorted.

"She-wolf Quinn is vicious in training," Vaughn said as she approached. "Strong build. You'd make good wife."

Quinn blanched as she dropped her sword against a nearby tree. "Uh … thank you?"

Siva—Thorne's wife—approached dressed in tight leather shorts and a small band around her breasts. Her bare stomach was toned, though it still bore the faint lines of having carried a child. She stopped before Quinn.

"Where did you learn to fight?" she asked, her Norcastan far better than most of the Cisean's.

Quinn shrugged. "Wherever I could," she replied vaguely. In truth, being a slave in Norcastan borders meant she wasn't without company. Soldiers from Jibreal and Bangratas were with her—and in return for her help translating, they taught her a great deal about fighting with more than hands and teeth. They taught her the sword, then the dagger, and before long she progressed onto weapons such as the halberd that the Cisean people so loved.

But the dagger was where her heart lie. One day she was going to return to her homeland for restitution, and when she did, she would skin the people who thought to sell her into slavery to begin with. But that was for another time. Another place.

Behind them, several women fought with halberds —the clattering of weapons echoing up into the tree tops. Siva looked Quinn over, her gaze assessing.

"Why do you ask?" Quinn continued, prompting her.

Siva reached behind her, retrieving a short rod that had been attached to the back of her belt. "You fight with this?"

Quinn took the offered rod. It was no longer than her forearm. She frowned down at it. "I suppose I could," she replied. She'd trained with a number of weapons, but never this.

Siva nodded and then gestured to another woman. A blonde with dark brown eyes approached and held out her own rod. Draeven moved to the other side of Dominicus, sheathing his sword and crossing his arms as he watched from the sidelines.

Quinn left her sword behind and took the oddly heavy rod, moving back to the area of the practice field she had occupied with Draeven just moments before. Siva followed after, stopping several feet in front of her and lifting a brow. She pressed her thumb into a notch at the tip of the rod and jerked it once.

Quinn watched as several sections of the rod slid free from the underside, sliding down and locking into place as the rod was transformed into a full staff. Siva held it comfortably at her side. This was a weapon she was well acquainted with, Quinn noted, as she looked down at her own rod. Her fingers ran along the notches that layered the wood. She'd thought them mere decoration before now. Finding the same notch Siva had used, she pressed it and swung her arm out and the sections hidden within the smaller rod slid out and clicked into place.

Quinn twirled the rod, frowning at the way it still had the same weight as it had before, but now felt more balanced. She swung it to one side and then to the next.

Siva, who had been standing and waiting for Quinn to start, spoke up then. "You are ready?"

"Nice staff," Quinn said in response. "Can I keep this after we're done?"

Siva lifted a brow. "If you can defeat me in battle, I will give it to you."

Quinn grinned. "Deal."

Quinn slid into position, lowering her shoulders and releasing a pent-up breath as Siva stretched back and stared. After a moment, Quinn lifted a brow.

"Are you going to attack?" she asked.

"No."

Quinn blinked. "I thought you wanted to see me fight with this thing?"

"I do."

"Then why won't you attack me."

"When you come to a practice field to fight, one is the aggressor and one is not. I am not."

"So, I take it I'm the aggressor. Fair enough."

Siva didn't respond as Quinn struck out, swinging the stick as though it were her blade, aiming for the other woman's head.

Siva lifted her staff—the long cylindrical rod blocking Quinn's and sending it up and over her head, then back down to land with a light thud. Siva looked up and locked her hands around her own weapon, standing between Quinn and hers.

"You fight as though this is a sword," she said. "It is not. Try again." Siva released Quinn's staff and stepped back, falling immediately into her original position.

Quinn stared at the other woman, this time curling her fingers around the mid-point and twirling it once. She strode forward—moving exactly the same as she had before, watching this time as Siva sighed and locked the end of Quinn's staff to the ground—but this time she didn't lose her hold on it. Quinn turned, elbowing the other woman in the face.

She stumbled back and Quinn gripped the staff lightly. Spinning around, she swung it at the back of the other woman's knees, but Siva saw her coming. She launched herself backwards, avoiding its stinging bite as she flipped in midair and landed once more, but Quinn wasn't done.

She swung, smacking away the other woman's weapon, and then striding forward for the win. She didn't see the satisfied gleam in Siva's eyes that would have told her something was wrong. She didn't consider the staff that came out nowhere and wrapped around her neck. Nor did she see Siva's hand that came up to hold it there as the wood rattled the base of her skull. She shoved Quinn's legs out from underneath her and the second jarring impact sent Quinn straight to the ground. She landed on her back, groaning as the bones of her spine protested the abuse.

Siva popped back to her feet with an air of ease while Quinn remained prone on the ground. Leaning over so that she could look Quinn in the eyes, Siva shook her head.

"You need more practice with the staff, but you are better than most."

Quinn stared back up at the older woman and

instead of feeling angry at having been bested, she felt respect. "Do you have any suggestions?"

"Suggestions?" Siva tilted her head to the side, confused.

"Advice. On using the staff better," Quinn clarified. She liked the weapon. It felt good in her hands, not as heavy as a sword, but still strong. The wood was agile. The weight of it was near perfect. As a bonus, she could carry it around even at its full mast and others would assume it was a walking stick, albeit one that could do some damage.

And best of all, something she hadn't mastered yet. The staff was a challenge.

Siva chuckled. "Learn to better use it as an extension of your body. You use it as you would a shorter weapon, but you're not so unwieldy that you haven't practiced with something like it before. You don't hesitate, nor do you pull punches—so to speak—but you ride your instincts and what you need is practice."

Quinn nodded. "Thank you."

Siva grinned, her chuckles fading. "My staff, please?"

"What?" Quinn frowned, her hand clenching around the wood she held within her grip. "I thought you said I could keep it."

Siva shook her head, wild strands of her blonde hair swaying with the movement. "If you beat me," she replied. "You did not beat me."

Quinn didn't think, but let her fear rise up. Siva's

eyes widened as if she saw what was coming. She stepped back just as Quinn swung, holding the end low to the ground. With her focus on Quinn, she didn't see the blunt end until it was too late. Siva grunted as she fell backwards and landed with an *umph*.

Quinn sat up and repositioned the staff at an angle, the end digging into the other woman's throat. Siva swallowed, a grin tugging at her lips.

"What was that?" Quinn asked, letting her power fade away just as quickly as it had risen.

Siva coughed, sitting up to watch Quinn's form. After a moment of tense silence, she nodded. "I stand corrected. You may keep it."

There was a twinkle in her eyes that told Quinn she wasn't *that* annoyed with being outdone. Besides, Quinn really wanted to practice with it more.

"Quinn!" Draeven's abrupt call drew their attention. Just behind the nuisance of a man was an even bigger problem Quinn hadn't wanted to deal with today.

Gritting her teeth, Quinn slowly stood up from the ground and reached down with her free hand to help Siva up as well. "Your master seems to be in a dark mood," she commented. "Thorne said he was seeing him today. Perhaps talks did not go well." Siva eyed Quinn as though she might have been the cause of the dark look Lazarus was shooting their way.

"I doubt it was Thorne," Quinn muttered under her breath as she strode back towards the group.

Lazarus stood with his arms crossed over his massive chest, watching her with cold, dead eyes. She had no idea why he seemed ... angry wasn't the right word, but perhaps heated. There was a fire burning in his cold eyes, and Quinn was sure if she put her hand out towards it again, she might get burned. She wouldn't. Not after the night they'd had because clearly neither of them had any plans on acknowledging whatever was building between them.

"What do you want?" Quinn asked sharply, glancing sideways as Siva pressed the notch on her staff and then pushed the wood back inward until the weapon was once again a smaller, forearm-length rod. Quinn manipulated her own staff until she attained the same result.

"We have business to attend to," Lazarus said. "Come with me."

Quinn moved to the side and bent to retrieve her practice sword as well. "Oh? And just where are we going, *your highness*?" she taunted.

Lazarus scowled at her but didn't say anything as he turned to Draeven. "Stay here. We will be a few days. No more. We'll be leaving for Ilvas when I return so make sure things are ready."

Draeven nodded. "I understand."

"I don't," Quinn snapped. "Where are we going?"

Once again, Lazarus didn't answer. He merely

looked her over as sweat sluiced down her skin and Quinn had no doubt that her cheeks had turned pink from the sun and exertion. "You may want to wash before we leave," he said. "It will be a short journey compared to our last few weeks, but we go on foot. No horses."

Glaring as Lazarus turned and strode away, Quinn only muttered under her breath as she followed at a much slower pace. "Thank the gods for that."

Bitter Truths

"It's better to be intimately familiar with pain and take the bitter sting of truth instead of the sickly sweetness of a lie."
— *Quinn Darkova, vassal of House Fierté, fear twister*

"How much farther?" Quinn groaned, wiping her eyes with the back of her hand. She'd bathed before they left, not that it did her much good once they began the steep uphill climb to the top of the mountain. Over half the day had gone and passed them by and Lazarus hadn't slowed for even a second of it.

"We're only a few hours out now," Lazarus replied. He'd been stoic since they had stepped foot on the rough but worn trail. She wasn't sure what brought on this dourness of his—whether it was the dream-not-dream or the things that occurred the night before that made him so short with her now—but he was keeping his distance. And she didn't like it, not one bit.

"I'm exhausted," Quinn panted, sluggishly dragging her legs upward. The burn in her thighs was real and made the hurt from riding a horse feel downright tolerable. "Can we break for a little—"

"No," came his reply. Quinn bit out a curse in N'skaran, not noticing the small rock that caught the toe of her boot and she went down. Her hands came up, protecting her face as it met gravel and stones. The scent of copper made her scrunch her nose as she groaned and rolled over. Despite the faint traces of pain in her hands, she was content to lie there for just a moment. Even with the pulse of discomfort and the slick feel of blood on her skin, it couldn't lessen the relief her legs felt as they were finally given the break they had been screaming for.

"Gods above—what the—" Lazarus' massive form filled her blurry vision as he kneeled down. "You did this on purpose, didn't you?"

"Mmm," Quinn groaned. "Of course," she coughed. Her lungs felt like they were bursting from all the exertion, but in actuality, it was simply the strenuous exercise and cold air. "I definitely did that intentionally, scratching up my hands just so I could have a break." She held up her hands and blood dripped down them. Lazarus looked past them, down at the girl lying in the trail.

"I never know with you," he muttered as he started to clean and bandage her wounds. If she were being honest, Quinn would have fallen sooner if she knew it would result in a break, but she kept that to herself as his calloused fingers skated over hers.

When her palms were cleaned and wrapped in dry cloth, Lazarus helped her up and they started again at a much slower pace. "So why are we practically running up this mountain like raksasas are chasing us?" she asked. Lazarus sighed.

"We need to test how strong you are," he said slowly. "And the Cisean's have a way to do that."

Quinn nodded. "So, it's true," she murmured, drawing his attention.

"What's true?" he asked, and she could tell it pained him. Whatever demons were chasing them this day, they weren't the raksasa of the dark realm.

"The Cisean's have a cavern that can reveal a Maji's strength … if you have the right tools. Yes?" she said, squeezing the sting in her palms by clenching her fists at her sides.

"You know of it?" he asked.

"I know of a great many things, Lazarus. Don't act so surprised." A slight smile curved around the corners of her lips and his expression darkened.

"Then you know how it works," he said. "Good. That'll make this easier."

She shook her head. "I didn't say that." She nodded up to where the trail disappeared over a ravine hundreds of feet above. "I said I know of the cavern. It's been rumored for years that they had a way to test magic, that it could tell if a person would survive the ascension..." Her voice trailed off and she didn't miss the way he stiffened. "That's what we're doing here, isn't it?" she asked. "You want to make sure that you're investing your time and resources wisely and that when the time comes, I can live through it."

She didn't say it, nor did she give it away, but the callousness of it stung a little. She had suspicions of what his intentions for her were, but still, there was more to them—more to whatever it was between them than this dispassionate indifference. Even if neither of them wanted to admit it.

"That's not exactly it," Lazarus said, his lips pinching together. "I need to get a feel for what I'm dealing with in training you, and the only way to do that is to have you tested. Unfortunately, we couldn't do it before we left Dumas—"

"—because you're the heir to the Norcastan throne and people don't like that," Quinn added before he could continue.

"Like I said before, there is more to it," he said eventually, and Quinn harrumphed because she knew he wasn't going to say more. "But yes, we had to leave in a hurry, and this is the only place that I can do it without too many eyes." Quinn frowned, crossing her arms over her chest.

"Why does it matter?" she asked.

"You're powerful, and power scares those who don't have it," Lazarus answered. She stumbled when the tip of her boot caught a rock and blinked twice as he continued past her. His long thick legs ate up the distance.

"You think people would try to kill me if they knew what I was," she said, not questioning, but in hopes to prompt some kind of answer from him. Lazarus stopped.

"For *what* you are? Without a doubt. That's why you tried to hide it." He paused, looking over his shoulder. Smoldering black eyes zeroed in on her. "But for how *strong* you are … some things are worse than death. You were a slave once. I'm trying to make sure it doesn't happen again."

Her heart jumped in her chest because he got it. For all his poking and prodding and herding and manhandling—he got it. "If the wrong people learn how strong I am before I can ascend, they might try to take me," she whispered.

He nodded. "Not that they'd be successful. I have a reputation for removing limbs when people steal from me." She might have shuddered if she were a lesser being, but the darkness in his voice had the opposite effect on her. Instead of feeling trapped, she felt safe. Protected. That shocked her to the core.

Quinn was always the protector, the guard dog, the weapon. Never once had she been protected.

Slowly she walked forward, coming to stand beside him.

"Will it hurt?" she asked. Her face gave away nothing. No shadow of doubt. No hint of feeling. It was the mask he wanted. The mask she needed.

"Yes," he answered honestly. "It's supposed to mimic the ascension and drain you completely so that it can measure what you'll be after it." Her eyebrows drew together as she stared at him. She understood the ascension in broad terms. She'd seen people go through it when she lived in N'skara, but Maji were rare in Norcasta. Partially because they were less frequent. N'skara bred for magic where as Norcasta didn't. It was also partially that most Maji, light or dark, chose to remain hidden from the prejudice they would experience otherwise in the southern countries. That was one of the reasons Quinn found Lazarus so interesting. Not only was he a dark Maji, but he was a nobleman *and* in line for the throne.

"Do you think I'll survive it?" she asked, shaking away her thoughts. She was not afraid, even knowing there was a chance she could die. There were worse ways to go. She knew because she planned to use them on those that had wronged her one day, if she made it through.

"I do," he said without hesitation. "Thorne said

this is going to be painful for you, but I truly believe you'll make it through. You're too strong not to."

Quinn stared at him, his features remained impassive, giving away nothing. She looked into his ebony eyes and saw the truth there. That he did believe that, but he was also worried.

Good, she thought to herself, striding past him and continuing up the trail. It meant he understood not just her past, but the value of her life. She could work with that.

"What are you going to do if I'm more powerful than you?" she asked absently after the sounds of his heavy footsteps sounded behind her, once again devouring the distance she'd created between them.

"I'm not sure you want to know the answer," he told her and Quinn lifted an eyebrow to urge him on. "If you're more powerful than me, I may not be able to let you go."

At that, she shuddered, but not in disgust, nor in fear. No, she shuddered because of something else. It wasn't that she wanted to be caught or trapped, but she knew that even when he held her leash, it was merely a facade. The way they were together was different than Lazarus among his other vassals. Where the others could complain but never received an inch, Quinn had learned how to take a mile. He gave her bits and pieces that he wanted no one to see, but she did. And with every piece he gave, she wanted more.

"What makes you think you'd be able to stop me

if I am?" she asked, not haughtily, but curious. His dark chuckle had her eyeing him as he strode by.

"You forget, Quinn. There's still so much about me you don't know."

She considered that and licked her lips as he continued on ahead.

No, perhaps she didn't know, but something told her she would.

If Lazarus' dreams were anything to go by, the man had demons—and much like her fear enjoyed the taste of him—she got the feeling that his demons rather liked the taste of her as well.

And that suited her just fine.

A Twisted Aberration

"To live life under the shadow of death is to not have lived at all."
— *Quinn Darkova, vassal of House Fierté, fear twister*

Quinn's legs burned as they ascended the last steps over a mound and around a cluster of trees. She was tempted to ask if they were almost there, especially since twilight had begun to spread its wings over the vast skies above them, when they finally stepped out of the tree line and came to a jagged dark hole in the side of the mountain.

"Is this it?" she asked as Lazarus approached.

He nodded. "I believe so."

Quinn moved to stand alongside him, just to his

right. "How can you be sure? There are a lot of caves in these mountains."

Lazarus lifted his hand and gestured to the top of the stone circling the entryway. Quinn's head tilted back, and her eyes alighted on the dark etchings that she'd just noticed. "What's it say?" she asked, narrowing her gaze as she looked up the side of the rockface for any hints.

"I don't know. Nobody does," Lazarus said. "It's an ancient language that died in the wars for the mountains." He paused for a moment, taking a breath as he glanced towards the darkening sky. Quinn started for the entrance when Lazarus put his arm out to stop her. "We can't enter yet."

She froze. "What? Why?"

"We enter when the moon is high," he stated, turning away. "For now, we will rest." Lazarus glanced back at Quinn. "You're going to need it."

Quinn frowned, but willingly turned away to follow him as he started building a fire. Several feet from the mouth of the cavern, Lazarus settled on the ground when the flames nipped at the cool mountain air, his back to a large oak as he waited for night to fall. Quinn plopped down across from him, letting the silence comfort her as they waited.

There was something off about the place, these mountains. Nothing substantial—nothing that could be seen—but her skin crawled with awareness, her power shivering under the surface. She couldn't quite put a name to the emotion in her mind, but felt it, nonetheless.

"So," Quinn began, tilting her head back on her shoulders as she eyed Lazarus. "You're going to be king, hmm?"

Lazarus shifted and then stilled against the oak once more, closing his eyes as he breathed deeply. "Perhaps," he replied.

Quinn narrowed her eyes on him. "Either you are, or you aren't."

Lazarus tilted his head back against the rockface without opening his eyes as he replied. "I'm not king yet, and the time for me to take the throne hasn't come."

"But it will, yes?"

"Only time will tell." Lazarus reopened his eyes, looking skyward.

Quinn wanted to say more but sensed that there was more going on beneath the surface of Lazarus' cool exterior. She bit her lip and stared at him— watching, analyzing, trying to dissect what it was about him that drew her attention. What it was that made a man like him falter. Fumble. What were his motivations? His dreams? Aspirations? *Fears?* She thought she knew the answer to that last one. The dream-not-dream had, at the very least, given her a hint.

But only that. The inked creatures that both came from him and desired to eat him made no sense. She didn't know what to think of it. Not yet.

As Quinn sat there, contemplating the secrets of the stone-faced man before her, the fire slowly began to die until only a small glow of red emanated from the ashes of the once roaring flames. The sky's blood darkened from bright orange to red and eventually to the ebony blanket that stretched as far as the eye could see. Lazarus sat forward as the moon peeked out from behind a few straggling clouds.

"It's time," he said, getting to his feet. He stomped on the already dying embers before turning and motioning to the cave. "Let's go."

Quinn stood and trailed after him as he stepped towards the cave. Together they entered, the cool night air dropping several degrees almost immediately. The sounds of the forest and the wind and the wildlife fell away as something *more* arose. Magic danced along Quinn's spine. This place, this cave, was *old*. Well beyond anywhere Quinn had ever been, and that included the temple in N'skara. Perhaps it was the oldest thing that existed on this plane, this realm. Not that she would ever know.

Quinn sucked in a breath as she felt venerable power infuse her limbs and she followed Lazarus farther into the recesses of the cave.

They came to the end of a short tunnel where another entrance stood, circled by the same strange lettering as they had seen outside. Lazarus shouldered through, but Quinn took her time examining the ancient script. Long blackened vines marked the path on the ground that crawled up the cracks in the rock to hang over the entrance—a curtain of sorts.

In barely a whisper, Quinn asked, "How will I know when it's over?"

Lazarus paused, his hand outstretched towards a section of vines that he meant to move aside. "When your magic has returned to your body," he answered.

Quinn considered that for a moment, then nodded as Lazarus finally pushed aside the last barrier to whatever awaited her. Quinn's lips parted as she stepped inside the sacred ground. The top of the ceiling had been carved upward so thinly that a small jagged hole about the size of a shield opened the cavern to the elements and beyond that, the moon. It hovered like an eye over the small pool of water, watching and waiting from above.

It was not the moonlight that lit the cave up, too dim for them to actually see, but the water itself. An iridescent glow emitted from the pools, shining faintly on lush ivory flowers that dotted the dark vines running along the walls of the cavern, reaching for the wet surface.

"Strip."

Quinn jerked and faced Lazarus. "What?" she demanded, crossing her arms.

Lazarus wasn't looking at her, though. He was staring straight ahead at the large translucent pool—

or really to the area up above it, to the smaller pool that fed into it by the means of a waterfall. "You can't wear clothes into the water," he said by way of explanation. He pinched the bridge of his nose. "Believe me, it's not my first choice but Thorne was very specific about what you have to do."

Quinn frowned, but he was not acting like a man interested in taking advantage. She had witnessed and dealt with far too many men like that. Lazarus was not them. While she knew he felt *something* towards her, she also had the distinct impression that wasn't what this was about.

Sighing to herself, Quinn walked toward the lower pool and began to undress. She stripped her weapons first—the rod-staff gifted by Siva, her sword she took from Draeven, and the daggers she'd collected over the years—leaving them, along with her clothes, on the edge. When she stood bare before him, she turned a fraction, glancing at the man over her shoulder as he rummaged through his jacket. Quinn knew she should be feeling some sort of anxiety, a faint inkling of fear for what may come, but the more she watched him the less concerned she became. It wasn't as if he was forcing her to do this, not really. She wanted to know about her power just as much, if not more than Lazarus did. And he was giving her the chance to find out. Beyond that, there was something about the cave that put her at peace. She knew pain was coming. That the magic in her veins had to leave her before it could return, and yet it was almost as if a part of herself was sliding into place this night.

A part that was always meant to be.

Lazarus retrieved a small leather satchel and tossed it to her. Quinn deftly caught it and untied the top, reaching inside to pull out a heavy palm-sized stone that was clear all the way through.

"That," Lazarus said before she could ask, "is a Servalis stone. It will be triggered when you go into the waters." He gestured behind her to the top pool. "You'll need to get to the top, and quickly."

Quinn sucked in a breath and nodded, turning for the lower pool. She was going to have to swim through the lower portion before she could climb to the top.

Tucking the stone close to her chest with one arm, Quinn entered the waters, letting the cold iciness wash over her skin, tightening her muscles as she moved. Lazarus shadowed the edge of the pool, a dark look crossing his face before he could slip into a mask of neutrality as she turned and dove under the water, careful to hold the stone up above her as she swam through the shallows until her feet found purchase on the underwater steps.

Water poured from her skin as she pulled herself out and climbed up to the top pool. A quick glance over her shoulder said nothing as Lazarus' expression was locked down tight. Their eyes met for a brief moment as she took a breath and stepped onto the ledge of the upper spring. The iridescent water glowing so bright it almost hurt. Immediately, Quinn stiffened as heat assailed her. It was so sudden she nearly fumbled and dropped the stone, but her fingers closed around it at the last moment and pulled it back to her chest before it could sink into the churning waters.

Across the cavern, Lazarus' face appeared as though it was carved from the same stone as the mountain while he waited for her to lower herself into water. Switching to holding the stone with two hands, Quinn lowered herself on the ledge and slipped into the clear blue as together—she and Lazarus—waited for the coming trial.

Quinn wasn't quite sure how long she had been floating in the upper pool; stone resting on her lower abdomen, held by stiff fingers, waiting for it to start … when she realized that it already had. Ever since she'd entered the high spring, her skin had slowly begun to tingle and sting. Everywhere the water touched felt like the edges of knives were pricking at her flesh. It just took her this long to notice. She shifted, moving to the side, jerking and crying out when one of the knives sank into her lower spine.

The stone started to slowly change from a color-less clarity to an opaque void as the nearly translucent liquid turned a murky gray before deepening further to a true black. Quinn shook her head as another blade slid into her abdomen, and she doubled over so rapidly her head nearly went under as the dark water turned ravenous. She squirmed, gasping as the pain mounted. Her flesh felt as if it were being peeled away layer by layer as invisible magic siphoned from her, swirling around her body while she remained in the center.

Magic began leaking from her limbs, beyond what was being pulled. It drifted from her mind on its own accord. Fleeing from her with the same strength of a riptide. With each passing moment, Quinn's body began to sag, and her breaths grew ragged. Aches cramped her sides as she used the last of her strength to remain standing. Despite the fire burning her, Quinn shivered as if cold. It was as if she had been drained of her blood, the very essence of life leeched away.

A bite of something sharp sliced open her insides and Quinn jerked one hand—the one that had inad-vertently pressed against her last invisible wound—out of the water only to see that she hadn't, in fact, been cut open. Her guts weren't swirling in the inky shadows surrounding her, though the pain in her flesh told her otherwise.

She choked when it came again and again and again—attacking every part of her.

Quinn sank her nails into the edges of the stone, trying to keep it with her as the agony became too much. Her lips parted in a silent scream as fire licked up her spine and then curled around her throat. Eyes wide, Quinn met Lazarus' indomitable gaze across the room. He stood on the very edge where she'd left him. Just a mere hairsbreadth from the actual water. He appeared, for all intents and purposes, as though he were merely waiting for her to stand up and get out. If it wasn't for the flash of fire in his eyes, she would think he simply didn't care.

Black dots filled her vision. She gasped, seeking air, but was too weak to inhale with her lungs. Her limbs were weak … too weak. Quinn pressed her back against the rock to keep herself upright. She couldn't sink, because she knew deep down she wouldn't come back up if she did.

She was so close to the end, she could feel it. Taste it. But it wasn't enough.

Because there was something else going on here … something she hadn't seen for what it was. Not until this moment. Not until it was too late.

Quinn didn't even realize when her eyelids had slid closed. She no longer had the energy to keep them open. Her awareness had whittled down to one single point. The Servalis stone that held the entirety of her being … *and then some*.

She had to keep going. She had to survive. She had to know she could survive and come out stronger. Squeezing the object between her two palms, Quinn silently demanded the truth.

And the stone answered.

A tendril of something dark reached from the

stone and into her chest, wrapping a vice around her life force. Her essence continued to rapidly drain away and Quinn felt it like a sword through her stomach when it started to pull more than just magic.

It was wrong. It was twisted—an aberration.

Her eyes shot open and she dropped the stone to the base of the spring whirlpool, but it was too late. Her arms wouldn't lift. Her legs gave way. Quinn's mouth opened but no sound came out as she was swallowed up by the black water and sank below the surface.

As her consciousness dispersed into oblivion, in her final thoughts, Quinn wondered … *was dying really this easy?*

Basilisk's Sacrifice

"Ordinary beings rarely make history. It is the abnormal, the aberrations, that change the world."
— *Lazarus Fierté, dark Maji, heir to Norcasta, Master of men*

Lazarus moved to the edge of the water, the toes of his boots barely skimming the edge of the still surface as he stared across the cavern. Leviathan's eye illuminated Quinn, transforming her pale skin to something otherworldly as she held the Servalis stone to her chest. Her eyes were squeezed shut, her lips pinched in agony.

Darkness leaked from her skin, staining the waters, churning them. Even as far from Quinn as he was, he could feel the sheer power that exuded from it. Concern began to fester inside his chest, eating away at his calm facade. Sparks of awareness prickled along his nerves, sending his senses into overdrive. He could hear every sharp inhalation of her breath, every shift she made to try and ignore the pain rapidly over-whelming her. He could smell the faint hint of salt on the cave walls mixed with the floral darkness of the moon flowers that stretched over the vines. There was something tainted about the scents, like a hint of rank blood was seeping from the petals.

Lazarus was fixated, his entire being focused on the woman across the space of water and stone. Quinn opened her mouth in a silent scream, her back bowing. Lazarus fought to not go after her. To not walk through the waters and pluck her from this nightmare—because he could not. Quinn would survive this. Despite the sharp gasps emerging from between her lips and the labored, sluggish movements of her body as she struggled to keep herself up, Lazarus would not accept any other answer. She would survive this and therefore, she would later survive her ascension. He couldn't doubt her. Not here and now when it would be too late.

And then the Servalis stone slipped from her fingers, splashing down into the oblivion of dark waters surrounding her. Lazarus frowned, his sharp eyes assessing Quinn's pale cheeks as she slapped her hands against the stone. She didn't appear to be aware of what she was doing. Her entire focus preoc-cupied. *Is she ... trying to get out of the water?*

Lazarus took a step forward, the clear water of the lower pool nipping at his ankles. Dread bloomed inside of him, reaching long tentacle like fingers up to squeeze around his heart and throat as doubt took form despite his best wishes.

Quinn looked up, her eyes meeting his. They were so hazy, so clouded, and he was no longer confident that she could even see him beyond that curtain of pain. Her lips, now nearly blue, parted and then she collapsed.

Lazarus cursed under his breath as she sank down beneath the surface of the opaque waters. He waited, hoping that she'd reappear within the next few moments. But when she didn't, he cursed again, turning and throwing off his cloak immediately.

Despite of Thorne's warning, he was going to have to take his chances and enter the pool. Quinn may not die from the pain, but she could certainly drown in the meantime, and Lazarus could not allow that. She was too important. Claudius had made it clear that without her this would all be for nothing. His entire future—his empire—his throne—depended on her.

And so even if no one had survived two people entering the pool before, they would now.

Because he would not let her die. No matter the price.

Lazarus dove through the lower pool, his muscles pushing him, his limbs cutting through the liquid with ease. His head resurfaced as he neared the higher spring and he took the stairs at the base to the top of the small well.

Pressing his palms on the ledge, Lazarus peered over into the blackened waters as they sloshed and churned. With a frustrated scowl, he reached down— trying to keep the rest of his body from the enchanted waters as much as possible. Already he could feel the strings of the stone's magic reach for the new energy source. It hungered, violently stabbing at his arm as he felt for Quinn.

Lazarus clenched his teeth and jerked his arm away. He reached for the one creature he possessed that could survive this magic and buy him some time. He needed to get her above the water so that when her magic returned, it wouldn't be trying to reenter a drowned corpse. The basilisk answered his call, sliding from beneath Lazarus' skin, the creature became tangible in the form of a long body with mauve scales. Stygian eyes met his gaze as the animal dipped its head. Lazarus sent a mental command and the creature curled its body around him like a shield, so that it moved with him as Lazarus heaved himself over the edge.

The siphoning that had assaulted him before remained, though it was muted by the basilisk's natural resistance to magic. Lazarus knew the creature wouldn't last long in this, but it was the more expendable of his possessions. Reaching down,

Lazarus found a slender wrist and gripped it between his fingers. Quinn's head emerged over the surface of the water as he dragged her up from the depths. Her limp body clung to the waters as he pulled her to him, fighting the waves that threatened to pull them both under.

Her lips were dark blue, the color of bleeding midnight. The same color was starting to sink into her cheekbones and under her eyes. She was cold to the touch, her skin a veritable frost. Lazarus lifted her, feeling for a heartbeat at her throat. It was there, but so weak and fragile, only a single small thump against his questing fingers every few moments.

He couldn't remove her from the spring. To remove her would be to remove all possibility of her magic responding. It needed to return to her body before he pulled her out, or else she would die all the same.

The basilisk curled tighter around Lazarus' muscles, letting him know that it was beginning to feel the pain of the Servalis stone eating at it. He had to find that stone. Heaving Quinn's prone body closer to his own, Lazarus angled down and searched for the floor of the spring. His fingers met and curled around a sharp point. What had caused the stone to change form, he didn't know, but he wasted no time jerking it back above the water's surface and pressing it against Quinn's naked chest.

"Breathe, Quinn," Lazarus ordered as he held her

to him and pressed his back to the stone walls of the spring to keep them both up. The basilisk squirmed around him, sliding between Quinn and himself as it shrunk to better suit its environment. The creature flicked its tongue out and hissed as a fresh wave of magic-depleting energy besieged it.

The pool began to settle as the churning and whirling went still. After several moments of calm, the water's surface became a mirror, reflecting their image back at him. Lazarus hoped that with the waters calming, the end of the ceremony would soon come. Quinn's magic would be returned and despite Thorne's warning, they would both survive. He refused to believe otherwise.

And then came the burn. Like fire in his veins, that dreadful magic shot down his spine. Sharp spikes of flame stabbed in a curved motion along his back, causing the basilisk to cry out in pain, its agony echoing up to the ceiling of the cavern. With wide eyes, Lazarus watched as the basilisk's scales grew pale and began to fade. He did not need to look at his back to know that the tattoo of the creature's soul was doing the same.

It was dying. A true death.

Flurries of dark purple ashes lifted into the air as the water's cleared in an instant, the absolute opaqueness of the Servalis stone began to dim slowly. The darkness returning to Quinn, crawling up her front like a cloud of smoke, into her nostrils and mouth and ears. As it did, her color began to return. The ivory of her skin, so unnatural before, began to pinken. The blue sheen to her eyelids and cheekbones diminished.

Lazarus bit the inside of his cheek as he waited. The magic needed to return completely, but the longer he remained in the water with her, the faster the basilisk deteriorated. Its cries teetering out into pathetic mewls and then only silence as Lazarus scooped handfuls of the still dark water and brought it closer to Quinn, letting the darkness lift away from the liquid and slide back to its home inside of the woman he held.

Lazarus' eyes narrowed as her hair began to soak up the darkness as well. He had heard rumors of the body changing when undergoing a trial such as this, but nothing compared to seeing it with his own eyes. Where her power was such a pure darkness, her hair was not. The silver strands slid against his palm as he reached up and shifted the locks to the side, pressing a hand to her face.

Her hair was still silver at the roots, but a faint purple color had bled into the ends and was steadily climbing. He smoothed her slick strands back as he watched the rest of it turn lavender. Her eyebrows followed suit.

He reached for the basilisk's presence, though its corporeal body had long since gone. It was there somewhere … but like smoke in the wind, not something he could truly grasp.

Lazarus shook his head as his eyes drifted down to the sleeping woman in his arms as the last of the dark water turned clear. But it wasn't only her magic she'd taken.

His basilisk was gone, and he knew without a shadow of a doubt that her magic had consumed it— she had not only taken back her own power, but she had devoured a piece of his as well.

Along his spine, Lazarus felt the emptiness, the lightness of being one soul lesser than he had been before. His muscles tightened as he lifted Quinn into his arms and out of the water, her legs over one arm and her back against his other. Her weight was slight by comparison to his own, but still, he took his time carrying her down the steps and through the lower pool. The translucent waters slid against his hips as he strode onto the rocky shore and placed her on the ground.

Lazarus bent over Quinn, pressing his fingers against her throat and sighing with relief as he felt the strong rhythm of her heartbeat returning. Then he backed up, waiting to see if she would wake up now that her magic had been restored. After several tense, quiet moments, Lazarus realized that was not happening.

He leaned forward, tapping her cheek lightly. Quinn's eyes drifted open, their depths murky and unfocused.

"Quinn? Can you understand me?" Lazarus

asked. Her body shuddered, shivers skating up and down her flesh as her lashes fluttered. "Quinn?" Lazarus repeated her name and once again received no verbal response.

Instead, she jerked forcefully as she turned her cheek and her back bowed. Water shot from between her lips, everything she'd eaten on the ascent up the mountain followed as it emptied on the cave floor. Lazarus attempted and failed to help her sit up, but shudders racked her body and she curled tight into herself before pressing against him—her mind obviously unaware of who she was touching as she sought out the only source of heat in reach.

Is this a result of the test? Lazarus wondered. He knew she was strong, that much was clear. The once smooth stone had turned pure onyx and grown crystals that still remained in the absence of her power— and what a magnificent power it had been.

As Lazarus lifted Quinn into his arms once more after retrieving her clothes and wrapping her in his dry cloak, he looked back over his shoulder. The waters of the spring had calmed, reflecting a now serene surface when just minutes before it had been a dark frenzied whirlpool. He had already known it, but this only served to establish and confirm Lazarus' suspicions. Quinn was no ordinary Maji.

She was so much more.

And true to his word—he was never letting her go.

The In-Between

"Sometimes the difference between real and fake is simply a change in perspective."
— *Quinn Darkova, vassal of House Fierté, fear twister*

Smoke and shadows surrounded her. Vastness and night. The pain had consumed her so wholly that she'd lost everything to hold on to, and yet still, she clung to that tiny scrap of presence inside her. That ember of life. She wasn't ready to die, no matter how fearlessly she faced the possibility.

There was still so much she had to do, so much she had to fight for. When everything was stripped away, she hovered on the edge of oblivion. There was only one thing that would save her now.

Spite.

Quinn had survived a childhood with monsters—not just with the creature that lived within her, but those that had raised her and then abandoned her in the worst possible way. She'd lived through her adolescence as a slave and eventually found freedom. She'd only tasted the briefest moments of independence before Lazarus had found her—and discovered that what she'd had wasn't freedom at all. Not like what she was gaining by being with him. An old woman not long for this world had told her that no one and nothing was ever truly free, but that they—people—could pick and choose the things that caged them.

Quinn was finally starting to understand, and she refused for her time to be up. No. She would hold on, because nothing in this world had yet to break her and nothing would now. Her vengeance for those who had attempted to destroy her still simmered in her veins, and one day, if she played her cards right, Lazarus would allow her the retribution she deserved. He would have no choice, because to be his vassal was to be protected from all, including the law. All but him, and he wasn't someone she needed protection from.

So, she held on and she waited.

The coils of black smoke drifted toward her, slipping beneath the skin. Dark shadows clung to her like droplets of water, seeking, searching for a way back in and she welcomed them.

She pulled and she plucked until every essence of

darkness that surrounded her had been torn from the air and returned to her, because if she was going survive—she was going to have to take it. All of it. Every last bit was hers to consume. She needed it if she wanted to live. And she did, more than anything.

Breath filled her non-corporeal lungs as the invisible cuts sealed and the pain faded.

There was something more, something that hadn't been there before. It slithered inside, having been absorbed along with the darkness.

In the void of her own mind, Quinn's lips parted as she whispered, "Who's there?"

A hissing filled her ears. A presence brushed against her mind.

She felt the cool hardness of scales sliding against her calves and when she looked down, she stared and blinked. A snake, easily twice the length she was tall began to curl around her feet and legs. Though there was nothing under them, no ground, no forest, no world to speak of—it still moved as if it did—much as she did here, in this place in the in-between.

She moved her foot, waiting to see what the animal would do, but it simply adjusted with her, seeking her out and curling around her limbs.

That's when she realized with a start that the beast was not here to harm.

No … it's protecting me.

Quinn leaned over slowly and the creature turned its head to stare at her. Eyes the color of onyx stones stared back, so clean and deep. It was chilling how they looked straight to her soul.

"Who are you?" she asked the creature. Her pale fingers touched the scales of its body and the snake shivered, but not out of fear.

The serpent opened its mouth and let out another hiss, but this time she felt it. That slight prodding against her mind. She didn't know how to open it up, only that she needed to if she was going to understand it. Sinking to her knees, the snake gave her space to sit before curling around her once more. She stroked its head and murmured soft reassurances.

Quinn couldn't explain it, but she felt connected to this animal. Something about the snake resonated within her, made her feel possessive of it, but for the life of her, she couldn't understand why.

"When we get out of here, you and I, we're going to do great things, aren't we?" she asked, leaning into the strong body that held her up. The beast's head came to rest on her belly and some part of her knew there was nothing normal about this. Most animals feared Quinn, but here, in the nothingness of the in-between, she was grateful to have something that didn't shy away.

She didn't think to look down as the snake's head slipped past her naked skin.

All she knew was that she wasn't alone. Then she heard him.

"Where are we?" As the voice spoke, Quinn noted

that it was distinctly masculine and raspy. It was old—
so very old.

"I'm not sure," Quinn answered. "I lost consciousness in the spring and woke up here. I think…" She
took a heavy breath. "I think we're in the in-
between."

"You are lost," the voice told her. She curled her
fingers around his scales as his body began to move
slowly, slinking under her skin.

"I am," she nodded, "but I'm not sure how to get
out."

Her fingers moved on their own accord,
smoothing over the scales until there were none left to
touch. Quinn blinked and realized the snake was
gone. *No—not gone…*

"I will show you," the creature told her. The edges
of her vision faded, and the only reason she grew
aware of it was because of the black consuming her
once more, but in the nothingness, there was no color.

"Who are you?" she asked again, stumbling for
something to hold onto as she began to fall.

There was nothing there, nothing to grasp but the
empty air.

"I am fear," the serpent told her. *"And you are my
master."*

COLD. IT WAS THE FIRST THING QUINN FELT WHEN her awareness began to rise. Her bones rattled as she shook, the hardness of the ground and the weight of her body dragging her back down from wherever her mind had been. She registered the chattering of teeth long before she realized it was coming from her. Something soft brushed over her skin and her fingers grasped for it, clutching the slight warmth of the fabric for dear life.

Time slowed as she drifted in and out. She felt when her body moved, and her bare skin pressed to another's. She sensed the warmth radiating from a body, but never felt more than the impersonal touch of fingers poking and prodding.

"Quinn?" a voice prompted, but it was not the one inside her, the one that called itself *fear*. She couldn't find the strength to move her lips, and so that voice went unanswered as she slipped back into the comfortable confines of the darkness. It was there that the snake wrapped around her battered soul, holding it close as she drifted through her daze of oblivion.

Quinn was so content in her darkness that when the cold faded and the heat came, it once again woke her. After so long of only cold and desolate, she flinched at the warmth of the burning heat. Her eyes fluttered open, searching for the source.

It was night, but the sky didn't seem as dark as it did in her restless sleep. Leviathan's eye shined down upon her and she followed that illumination to the burning fire only feet from where she lay. Tendrils of orange and red twined together in a lover's dance as embers sparked and took to the wind. She stared at the fire, still groggy and disoriented, when she saw another figure just beyond it.

He stood with his naked back to her, a shadow outlined by moonlight and trees. Creatures painted in colors of black and blue, the purples of dusk and the yellows of dawn, crawled over the taut muscles of his back, between his shoulder blades and down his arm. Quinn blinked as what she could have sworn was a firedrake stared back at her, its evergreen eyes so unbelievably life-like that she gasped.

Lazarus stiffened as she kept blinking in confusion. She felt scales beneath her fingers, not cognizant enough to understand.

"*I am here,*" the ancient voice of a man whispered through her mind. She blinked, transfixed as Lazarus turned towards her, his eyes going wide. It was then that she realized the beasts she saw weren't *on* his skin, they were *under* it, crawling and sliding beneath his flesh as though they weren't mere images, but living, breathing creatures.

"Quinn," he spoke her name and there was a familiarity to it. A relief that she only barely grasped before her vision began to darken again. Her skin was slick with sweat and far too hot, but the snake … its scales were chilled. She relaxed into its cool embrace as once again she drifted thinking about what she saw.

Vow of Silence

"Friendship was just another word for favor, and neither were granted without reason."
— *Lazarus Fierté, dark Maji, heir to Norcasta, Master of men*

Lazarus froze, watching as the basilisk curled around Quinn's prone form. It stared at him with its deep, knowing eyes. The creature had not forgotten its previous master, but it seemed that it had found another. One that Lazarus noted with no small annoyance, that it was more than happy to serve— loyal in a way it never had been with him.

"You answer to her?" he asked the snake, knowing full well that if the beast wanted to communicate with him then it would.

"Yes," came the serpent's reply. Lazarus nodded.

Just as he'd suspected, the basilisk hadn't simply died or disappeared. It had been consumed … but not in the same way as Lazarus had consumed the animal before. Somehow, the basilisk had merged with her, taking the smallest sliver of his magic with it. The single strand that held its soul together, keeping it from disintegrating without its original body.

Lazarus took a step forward and the snake hissed, cocking its head and baring deadly fangs. "She's sick, creature. I cannot help her if I can't touch her," he said, staring down the massive snake as it slowly began to recoil and shrink.

"*I am watching,*" it said in his mind, the warning imminent. Lazarus nodded as the thing began to slink back into her, leaving her fevered skin bare to the elements. She'd gone from shivering to catatonic that first day, where she stayed for another one, but then the fever hit…

Three days and they hadn't been able to make it back down the mountain. She'd fallen ill in that time, and while he was certain her body had retained its magic, he wasn't certain her body would survive whatever illness plagued her now if he pulled her from the fire for too long.

So, they waited, but Lazarus knew they were running out of time. What food and water he did bring was growing scarce after so many days. He'd filled his flask at the spring but only made it a quarter of the way down before having to stop.

He smoothed a hand down his face before pinching the bridge of his nose and exhaling deeply. A moment or two was all he allowed himself before attempting to make her drink water. He'd had varying success the past three days, but this was the first time she'd woken with any sort of clarity. He had to hope that meant the fever was coming to an end, for both their sakes.

Her lips parted as he lifted her front half and settled her against his thighs. A sigh escaped her as he unscrewed the flask and placed it to her lips. Slowly, he tilted it, allowing the smallest trickle of water to flow between her lips. Quinn moaned, swallowing before she began to guzzle more.

Lazarus sighed. He would never believe that relief was what lessened the tension in his shoulders as Quinn's fingers came up and closed around the flask as she downed the rest of their remaining water.

He wouldn't admit to the worry that gripped him. He wiped her sweat slicked skin and dressed her in the only clean clothes she had. Like it or not, they had to make it back down this mountain today. She needed proper nutrition and real rest to overcome the last of the effects of the spring, and he needed to talk with Thorne about what had transpired.

Pulling the clean burlap shirt over her bare stomach, his knuckles tightened as he pulled away. Quinn was unquestionably a woman, one that he'd been taking more and more of an interest in whether he wanted to or not—and it wasn't because of her body, though he had noticed her slight curves and pale skin more than he wanted to admit during the past three days. She was sick, and the Quinn that intrigued him was not an unconscious woman without bite.

Turning away, he dressed himself, strapping on both their weapons before hauling her into his arms, cloak still tight around her shoulders. A few kicks of dirt smothered the remaining fire and then they set out.

Lazarus carried her, one arm wrapped tight around her back and the other under her knees as he started down the mountain. The winds whipped against his skin and flipped up the cloak he had bundled her in, and he sent out a silent command for them to settle. Before long, her weight began to take its toll, and he had to call upon another of his creatures. He let the stone like strength of a troll flood his veins, hardening his skin and keeping him going. Funneling his magic to control the beasts beneath his skin was very little compared to the physical strains wearing on him in that moment.

But he had no choice.

Desperation and drive employed him, compelling him forward. With every step that drained a tiny bit more, the sheer force of will pushed him to continue onward down the mountain and not falter, not even for a moment.

Cisea came into sight after far too long. Shouts

rang out across the village as Lazarus stumbled through, masking his exhaustion with slowing footsteps. An ash-blonde head appeared in the crowd forming around him as cries about the she-wolf met his ears.

Draeven stepped forward, his face paling when he took in Quinn's unconscious form.

"What happened?" he demanded, his eyes narrowing on Lazarus with suspicion.

"She's alive," Lazarus replied with a growl, answering the unspoken question in his eyes, but not the one in his left-hand's mind. He still wasn't sure how to answer that just yet, not when he barely understood it himself.

"Only just," Draeven replied tersely. He stepped forward, just starting to lift his arms to try to take her from Lazarus when Lorraine came hurrying through the crowd, Dominicus not far behind.

"Gods above," the older woman proclaimed. She pushed the cloak out of Quinn's face and pressed a small hand to her forehead, then her cheek. "She's with fever. We need to get her inside—"

"Dominicus," Lazarus said, turning to his weapons master. He lifted his arms to hand her over. "Take her up to their room and keep guard. Lorraine, she's sick but she's on the mend. She needs to get more fluids and a healing brew. Think you can handle that?" he asked as Dominicus took Quinn and started walking.

"I'm a healer, for Gods' sake, Lazarus—of course I can care for her," she snapped, turning on her heel. He didn't like the way his people were looking at him, like Quinn's condition was somehow his fault, but he didn't have time to coddle them either.

"Oh, and Lorraine…" He waited for her to pause. "Keep your questions to a minimum if she wakes up. She's been disoriented and might not respond well."

Her response was a cold laugh he'd only heard a handful of times over the previous ten years. "It's Quinn. When does she ever respond well?" Lazarus didn't bother with a reply as she turned and hurried after Dominicus. The Cisean people made way for them, their jewel-toned eyes turning from the sleeping woman to him—frigid hostility only barely concealed.

Thorne appeared around a crop of trees. He walked by Quinn, narrowing his eyes on her as Dominicus carried her away, before turning to Lazarus and motioning for him to join him in his hut.

"I'm coming with you this time," Draeven declared and Lazarus only grunted. Having his second-in-command might go over better given Draeven's affinity for people. It would at least keep Thorne off his back for the time being. The man wasn't nearly as forward when others were around.

Lazarus turned through the crowd and Draeven followed close behind. Thorne was already up in the tree hut by the time Lazarus made it there, exhaustion making him drag, not that he showed it as he started up the rope ladder. His large hands closed around the edges of the wooden floor and he pulled himself up.

"You were gone longer than expected," Thorne said before Draeven had even joined them. "My friend…" he added slowly, as if that title might be in question.

"There were complications," Lazarus replied as he folded his hands behind his back. A picture of perfect authority and control were it not for the wrinkled tunic and dark circles beneath his eyes.

"I can tell," Thorne said slowly, his eyes drifting from Lazarus to Draeven and then back. "Her hair and aura have changed color."

Lazarus nodded because he'd suspected as much. Her magic had consumed the basilisk and his own when the stone returned her power. Only time would tell how much, but the lilac strands of her hair made him think the snake wasn't going anywhere. It had chosen her to be a true master, and whether she realized it or not—she had chosen it too.

"Does that not often happen?" Lazarus asked, wanting to test the waters and see how much Thorne might say before demanding some answers of his own.

He hesitated before saying, "In the past, it has only happened twice. Both times when someone entered the waters…" Thorne shook his head as if troubled by those memories. Lazarus could understand why after seeing Quinn nearly die in the way she had. "In both cases, the Maji who entered were drained completely of their magic and the person who held the stone received both. Our bodies are not meant to hold so much, and nature intervenes. They both succumbed to sickness and perished within days." He wouldn't say it, but ice froze around his veins and followed them straight to the center of his chest.

"Quinn is improving," Lazarus said, not sure whether he was trying to convince the other man or himself.

Thorne nodded. "If this is days after, as I suspect it is, I think your vassal might be the first to survive such an encounter. The question I have is: how did you?"

Lazarus looked away, nodding slowly to himself as he toyed with how to answer that question. Thorne was not an ignorant man, nor was he blind.

"If I tell you what happened and how I saved her, you must take a vow of silence—to keep that information between us ... *my friend*," Lazarus said, knowing that this small sliver of truth would go a long way in keeping Thorne appeased.

The red-headed bastard let out a chuckle. "Alright, Lazarus. What is said between us will stay between us, or may Ramiel strike me dead." Lazarus hid his smirk as Thorne invoked the vow of silence by the God of balance and justice. While the immortals that created this realm and its Maji might not walk amongst them, they still had a presence here—still had power. To invoke Ramiel and then ignore a vow was asking to be struck by lightning where you stood.

No matter what Lazarus told him now, Thorne wouldn't breathe a word—not at the risk of angering a God.

"Quinn did everything you told me. She stripped and took the stone into the water under Leviathan's eye. The waters turned black and began to churn, then the pain came, and she lost consciousness after a few minutes—"

"Minutes?" Thorne interjected.

"Yes."

The other man's face turned flushed as he looked first to the ceiling and swore and then looked to the ground, before saying. "It shouldn't have lasted that long. The ceremony is typically measured in seconds, not minutes." Lazarus shook his head, not terribly surprised given how her power seemed to astound them at every turn.

"Well, it did, and she fought through it up until her body was too weak to hold herself up anymore. I feared she was going to drown and so I took the chance and went after her." Behind him, Draeven had been awfully silent for the whole of the conversation, but he sensed his second brewing. The rage Draeven usually worked so hard to keep in check was simmering beneath his skin. They were going to be having their own talk shortly after this.

"How did you get into the water and survive?" Thorne asked, leaning forward.

Lazarus stepped forward and lifted the hem of his tunic to show his chest. Draeven didn't make a sound, though Thorne's eyes went truly wide at what he saw before him.

"*You're a*—"

"Yes."

The other man blinked twice and settled back, not nervous, nor afraid, but unsettled. "I had a basilisk in my possession until three days ago," Lazarus started. "I used it to stave off the power of the stone, but it was stronger than I anticipated and the basilisk was consumed by its magic." Lazarus paused, knowing whatever was said here and now Thorne could never speak of again. It was best to get it all out and see if he had any information to share about what would become of her. "That same basilisk came out of Quinn's skin last night when it thought I might try to harm her."

"She's now the holder of its soul?" Thorne asked, looking older, more haggard and worn than he had when Lazarus had entered his tree hut mere minutes before.

"And its loyalty," Lazarus bit out. "They are bonded … deeper than I am with my possessions. I think that when she was dying the basilisk somehow merged with her." Thorne seemed to consider this for a moment before nodding.

"It would make sense," he began. "The Servalis stone is intended to absorb all magic before returning it to its holder the same as it was before. A Maji's magic is as vital to them as air or water. To be stripped of it would mean death, and so if the snake was drawn into that before it was put inside her, I suspect they have become something that ... if not new, then something that has not been seen in this world for a long, long time."

Draeven stepped up then and asked, "And if the snake dies—what would become of Quinn?" He turned to look between Lazarus and Thorne, but they both shook their heads in answer.

"There's no way to know for certain without killing it, but she would likely die too," Thorne answered slowly. Draeven's eyes flashed from a violet hue to maroon, but he continued. "Everything has a price, young rage thief." He tilted his head towards Lazarus' second-in-command and Draeven clenched his jaw. He didn't like anyone mentioning who or what he was, for any reason. "She stole a piece of magic that wasn't hers to behold and nature finds a way to balance that. Fortunately for you both, basilisks are one of the hardest creatures in this realm to kill due to their natural resistance to magical forces." Draeven didn't say anything, but the glare he shot Lazarus made it very clear that the coming conversation would not be pleasant, even if he wouldn't say so in front of Thorne.

Lazarus pulled the Servalis stone from the satchel hanging at his side. The clear-cut stone that was once smooth had grown into jagged points with tips sharp enough to cut through skin. Lazarus lifted it to the light, and the stray rays of sun caught it just right, throwing off a series of smaller beams of light around the room.

"Do you know what to make of this?" he asked. Thorne stood from his throne and stepped forward to examine the crystal from every angle.

Silence filled the room for several moments when he finally stopped and returned to his throne without a word. There was a grimace to his face, his lips set in a line. "The kind of power that girl holds is immeasurable. There are only rumors of this happening to the stone. Stories ... or so I had believed. I've heard tales of Maji from Cisea that went through the process and the stone itself changed as it did with her ... and after all I've seen now, I know better than to dismiss those legends." Lazarus couldn't help the prickle of unease that went through him, followed by a shiver of delight. He knew that day he saw her in the market she would be something to behold, but he was not prepared for the conflicted emotions that ran through him which he couldn't—wouldn't —understand.

"She may be a fear twister, but whatever happened in that spring has made her more and it won't be long before my people take notice. Her hair has already changed, and if my suspicions are correct, her powers may grow more volatile after this. She's going to need guidance if you don't wish to lose her to the darkness, Lazarus. Otherwise, she'll begin to walk paths not even you or I would dream of." Lazarus tucked the stone away again while Thorne spoke, confirming all of his suspicions and more.

"Quinn has always been volatile," Lazarus said slowly. "The key to her is not restraining that power but learning how to redirect it so that it doesn't destroy her or anything I don't want it to." Draeven shook his head and Thorne's jaw tightened. Neither of them cared for his methods, but that was not his concern. That was why they weren't the ones who had signed a blood contract with her.

"Regardless of how you choose to handle her, I'm going to have to ask that you and your party leave soon. The girl's changes are going to draw unwanted attention towards me and those allowances I've given you. While my people seem to be quite fond of her, that might not be the case if they realized what you've done." Lazarus tilted his head forward, his chin dipping.

"That won't be a problem," he said.

"Good," Thorne replied, holding up a hand for Lazarus to pause when he turned to leave. "The other reason you might want to get moving sooner rather than later is that my men found evidence of others moving through these mountains. They've done well to stay concealed, but their tracks lead me to believe it's not a small party—and they are likely not here for amicable reasons." Lazarus sighed and cursed the damned noble brats. He had no doubts in his mind that if another group had entered these mountains, it was because they'd sent a hunting party straight for him. Claudius must truly be deteriorating for them to grow this bold.

"Thank you for the warning," Lazarus said. "We'll be leaving soon. Make sure the boy is ready if you still want me to take him." He was already contemplating how fast he'd be able to get Quinn on a horse before this meeting; talking to Thorne only solidified that it was time. They'd gotten what they came here for and then some, but in Quinn's condition, the journey out of the mountains wasn't going to be easy.

Thorne chuckled. "I know your dislike for him, but he will serve you well in the coming trials." He paused. "Take care with the girl. I don't know how this will play out, but I'm interested in hearing Vaughn's reports of what becomes of your situation."

That's one way to put it, Lazarus thought dryly. Draeven stepped around him and moved to leave without needing to be told. Lazarus held up a hand for him to pause.

"I need you to send a message out to Tritol. I have a feeling we'll be bringing some unwanted guests to their doorstep," he said.

"Consider it done," his left-hand replied,

descending down the ladder without another word. While his anger about Quinn's situation might be problematic, his second knew where his place was at all times.

"We appreciate your hospitality this past week," Lazarus told Thorne, and the other man only shook his head.

"Don't forget our alliance," he said. Lazarus nodded and began to descend when he spoke again. "And Lazarus"—Thorne paused—"may the Gods be with you, my friend." In a whisper so quiet Lazarus hardly heard it, he added, "for both our sakes."

Neiss

"People say to never trust a snake, but it is not the animal itself that is at fault—but the man who chose to back it into a corner."
— *Quinn Darkova, vassal of House Fierté, fear twister, Master of fear*

Quinn's eyes opened and focused on the patchwork of straw-like greenery that was the ceiling. Her muscles screamed as she groaned and moved to sit up.

"Oh no, dear, don't move so fast." Lorraine, who'd been across the tree hut quickly packing her things away, turned and rushed to Quinn's side.

"What—" Quinn stopped and licked her dry lips.

She felt like her tongue had swollen to the size of an andafruit.

She felt a hand pressing to her forehead and then heard Lorraine's voice. "Your fever has broken," she said with a sigh of relief, "and just in time too."

"Just in time for what?" Quinn asked, blinking furiously, trying to bring the rest of the ridiculously bright space into focus. The more she did it, the less the light seemed to bother her.

"We're leaving Cisea," Lorraine said. "Master Lazarus came down from the mountain with you early this morning. He's been with Thorne and Draeven since. Dominicus just got word that we're leaving before twilight."

Quinn shook her head and then moved her legs out from under the covers they'd piled on top of her. "Oh no, don't get up just yet. Rest as much as you can," Lorraine said quickly, pushing the covers back over her body. "We'll be riding on horseback for several hours today before we break. It'll take us a few days, at least, to get back out of the mountains."

"I'm fine," Quinn insisted, pushing the covers back once more and getting to her feet. She stared down at the burlap shirt and loose black trousers. Shooting a look Lorraine's way, the other woman sighed and nodded.

"Yes, I changed you," she said, answering Quinn's unspoken question.

Quinn narrowed her eyes and shifted on her feet. "Thanks," she replied, unused to saying the word.

Quinn sensed Lorraine's attention on her as she untied the laces of her trousers and redid them tighter so that they cinched to her hips. As she moved, the oddest sensation came over her ... like there was something under her skin. It prickled along her spine with unrest. Quinn shifted, noting that along with that itchy sensation, there was something else that felt sore and achy. Almost as though she'd been burned and then healed. She knew that feeling all too well. After all, she had been a slave, and as such had been branded seventeen times with hot irons pressed to her skin to mark her as nothing more than cattle. Quinn held her breath for a moment, trying to recall everything that happened up the mountain.

The skin below her abdomen twinged, just to the left of her navel, sending a jolt of pain through her. Quinn clamped her teeth together, her jaw tight as her hand dropped to the edge of her shirt. If she saw a brand there after everything she and Lazarus had been through ... Quinn didn't let herself finish that thought even as dark and pungent magic began to saturate the air.

Lifting her tunic, Quinn held her breath, and then let it out in a huff. Though the small stretch of skin hurt when she moved, there was nothing there, brand or otherwise. "How long was I asleep?" Quinn asked, releasing the material and trying to put her strange physical feelings aside.

"I don't know. You and Master Lazarus were up in the mountains for days," Lorraine replied. "You only got back just this morning."

"Days?" Quinn gaped. "How many days?"

"Almost four," Lorraine said.

That wasn't right. If that were true, then Quinn would have been unconscious for ... at least three days. Something fluttered at the edge of Quinn's peripheral, she turned her head and tried to make sense of what she saw. Grabbing a hunk of her hair, Quinn pulled it fully over her shoulder and held it up to the light. "What in the dark realm..." It was purple. Not a deep purple, but still a light lavender, and not the silver-near-white it had been.

"You showed up like that," Lorraine said quietly. Quinn looked between her hair and the other woman who stood somewhat uneasily, shifting side to side. Lorraine looked to the door where Dominicus stood and Quinn sensed she wanted to say more but wasn't supposed to.

"What happened to me?" she whispered. No sooner did the words leave her lips and it all came crashing in. The memories, the dreams, the pain, the voice...

"You were dying," a voice said in her mind. The same ancient one that held her through that fevered delirium. *"We both were."* Quinn's breathing sped up as

317

she waited for Lorraine or Dominicus to respond, but neither seemed to notice the voice at all.

Can they not hear it?

Quinn looked between them wide-eyed, wandering perilously close to the edge of crazy. *If they can't hear it, then that could only mean—*

"I don't know," Lorraine said, her worried expression flitting between Quinn and Dominicus. "Lazarus only told us he had to test your magic. He didn't say how." Quinn swallowed hard and looked away.

She'd walked into the spring knowing what might happen. She didn't blame him for the outcome because deep down without a shadow of doubt, Quinn knew—despite what he'd told her—he had also saved her. The pain had become too much and when she couldn't handle it, she had finally given in to the waters, and somehow, someway, her body had been pulled out and brought back here. The rest was a bit hazy … but those memories still lurked.

As did the voice inside her.

"What are you?" Quinn whispered.

"Who are you talking to—" Lorraine started, but Quinn held up a hand to hush her.

"I am fear," the voice answered, repeating what it had told her before. *"And you are my master."*

Quinn turned away from Lorraine, facing the window that overlooked the forest as she said, "But that is not your name. What do I call you?"

"Quinn, what are you—"

"I do not have a name. I did once, but it has been so long since the God that created me has spoken." Quinn pondered, ignoring Lorraine's prattling as she lifted her hands and pushed up her sleeves. A thick purple tail wrapped around her wrist and circled up her arm. It was the body of a snake, and it moved.

Quinn lifted her hand and turned to Lorraine.

"Do you know what this is?" she asked in a voice of deadly calm. Lorraine's eyes widened and Quinn looked to Dominicus who appeared equally at a loss for words.

"I have a feeling," she said eventually. Quinn nodded.

"Lazarus did something to me, didn't he?" she asked, not quite an accusation but still a demand for answers.

"I—" she broke off as the shadow man himself appeared through the doorway where Dominicus stood. The guard stepped aside without a word to let Lazarus through. Draeven wasn't far behind.

"Quinn," Lazarus said slowly. Her eyes flashed as the tail of the snake began to break away from her flesh.

"What happened to me, Lazarus?" she asked as the serpent slipped completely from her and yet still coiled around her body. The sudden weight of it winding up one arm, over her shoulder, and down her back was more than she was expecting. Quinn stumbled and the creature that called itself 'fear' darted out from under her shirt, moving to place itself in front of her and swelling to more than double its size as Lazarus and Draeven stepped forward—whether to help or not, she didn't know, which meant that neither did the snake. The animal eyed them in warning.

"Tell the basilisk to stand down," Lazarus ordered instead of answering her. She stumbled into the side of her cot, placing a hand on the wall to keep herself from falling onto it. Like it or not, she was still weak from the spring.

"How do you know I can talk to it?" Quinn snapped back, running a sweat-slicked hand over her wrinkled shirt before rubbing her eyes. A thick end of a tail wrapped around her ankle, and Quinn blinked. The snake was stroking her, almost affectionately.

"Do not worry, master. I will protect you."

Lazarus gave her a look, then pointedly glanced at the snake as if making his point clear. Lorraine, who had been only feet from her before, stepped back, as did Draeven. While they might have gotten used to Quinn, it appeared the basilisk—as Lazarus referred to it—was too much for them.

"It thinks I'm its master," Quinn said in a weary breath. "Why does it think that?"

"Because you are," Lazarus said in an exasperated tone. She narrowed her eyes on him and the snake took notice, growing in size once more until the full width of its body pressed against her lower legs and it released a hiss.

"I'm with the snake on this," she said, righting herself and stepping away from the bed.

"Something happened when you went into the pool, and I had to use the basilisk to save you. The stone ripped away its soul, and now it resides in you. For all intents and purposes—you are its master," Lazarus growled, the muscle in his jaw ticking.

The words the basilisk told her came back. *You were dying ... we both were.*

And yet they both survived. Somehow.

"Wait a moment." Quinn shook her head. Her mind catching the one thing she was pretty sure he didn't want her to notice. "You *used* the basilisk? How? Are you a beast tamer—"

"No," Lazarus said, cutting her off. A chill washed over her, a hint of that errant wind that caressed her bones those weeks ago—on the day they first met. *If he isn't a beast tamer but he can control a basilisk, what is he?* "This isn't a conversation I want to have here, Quinn," Lazarus told her. His eyes flicked to the open window behind her, and she understood. "We need to talk about what happened, and I'll answer your questions—but first, we need to get out of these mountains."

She waited. They all did, standing tense as the basilisk reared its head, waiting for a command from her, ready to strike. The exhaustion in her bones ran deep, and despite her suspicions—Lazarus did save her, and he did carry her down the mountain.

"It'll be a week in two days. I expect my answer whether we're out of the mountains or not," Quinn replied, stepping up beside the snake.

"Fine, but you tell the basilisk to stand down, and since you're feeling well enough to be a pain in my ass, get yours downstairs and on a horse. We're leaving now."

Lazarus turned and stalked to the door in the floor, sliding down before slipping out of it entirely. As one, Draeven, Lorraine, and Dominicus turned to look at her and the snake as it wrapped itself around her trembling form. She'd held out until Lazarus left, but her body couldn't handle it much longer. While she might have been awake and able to move, she wouldn't be training for a while yet. Even Dominicus, who's blue eyes were always so piercing when he watched her, sighed and shook his head.

"You're something, girl. I'll give you that," he said as he brushed his light brown hair back from his face. Quinn sighed, shuffling over to the bed before sinking down onto it.

"Things would be a lot easier if he wasn't keeping secrets." Quinn sighed, numbly noting how the basilisk curled around her waist as it shrunk in size again.

Soft footsteps approached, as Lorraine slowly came to kneel by her feet—a steaming cup in hand. "Drink this," the older woman said. "It'll help you regain your strength faster."

"You might not want to do that—" Draeven started as Quinn took the cup and downed it in one go. Her chest racked itself as she let out a spluttering cough.

"What's in that? Poison?" Quinn croaked as Lorraine gave her a slight smile and took the cup.

"Medicine," she answered.

"Same thing," Draeven bit out from the other side of the room where he watched her hesitantly.

"You're scared of him, aren't you?" Quinn asked, petting the sleek mauve scales. She liked the feel of them.

"Eh…" Draeven tilted his head side to side. "I'm not a fan of creatures that could eat me, or in its case, kill me with a bite." Quinn shook her head, a slight upturn to the corner of her lips. "Are you going to make it on a horse this afternoon?" he asked.

Quinn sighed and the slight smile slipped from her face. "I don't have much of a choice now, do I?" He nodded, understanding shone in his violet eyes.

"Lazarus won't say it, but he has a good reason for leaving today," Draeven said as Lorraine moved around her to begin packing up both their things.

"He always does," Quinn replied.

"Yes, well"—Draeven looked away from her sharp, crystalline eyes—"you let me know if you need a break and I'll see what I can do."

With that, he disappeared, followed by Dominicus who shouted from the ground, "It's time."

"We're coming," Lorraine called back, turning to give Quinn a sympathetic smile. "Do you know how to put the snake back?" she asked her.

Quinn blanched. "I…" She paused. "I suppose I could just ask him." Lorraine, may the Gods bless her, she didn't look at her like she was crazy this time. She just smiled and nodded, encouraging her the only way she knew how.

"Why don't you try that," she said, stepping back.

Quinn nodded and turned to the snake. "We need to go now. Can you … um … return…" She hesitated to say *under my skin*, but the basilisk seemed to understand. His head slithered under the hem of her shirt, his tongue briefly flicking at her bare stomach, making her jump before he melted beneath her skin. Quinn shivered as goosebumps broke out across her arms.

"Are you alright?" it asked in her mind. Quinn nodded without realizing it might not know if she didn't speak. *"I can hear your thoughts, young one. Words are not necessary."*

"I see…" she thought, testing it out. The low, raspy hiss of pleasure surprised her. It sounded almost like a laugh. *"You said you don't have a name, but I think if you and I are going to be together now, you probably need one. Can I call you Neiss?"*

There was a pause as the snake seemed to consider her request.

"I would like that," it told her. She smiled and got to her feet. Lorraine kept giving her perplexing looks as

they climbed down the tree hut and started toward the waiting party.

Four heads turned in their direction as Lazarus, Draeven, Dominicus, and Vaughn stood waiting. "You ready, she-wolf?" the latter asked her. She glanced at Lazarus who stood tight-lipped and proud, holding Bastian's reins.

"I'm ready," she said, and this time she meant it.

Veracity's Compulsion

"Fear does not fear itself."
— *Quinn Darkova, vassal of House Fierté, fear twister,*
Master of Neiss

Q uinn's spine ached and jolted with each clomp of the horse's hooves. The trees grew thicker around them before they grew lighter, and still they weren't out of the mountains. When Lorraine said that it would take them days, she hadn't been overexaggerating.

Ahead, Lazarus and Vaughn pulled their horses to a slow halt and Lazarus called back, "we're stopping here for a rest!"

The longer that passed by, the sorer Quinn felt, which meant the more her patience was running thin with people, especially Lazarus. He'd been awfully stoic since they set out from Cisea, no words or sly glances, and she'd been put back with Lorraine. That partially had something to do with Draeven and Dominicus being anxious about Neiss. They were scared of the basilisk, whereas Lorraine, if she was—she didn't show it. It was going a long way towards increasing Quinn's tolerance of her, that and her silence. She hadn't muttered a word of propriety or manners, though her lips thinned when Quinn slid down the side of the horse ungracefully.

Dominicus, Lorraine, and Draeven took the horses off to the side while Lazarus and Vaughn spoke in low tones. It was obvious that Lazarus was unhappy about the arrangement with Vaughn joining their group, but he relied on the Cisean warrior for information in the mountains. Quinn got the impression this wasn't his first time through these parts, but he didn't have the same sort of intimate understanding that came with being raised here. Only someone with that sort of knowledge could navigate these twisting woods in the time they needed to.

"—another full day's ride before—"

"Lazarus," Quinn snapped as she approached, disrupting whatever Vaughn had been in the middle of saying. Staring, Vaughn turned and looked down at her as she focused on Lazarus. "We need to talk," she said.

"Not now," he said without looking at her.

"Oh yes, now." Reaching up, Quinn grabbed his arm. "I don't like being ignored, Lazarus. We will talk and we will talk *now*. I've waited the two days. Your time is up."

Silence fell over their group. Quinn didn't need to look over her shoulder to know that the others had all stopped what they were doing. She could practically feel each and every one of their eyes boring into her. She didn't care. This was important. Lazarus needed to know that she wasn't going to lie down and allow him to put it off. She had let it go while they'd ridden hard to get out the mountains, stopping only for brief bouts of rest, food, and sleep, only to start back up again. Not once did she complain despite the fatigue that plagued her. Not once did she ask for a break, even when the cramping in her side became so intense she worried she would pass out. She simply leaned forward into Lorraine and prayed to the Gods that the weakness in her bones would leave her.

Today was the day. Today, she would demand her answers and he would give them to her.

Lazarus leveled her with a cool detached look, a moment of silence spanning between them before he nodded, turning back to Vaughn. "Give us a moment," he said.

Vaughn frowned between the two of them, but did as he was asked and stepped away, heading over to help Draeven with the fire. Lazarus turned the full force of his gaze—disapproving as it was—on her.

Quinn released his arm, turned, and strode into the line of trees. She knew that he would follow and a moment later she heard the telltale sound of his boots crunching dry leaves under his feet.

When Quinn felt as though they had gone far enough, she turned on her heel and faced the man that both tempted her and frustrated her. There were dark, dark feelings in her chest when it came to this man. There were also lighter things, though not truly light. Everything about Lazarus was a mystery. A man broken up into so many pieces that she had only just begun to start putting those fragments together. "I want answers," she stated, crossing her arms over her chest.

"Ask your question, then," Lazarus said, stopping a few feet before her.

Quinn looked him over and then dropped her arms. She began to circle him, moving leisurely, if not for the predatory way she watched his reaction—or lack thereof.

"What are you doing?" he demanded when she didn't immediately present him with her inquiry. Quinn wondered if it was getting to him. She hoped so. He was getting to her in ways she didn't want to admit.

"Debating," Quinn replied drily.

"And pray tell, what are you debating?"

"Is that your question?" Quinn asked.

"Is that yours?" Lazarus shot back.

She stopped when she was in front of him once more, this time close enough to smell the sweat and dirt on his skin. "You saved me," she stated.

Lazarus' jaw hardened. "That's not a question."

"You came in the spring and you pulled me out," Quinn continued. "From what I hear—"

"From what you hear?" he repeated, his eyes narrowing on the woman in front of him.

She rolled her eyes and waved her hand. "You weren't supposed to," she pointedly ignored his previous question and loved the way the muscle in his jaw ticked with frustration. "The spring can't hold two people at once and let them live, except I did—you did."

"Is there a point you're getting to?" Lazarus asked. "A *question*?"

"I want to ask you what in the dark realm happened on top of that mountain—in the spring," Quinn said.

"If that's your question, then I'd be obliged to—"

"But I have a more important question to ask," Quinn snapped, interrupting him.

Lazarus froze as her hand lifted and her fingers traced down the middle of his chest. She had been delirious, hot with fever, but Quinn had a feeling that what she had seen—Lazarus without his tunic—it had been real. More real than that dream—or rather not-dream—she'd had about him. Lazarus clenched his teeth. It made her want to feel the skin of his jaw, touch the muscle and strength there and marvel at it.

"Ask. Your. Question." He hissed the words out as though they were painful.

"I ask it," she started, "and this time you don't give me some blasted non-answer, got it?" Her crystalline eyes met his dark gaze. He nodded once. "What are you?" she asked.

Lazarus stared back at her, and Quinn could feel the whole world fall away—the forest, the ground, the soft sounds of their group in the distance setting up a temporary camp. Her breathing slowed. Her heart rate sped up. Finally, she would have this from him. She would know.

"You wish to know what I am? What kind of Maji you've tied yourself to for the next five years?" he repeated. Quinn didn't answer. He already knew she did. "Very well."

Quinn's hand dropped away from his chest as he moved closer until her slight breasts brushed up against him. She kept her gaze steady on his. He leaned close, his mouth a mere inch away from her ear as his lips parted and his warm breath brushed over her flesh, sending shivers down her spine.

Quinn could feel Neiss slithering under her skin, but the creature sensed no danger and quietly fell back into slumber, its presence receding to the back of her mind.

"I am what they make legends from, little fear

twister," he whispered. "I am that which consumes the living. I am a soul eater."

All of the breath rushed from her chest and Quinn blinked hard as her mouth fell open and Lazarus slowly moved back to once again meet her gaze. Her throat was dry. Her eyes wide. Prickling numbness stretched along her limbs.

"A s-soul eater?" she repeated. Even when she had lived in N'skara, one of the premiere places to learn of all types of Maji, soul eaters had only been talked about in hushed whispers. They were myths—legends, as Lazarus had said. Not real. At least, she hadn't thought they were. Until this moment.

"I am," Lazarus replied darkly. "Are you afraid of me?"

Quinn tamped down her shock and lifted her head. "Is that your question for me?" she asked. He nodded once, keeping his expression stoic and impassable.

Moving closer, impossibly closer so that their chests were pressed together again, Quinn leaned up on her tiptoes, and rested one hand on his shoulder as she whispered, "I *am* fear." The muscle in his jaw worked as her breath fanned over him, making her grin wickedly. "I do not fear."

With that, Quinn pulled away from him and brushed by his shoulder, the ends of her now lavender hair lifting at a slight wind as she walked away. Anger seethed within her veins. Soul eater or not, Lazarus should have answered that sooner. It explained so much. Too much. His silence might not push her away, but she could be angry with him in the meantime for it. Quinn paused on the edge of their secret clearing as Lazarus spoke once more.

"I would assume you know that releasing that information will nullify your contract with me and the protections it affords," he said tersely.

Quinn turned and lifted an eyebrow at him. "And I would assume that you would know me better than that by now," she replied. "I'm a fear twister, not a canary."

Lazarus relaxed his shoulders.

"However," she said. His shoulders tensed once again. It amused the dark depraved parts of her soul to see him on edge, even if only for a moment. "In the future, it might behoove you to share important details like that, or the full scope of both your intentions and actions where I'm concerned. I can't very well circumvent your stupidity if you don't inform me."

Lazarus was still gaping when Quinn twisted back around and strode away.

Phantom Inklings

"Emotions are fickle beasts, untamable by even the greatest of masters."
— *Lazarus Fierté, dark Maji, heir to Norcasta, soul eater*

She'd barely spoken a word to him in days and the voices were driving him crazy.

Their last conversation played over in his mind. Draeven hadn't ever spoken to him that way. If the man had, Lazarus would have had him dragged through the mud by his own horse. It was much the same for any other man or woman. And yet, he couldn't do anything more than watch as Quinn left. A woman like her would either make him the greatest king in the history of the Sirian continent or be the death of him.

He hardly missed the basilisk's presence, especially when Quinn's mere scent had the souls he held within him so impassioned that they pushed and pulled every minute she wasn't near him—and when she was, it was other urges—the darker ones—that pushed him. The last words she'd spoken to him still played over and over in his mind each night they camped, and she went about her business without paying him any mind. He respected her for it, though it made his growing need for her worsen.

He felt a hunger in his veins that made him restless, almost like his inner predator was craving a wild hunt—except the prey he so wanted, he couldn't consume. Much as he might like the idea of having Quinn under his thumb, he didn't want her in that way *ever*—not as a mindless creature without will. That's exactly what she would become if he ever took her soul, and he doubted he would survive the encounter, even if that was his intention. No, his actual desire was so much worse, and watching her train with the *boy* killed a part of him.

"He's skilled," Draeven remarked beside him. They stood just on the other side of the tree line that Quinn had insisted they practice behind. No doubt wanting to escape his ever-watchful eyes.

"He is," Lazarus agreed begrudgingly as the warrior circled her, halberd in hand. They'd put a blindfold over Quinn's eyes this time, and when Vaughn swung his weapon for her head, Lazarus had to fight the souls as they reacted with vehement outrage.

Quinn didn't need his assistance, though.

"Gods above," Draeven muttered as she jumped, twisting her body mid-air to bring her foot down on the hand in which Vaughn held the halberd. The Cisean winced, releasing his weapon immediately as she landed, pivoting to give herself the room she needed to bring her opposite foot up. She struck him in the throat with enough force to send the warrior reeling—all without use of her eyes.

"But not good enough, it seems," Lazarus remarked with no small amount of satisfaction. A smirk tugged at his lips as he watched her move back to where she stood before without removing the blindfold.

"I'm not sure any one man would be enough to handle that woman," Draeven murmured. The smirk dropped from Lazarus' face before his left-hand could see it. He had very different thoughts on that matter, but he wasn't about to disclose them to anyone—not even Draeven. "She's vicious, even in training. I don't know if she realizes one of these times, she might actually kill him," Draeven continued.

"If she wanted him dead, he would be," Lazarus replied, not all that concerned.

She was too fond of him anyway, even though half of it was a farce only meant to piss him off—he was sure. He would have put an end to these little sessions if it were anything more.

The Cisean moved again, this time dragging the end of the halberd six feet behind him, trying to throw her off. Quinn stood, her back straight as the weapon itself as she pulled out the rod she'd taken from Siva. Her hands moved, and he could tell she'd been practicing when she found that notch on the staff immediately and the second half of the weapon slid out. She began to twirl it between two hands and Lazarus squinted.

Vaughn stilled, lifting the halberd from the ground silently—only to bring it down on top of her head.

Or try to, rather.

The spinning staff had picked up enough momentum that the hook on the end of the halberd caught, twisting away from her body and out of his grasp. She brought the staff to an abrupt halt, stamping her boot on the end of weapon, only inches short of the deadly twisted metal end.

"There's no way she could have stopped that without knowing where he was," Draven commented.

"Perhaps she heard him," Lazarus remarked.

"Not with him dragging the halberd behind him she didn't. That's the first time he's tried that, and it didn't throw her in the slightest. She's using the field of vision," Draeven said. His second-in-command crossed his arms and leaned forward, squinting. "But I can't see her magic."

Interesting, Lazarus thought. He could see the wispy strands of fear and ashen footsteps she left in her wake, but no field. He had assumed that meant she either wasn't using it or had already placed it, but Draeven couldn't see anything.

That made him wonder. *Was it possible she...? No.* He wouldn't even entertain the thought.

But her control, he couldn't deny, had improved tenfold.

Vaughn advanced on her and she moved with steady limbs as she stepped one foot back and thrust the staff forward. The boy caught it between two hands, just a breath before it slammed into his face. They stood at an impasse, but not for long. Quinn twisted to the side, keeping a firm hold on the staff as she moved to kick him in the chest. Vaughn saw it coming this time and released one hand on his end of the staff to catch her boot, holding her there. He forced her off her footing, causing her to lose her balance as he pushed her back.

Somehow, the warrior either didn't see or didn't think about the cruel twist of her lips and the way she smirked as she fell. Her back hit the ground hard, but Quinn didn't crumble. Vaughn still held her foot, and she used that to rock him forward, attempting to either force him down towards her or to throw him over her head.

The warrior was smart enough to let go, but not

before he lost balance and control of the staff. She swept her other leg under him, and he went crashing onto the ground beside her. She rolled, bringing the staff back up as she straddled his prone form—and then widened her grip to bring it down on his throat —holding it there to block his airway.

Vaughn rasped something between his lips that sounded suspiciously like, "mercy—my she-wolf." Quinn smiled, sitting back and lifting the rod away. She laid it to one side of her and pulled the blindfold from her eyes. Those crystalline gems glimmered with amusement and the thrill of the fight.

"You alright there, Laz?" Draeven asked lightly. Lazarus turned his eyes away from Quinn and towards his best friend who watched him with delight.

"I'm fine."

"Mhmmm." His second nodded, though from his tone it was obvious he didn't believe it. Draeven looked him up and down, from the incline of his neck to the taut muscles of his arms, and finally the white-knuckled grip of his fists. "I hate to tell you this, but you brought this on yourself. Quinn isn't like your little passing fancies. You brought her with you, intending to make her a weapon—and while she might be one—she's different. *You* see her differently."

"Draeven, I am not in the mood for your—"

"I'm well aware," his second replied with an edge to his voice. "She woke up in a fragile state and you pushed her—right to *him*—so whatever you do, don't kill the boy. Not only will Thorne be pissed, but even worse, she will be too." Lazarus gritted his teeth, fighting to keep his mouth shut. Quinn hadn't been the only one stewing in her thoughts as they traversed the expansive region of the Cisean mountains down into Ilvas—but Draeven, unlike her, had the control for when and where to choose his battles. "If you kill him, I am not cleaning up the mess. You get to deal with her if she loses her shit and sends the basilisk after someone."

Lazarus sighed. "I'm not going to kill him."

"Good," Draeven said, "because I haven't seen you like this before, and when you're unpredictable, people tend to die." They held eye contact for a stretch of a moment before Lazarus nodded and Draeven turned his head back to the session. The tension between them dissipated as Quinn climbed off Vaughn and reached for the blindfold that now dangled around her neck, pulling it back up.

"Again," she commanded the Cisean and the boy fell in line.

He and Draeven stood there as the sun dipped low, disappearing under the horizon. When the sky turned from cerulean to gray, and to the midnight blue with only Leviathan's eye for light, Quinn finally called an end to the training session and started back for camp. The boy— Vaughn—simply stood there and then turned, looking at both Draeven and Lazarus with knowing eyes. He strode forward, his halberd leisurely at his side as he stepped through the line of trees.

"Remember what you told me," Draeven muttered as he turned for camp. Vaughn watched him go, none of the playfulness or light in his face he held when dealing with Quinn.

"You watch she-wolf Quinn—even when she doesn't want you to," the warrior said. His Norcastan was broken but improving slowly the longer he was with them.

"I watch all of my vassals," Lazarus replied.

"Then you know she has changed," the warrior said. His pale green eyes watched Lazarus with an intensity that few would. "The darkness in her grows."

Lazarus' eyebrows drew together slightly as he pressed his lips together before saying, "What exactly does that mean?"

The warrior looked away, swallowed, then stared down at the ground for a moment before swinging back to him. "I don't know," he answered. "But I am"—he paused, searching for the words. "I am worried about her." Lazarus blinked, but Vaughn continued. "I think you are too."

And with that, the boy—the man—walked away, leaving Lazarus in the cool night air alone with his thoughts to try to make sense of what was going on with Quinn.

But for the life of him, he didn't know anymore than she did.

Even if the whispers inside were telling him that something wasn't right ... something had changed.

Depravity's Spark

"The painful past of a tortured soul can shape the future of a man with the desire to be good."
— *Quinn Darkova, vassal of House Fierté, fear twister, Master of Neiss*

Darkness had fallen rather quickly. Quinn wiped away the worst of her sweat and took a seat by the fireside. Lorraine waited with bowls of stew filled with freshly caught rabbit, Quinn took one and turned her eyes back to the surrounding area. For the last week she'd been training every spare minute she had, ever since they left Cisea and she recovered her strength. Lazarus watched her, though he tried to stay far enough back so she wouldn't see.

Stupid man, Quinn thought to herself. *Of course, I see*

you. She always did, because she kept her field of vision up as a constant companion. For days there had been something on the periphery of it that left her edgy, but as she took a bite of her stew and turned to where Vaughn and Draeven stepped through the trees, she noticed that Lazarus hung back from them this time and motioned for Dominicus to join him.

Neither of them flicked a glance at the fire or the people surrounding it as they disappeared beyond the trees once more. Quinn wondered if it was their immediate absence that made her feel off—as though there were eyes on them—or if it were simply her paranoia. Before she could think too hard on it, Vaughn crouched down at her side.

"You did good, she-wolf Quinn. Good training. You are getting used to staff," he said, taking his seat.

"Thanks," Quinn replied, nodding his way as Lorraine shoved a bowl and spoon into his hands.

"I agree," Draeven commented as he sat down. "You seem to have mastered your field of vision, that's for sure."

"Yeah. I think the training is helping," Quinn said vaguely as she lifted the spoon to her lips. That wasn't the only thing she had gotten the hang of. Despite how hard she had pushed herself, Quinn hardly felt the day's exertion. Before Cisea, she had felt strained and bone-deep exhaustion by the time she had called it quits. Today, she had pushed herself far beyond what she ever had before and still it felt as though she could stand up and go again. Her nerves and muscles and bones were alive with energy, and ever since she came out of the strange sickness, she felt better than she ever had.

The only thing still bothering her was the sore spot on her abdomen. Even as Quinn sat and ate her dinner, she recalled checking it just that morning. Something dark had started to form there. It wasn't a brand—she knew that much—but she also wasn't quite sure what else it could be.

There was a dark outline of a circle with blotches of that same darkness creeping towards the larger one, but it wasn't complete.

The group ate in relative quiet—a few thanks to Lorraine and comments about the day as they all consumed their meal. And as they ate, Quinn eyed Draeven. Unlike the others, he would probably be more aware of what her body was going through if what she suspected was true. But how could she ask him without ringing any warning bells? Quinn chewed on her lower lip as she observed him quietly.

With a sigh, Draeven finished his stew and set his bowl down, lifting his head to stare at her. He had obviously been aware of her keen glances and Quinn wasn't the kind of person to hide what she was doing without good reason. At the moment, she didn't have a good reason to hide her interest, so she simply stared back, waiting for one of them—likely him—to break the silence.

"What?" he finally caved.

Quinn continued to watch him. "I'm just wondering something," she admitted.

"And that is?"

Lorraine and Vaughn's eyes bounced between the two of them.

"You're a Maji, right?"

Draeven stiffened but nodded in answer. "I am," he said.

"What kind?" she asked.

"Does it matter?"

Quinn shifted and leaned back on the log she was perched on. "No, I guess not," she said. "But I'm just wondering what your ascension was like—you've had it already, yes?"

His eyes widened and then narrowed in confusion, as though he couldn't quite understand why she was asking about that. "Yes, I had my ascension several years ago," he replied.

Quinn fiddled with the spoon in her bowl before moving it to the side and handing it off to Vaughn, who passed it to Lorraine—before returning his rapt attention to the two of them. "When I lived in N'skara," Quinn started, "I was taught a little bit about it, but most Maji that live in N'skara are light Maji. I'm wondering if it's any different. That's why I asked what kind of Maji you are."

Draeven shifted again, looking decidedly uncomfortable as he answered her. "Gray," he said sharply, as if the word itself was dragged from between his lips.

"And what was the ascension like for you?" Quinn asked, keeping her face neutral—void of any hints or signs.

Draeven looked away, saving Quinn the task of keeping up her impartial facade as she turned completely towards him and away from Lorraine and Vaughn. "The ascension is ... difficult on any Maji," Draeven started. "There are many who do not live through it. Your body is either strong enough to withstand the full potential of your magic, or it is not."

Quinn nodded. While she had never witnessed an ascension in N'skara, she had heard that some had failed to survive—those that hadn't lived had been weak to begin with, their bodies frail or even sickly.

"The ascension acts as kindle to a flame, it ignites the truth of a soul." Draeven turned his face back to Quinn and he stared somewhere beyond her, at a place she couldn't see. "It is a painful process," he said. "Some people believe that it is a test of the Gods to see if we are worthy of such power." Draeven sighed and leaned back, craning his neck so that he was looking at the night sky through the treetops. "That's why there are physical changes to a Maji's ascension."

"Physical changes?" Quinn asked, hunching forward intently. "What kind of physical changes?"

Draeven dragged his gaze away from the sky and

looked at her curiously. "Why do you want to know?" he asked, his eyes narrowing as suspicion finally edged into his expression.

Keeping her own face impassive, Quinn shrugged. "I'm past the age of normal ascension; I'm just curious. I expect I'll hit it soon."

Draeven eyed her for a moment more before he huffed and went back to staring up at the trees and stars. "Before I ascended," he said, his voice low, "I wasn't very big." Quinn raised a brow, looking him over. Out of the corner of her eye, she saw that Lorraine looked just as befuddled.

"I was actually a pretty small kid. Scrawny, some might say," Draeven continued, ignoring the rest of his audience. "One night in my late teens, the ascension hit me like a wild boar. I thought I was dying. The pain ripped me apart and rebuilt me into a new man. After that, my body put on muscle like nothing I —or anyone in my village—had ever seen. One day, I was small as an undergrown, half-starved kid, and within the following month I could run and keep up with men who'd done nothing but hard labor their entire lives. Within the following six months, my height shot up. I felt invincible." His tone might have been wistful if there wasn't a sharp bite of animosity Quinn couldn't understand the reason for. "The only difference with me was that my magic didn't really start to form until the year before my ascension."

Quinn frowned. She wanted to say that wasn't normal, but judging by his expression he already knew it. "Was your ascension difficult because of that?"

She was also a late bloomer. While her magic had shown up before either of her sisters and she'd been toying with it for years … she was also years past the age Maji entered their ascension. Would that cause it to be more painful? Perhaps even…

Draeven's shoulders stiffened, drawing her back. "During it? No. My family suspected what I was because they both were—though magic runs in the blood, magic doesn't always choose the children of Maji. Sometimes it may choose the grandchildren or great-grandchildren. My mother was a potion master, my father a light whisperer. They knew what to expect, and when I finally did start showing signs—though we couldn't tell what I was yet—" he paused, grinding his teeth for a moment as he inhaled through his nose. A sharp spike of heat filtered through the camp and Quinn was sure it didn't come from the slowly dying fire.

"The ascension itself, while painful, I knew how it would affect me," he finally continued after a brief, but tense moment. "It was what happened afterwards that I didn't expect." Draeven dragged his eyes away from the sky and looked directly at Quinn. "Unlike you, I didn't receive my magic until that previous year. I was in no way prepared to control it. That's why you need to learn to control yours sooner rather than later."

Quinn opened her mouth to reply, but it was Vaughn that leaned forward and spoke next. "Did you not yet know your master?" he asked.

Draeven twisted his head, blinking as if he had just realized that Lorraine and the Cisean were still there with them. "No. Lazarus didn't find me until a year or two later."

Vaughn's brows furrowed. "A year or two? Do you not know?"

A dark shadow fell over Draeven as he stood up and moved away from the fire, finding his pallet on the far side of the clearing. "The years between my ascension and the beginning of my employment with Lazarus are eclipsed in my mind," he said, his voice dripping with darkness. "Don't ask again."

The conversation died there as Lorraine went back to cleaning up the mess of dinner. Vaughn stared at Draeven's unmoving back with a pinched look of regret. Quinn sighed and stretched her limbs. If nothing else, Draeven's story had given her another hint.

She leaned back on her palms and closed her eyes. The darkness of the night called to her, and she let the tendrils slip from her skin and slither free. It was almost too easy for her to bring up the field of vision. She didn't expect to find anything, but she was curious—Dominicus and Lazarus had yet to return.

What she saw in her mind's eye, however, had her stiffening. Without wanting to alert Vaughn or Lorraine, she slowly got to her feet and stretched again. When Quinn began to make her way to the edge of the clearing, Lorraine called out to her, wanting to know where she was going, and Quinn surprised even herself when she lied without thinking. She said something quickly about relieving herself before bed and then ducked under a low hanging branch as she strode away.

She needed to relieve herself, alright. She needed to relieve the slowly building malevolence in her system and she suspected Lazarus had just the thing she needed.

Unlikely Tormentor

"It's not the words of a dying man that speak volumes, but the eyes of one as they stare out into oblivion."
— *Lazarus Fierté, dark Maji, heir to Norcasta, soul eater*

Watching. Waiting. For once, it wasn't the voices of souls he'd eaten that stalked him, but the enemies who thought to slay him while he slept.

"Fools," Lazarus muttered to himself. As if he wouldn't notice the eight men that lurked in the shadows around the camp. He'd have picked them off while Quinn was training, but they were still too far out. One of them might have escaped, and with him, word of the very woman he was trying to keep under wraps. No, he needed to lure them in. Let them think that they'd all gone to sleep. He needed them to think that they were easy. That *he* was easy. And then, when they least expected their demise, he would slit their throats and let them choke as they bled to death.

And that's just what he'd do.

With a nod to Dominicus, his weapons master took to the woods under the veil of night. His stealthy form slipped in and out of trees, far beyond what Lazarus could see—though he still felt the man's presence. He sensed each of the enemy souls as the ex-mercenary quietly slipped close and then divested them of their life. There was no whisper of their last goodbyes in the dark, no cries of outrage. They merely ceased to exist—just the way rats should be dealt with.

One by one they dropped, and the feeling of their souls blinked out—until there were only three: Dominicus, his target, and the unlucky bastard who drew the short stick and would feed Lazarus' demons that night.

He went for the latter, trailing through the woods with the same silence his assassin had helped him hone years ago. *The darkness was a void he knew well,* Lazarus thought as he pulled the wraith from his skin.

The vile creature was once a man, a rage thief gone mad. He'd killed himself, but his magic hadn't been ready to return to the Gods and a wraith was born. A creature of pain that existed in-between, created from the harvested soul of its owner that wasn't strong enough to hold all the rage it had consumed. This one had the ability to blend shadows and sense misery.

It suited Lazarus quite nicely as he wrapped it around him like a cloak and took to the darkness. Animals scattered, unable to see him, but sensing his presence and the vileness of the wraith. They had an uncanny way of grasping what their human counterparts could not.

As if to prove his point, the enemy mercenary came into view. He was stout man, but thickly built. The top of his head was balding, and his goatee was dark and well-kept. Lazarus hadn't seen the man before, which meant he was either new or too incompetent to warrant notice. Lazarus had a feeling it was both. Not many would take a contract on him these days. There was a reason for it, and he planned to remind whichever royal brat that sent him of that.

He moved like a shadow, his thick, calloused hand already wrapped around the back of the man's neck before the fool could utter a word.

"Let's take a walk," he murmured into the would-be killer's ear. "Shall we?" The wraith curled closer, reaching for the fiend as he attempted to struggle before finding it futile.

He didn't open his mouth to plead or beg or cry as many did when caught, Lazarus noted with a sliver of respect. He'd meet his death either way. It was the ones that stuck to their word that were the hardest to break. This would not happen quietly.

Lazarus looked to the trees and the sky, recognizing that while it might be night there was another moving toward him from nearby the camp. He stopped in the clearing where Dominicus awaited him.

He thrust his chin towards the woods, still not recognizing this soul just yet. Dominicus followed his command and started for the tree line just as Lazarus pushed his prey to his knees. The other man went to the ground easily, and when he looked into his eyes, Lazarus could tell that he knew his death was coming. He'd accepted it.

How refreshing, he thought.

"You know how this goes," Lazarus started. "You can either speak and die swiftly, or draw this out and learn how unpleasant I can be. The choice is yours." The man's lips pressed together and he lowered his gaze from the tree line, and Lazarus sighed. "So be it."

He commanded the wraith away and shifted to call forward a different beast when a thump and a curse stole his attention. Lazarus clamped one hand around the man's shoulder and half-turned to see Quinn striding forward, followed by Dominicus who was rubbing his jaw.

"You pack a mean right hook," his guard grunted.

"You held a sword to my throat, what did you expect—" Quinn's voice stopped short when she saw him. Her eyes dropped, and she tilted her head—getting a peek of the man he needed information from. He could sense the shift in her … not of revulsion, but something far more interesting.

"What are you doing here, Quinn?" he asked her. The woman's eyes never left the man kneeling at his feet as she slowly walked forward. A certain dark gleam entering her gaze.

"Quinn…" Dominicus started, more hesitant than he was only moments before.

It happened fast then. In the corner of his eye, Lazarus saw a flash of metal and shifted to escape it, knowing that he wouldn't. He'd been too distracted by her.

Then she did the unthinkable.

Her hand twisted and darkness shot forward. Lazarus froze, taking a step away to see the inky tendrils coiled around the man's arm. The dagger he held falling uselessly to the ground as those tendrils tightened, and a sharp crack filled the clearing as the bones of his wrist snapped.

Quinn tsked softly as she kept moving at a slow, meandering pace. "You go into the night to kill a man, not knowing what awaited you."

Lazarus stepped back, unable to look away just as much as he was too enthralled to stop it. He had no idea what Quinn planned to do. She was far too unpredictable, but something about that gleam in her eye told him that a piece of her was shifting—falling into place.

Her lavender hair reflected silver again in the moonlight as she came to stand beside him. Quinn squatted down, leaning forward so that her face was only inches from the mercenary's and Lazarus got the impression that, despite the pain that flushed his cheeks and the way he was biting his lip, he might very well be just a tiny bit hypnotized by her as well.

"Lazarus, I don't know if you should let her—" Dominicus broke off when Lazarus lifted his hand to silence him. He had this burning need to see what exactly she would do.

This torturous desire that was so perverted and wrong in every sense and yet he couldn't find it in him to care.

"Tell me," she whispered, "what is it that you fear?" There was a haunting edge to her voice. As if something else were riding her, but Lazarus knew that wasn't the case. He'd seen her in this place only once before. It was what drew him to her then, at the market.

"I-I…" the man on his knees started. "I…" He was trying to hold those words in. Those secrets. Quinn smiled like she knew it, and a pale hand caressed the man's dirty cheek.

"It's alright," she whispered softly. "I'll find out all the same."

Her fingers twisted a fraction and the tangible tendrils of fear snaked up his arm. The mercenary froze, whether in horror or shock, Lazarus wasn't sure, but it took great effort for him to look away from Quinn and stare at the tendrils slowly slithering over his shoulder.

"What dark magic is this?" the would-be assassin whispered. The peals of a soft laugh, tinkling like windchimes filtered through the air. It should have frozen Lazarus' blood instead of heating it. The tendrils crept over the man's collar and up his neck. A real terror began to root itself.

Quinn clicked her tongue against the roof of her mouth. "You should have asked more questions before coming after me and my friends, and now you'll pay the price." The coils of fear twined together as they skated over the delicate flesh between his neck and ear.

The mercenary's chest rose and fell with great exertion as he tried and failed to calm himself as the darkened strands slowly crept into his ear and continued to burrow.

"No," he said as his shoulder twitched. "*Please don't* —" His chest spasmed as his eyes began to roll back in his head before screwing shut. "No, no," he moaned.

"Shhhh," Quinn whispered, her fingers curling

around his chin. "You didn't want to talk to me before. It's too late now." And it was, judging by the blood that dripped and then ran from his nostrils. He let out something between a groan and a scream, the noise born of unspeakable pain. Quinn only blinked, not phased in the slightest.

"Ahhh," she murmured. "You've been a very bad boy, Gadmor. So bad."

His lips parted and the mewling sound that came out only made her laugh more.

"Sto—" He couldn't even finish the word before the thrashing started. Quinn's nails pierced the flesh of his chin, forcing his head to remain still.

"Would you like to tell them?" she asked. "Or shall I?" The only response he could give was a broken gagging sound as blood began to leak from his ears.

"They'll—kill—th-them," he choked out as his body convulsed.

Quinn rolled her eyes and released her grip. His entire frame veered away and fell back into a twitching pile of limbs. "I know," she murmured, the first hints of clarity entering her voice. "But you made your bed when you chose to come into these woods. Now, it's your wife and son that will have to live with the consequences of your failure." Her voice had gone from playful and deceptively soft, to hard and clear as the Servalis stone in his satchel.

Quinn rose to her feet and extended a hand. The

tendrils of fear crawled back out the other ear and slithered over the husk of a man that lay prone and moaning in her wake. They drifted into the air, settling on her skin before slinking under. Only then did anyone speak.

"We won't be able to interrogate him now," Dominicus started. His tone was frustrated, but the careful glances in her direction meant he did not want to push her when she was like this, no matter the consequences.

"You won't need to," she replied. "He feared for his wife and son. Gadmor was a dead man that couldn't provide, so he traded all he had to give. His life." Her hands fell to her sides and she clenched them into fists. "He and the other seven didn't come into these woods to kill you—though they would have, given the chance. They came to distract you, so that the real threat had time to find us before we reached Tritol." Quinn paused. "And before you ask, no, they weren't given knowledge of who sent them. Whoever it was at least had the forethought to not leave a trail."

Lazarus let out a curse, but all Quinn did was turn on her heel and start for the camp. "We need to leave. Now. So we stand a chance of crossing the rest of Ilvas before they find us," she said over her shoulder.

Dominicus slit the suffering man's throat and turned to Lazarus. "I don't know what's going on with her, but that wasn't normal. We need to talk about this when we get to Tritol. I don't know if bringing her to N—"

"We'll talk, but for now, she's right. We need to go," Lazarus said before he followed after her into the darkness—where they both belonged.

As the Sun Rises

"A creature who does not need a weapon is one."
— *Lazarus Fierté, dark Maji, heir to Norcasta, soul eater*

Bastian carried its master as Lazarus leaned forward over the horse's neck, urging the beast to go ever faster. Hours they had ridden through the night. Even for an experienced rider it was a difficult pace to set. He could hear the heaving of the others, and though they struggled to keep stride, none spoke a word of complaint. They, too, could feel the rising urgency as if the dark realm's shadow wolves were upon them, ready to tear their bodies limb from limb and feast upon their flesh.

The land shifted as they rode, changing from

narrow passages through forests to open plains as they exited the woods. The tree line still stretched alongside them as the roads widened, obviously built in a way that was meant for carts and coaches rather than lone riders. As everyone spread out, in Lazarus' peripheral he noted that Quinn was riding just as hard as the others, her skills on a horse having grown significantly since their first encounter. So much so that Lorraine was now to the side, riding along with Dominicus.

His newest vassal had certainly changed. When he had first met her, Lazarus had thought Claudius already mad for possibly thinking that such a small, inexperienced Maji could be what either made or broke his empire. But now, he saw something different in her. A darkness had risen to the surface, one that she fully embraced.

Across the plains, the sun slowly began to rise, bleeding out the new day across the skies as the night receded. The land spread far and wide, and beyond it the ocean lashed against far off cliffs. The air was thick with the scent of salt and sea.

Had they taken their time as travelers normally would, it might have taken them another full day to reach even this far. They were getting closer. It wouldn't be long now.

"There! I see it!" Draeven called out. Lazarus turned his head and noted that he was correct. The capital of Ilvas rose, a single shining city along the flat lands bordering the edge of the ocean and the wide mouth of a river.

Tritol was the gem of Ilvas with capped golden rooftops and wide pillared buildings, all surrounded by a sandstone wall meant to protect the city from land marauders. Lazarus nudged Bastian in the side with the heel of his boot, kicking the horse's speed up a notch.

"When we get to the city, I want you to take the others and find lodging. I will want to meet with Imogen myself," he said.

Draeven jerked his head to the side. "I will accompany you," he replied.

"No." Lazarus turned his gaze forward once more. "Quinn will accompany me."

"But—"

"What's that?" Dominicus' voice rose above the clomping of their horses' hooves in the dirt. Both Draeven and Lazarus scanned the horizon for whatever he had seen.

Up ahead, riding towards them at a more sedate pace was a small battalion of white and blue clothed Ilvasian soldiers. Lazarus sat up and Bastian slowed beneath him.

Draeven shot his master a look. "They must have received your message," he said. There was no hiding the small hint of relief in the man's voice.

Lazarus stared ahead, watching the approaching soldiers. "Yes," he said. "Thorne came through."

"Did you doubt my King?" Vaughn asked as he approached the two of them. Lazarus' horse came to a stop and with it, the others followed.

Beyond the advancing troupe, the flags of Ilvas fluttered in the early morning wind. A horse neighed. Several of Lazarus' group panted with the force they had exerted to get this far, though not Quinn, he noted, keeping his eyes on the horizon, watching the men in uniform. Something felt off. Had he and the others truly outrun the enemy?

Quinn's horse pushed between him and Vaughn as she came upon his right side. He turned his gaze and examined her. Her eyes, however, remained trained forward, her back straight. *Is it just her?* Lazarus wondered. Something was putting him off...

The Ilvas guard was approaching, likely to offer them the assistance he had requested of Imogen.

"Something isn't right." Quinn's voice was like silk in his ears—silk stained red.

"What—" Before Draeven could finish asking her what she meant, an arrow was released and flew right between him and Quinn. It slid perfectly between the spaces of their bodies—a warning of their impending altercation.

Quinn growled low under her breath, taking up the reins of her horse. The creature neighed and stomped its hooves beneath her, obviously still uncomfortable with its rider, but Quinn's body slid along the horse's back as though she were one with the animal.

She remained unphased by its reaction to her, ever in control. A control she hadn't possessed not long ago.

"Go!" Quinn shouted. "If we all group together we're one giant target!"

All at once, as though everyone had just realized the truth behind the loosed arrow, they did as she said. Lazarus urged Bastian to follow after her as she kicked the sides of her horse and sent the creature rearing back and then forward.

"Lazarus!" Draeven called after him.

Lazarus turned his head, replying to the man's unspoken question. "Span out," he called back. "This is the only way to Tritol and turning back isn't an option." Lazarus' eyes met Dominicus' and the weapons master nodded. He would protect Lorraine with his life. They could not lose a good potions expert and healer.

"Quinn!" Lazarus' horse lurched as he converged on her. "Follow—"

"We have to break through them," she interrupted, her eyes focused. "It's the only way." Already the tendrils of fear began to seep from her skin, forming around her like snakes coiled to strike, ready and willing to protect their master. Like the basilisk.

Another arrow released and Lazarus and Quinn both swerved to avoid the oncoming bolt. Quinn growled low in her throat, the sound violent and angry. And just as the new day was lit aflame by the rising sun, it was blinked out of existence. One moment the skies were pinkening into the morning blue, and the next a vast ocean of black sky spread, descending over them, blocking out all light except what was left to visualize the enemies at their front.

As the sun rose, the darkness fell once more, conjuring a premonition of the imminent oblivion approaching their enemies.

Blood in the Dirt

"And once the flames of ascension consume you, you will be reborn anew."
— *Quinn Darkova, vassal of House Fierté, fear twister, Master of Neiss*

Quinn called to the fear inside, letting it out to slip over her flesh. It tingled along her nerve endings. She was almost sure of it now—after her conversation with Draeven and the things she'd done after that. Her control over the fear was near perfect. In fact, the tendrils no longer felt separated from her at all—as though they were a different entity entirely.

The tendrils that ran along her arms and stretched out across the sky—blackening it, rousing the fear in her enemies—was now like another limb to her. The horse between her thighs trembled, its own emotions fueling her power as she surged forward.

Arrows fell upon them in rapid succession, forcing her to swerve or pick up the speed again and again. Lazarus raced alongside her, the scent of salt and desperation was like kindling to her flame. She shuddered in delight at the dread that stemmed from up ahead, rising in waves, crashing down over her senses —as it completely and utterly rode her.

Adrenaline in its purest form flooded her system, and in that moment, Quinn never felt so alive. So very powerful. She and Lazarus ate up the distance between them and their enemies, and in a clash of metal and booming thunder, they struck. The skies, now blacker than night, made it difficult for them to see, even though they carried torches. That orange flame only did so much when Quinn swung clean through the arm holding it. The flame hit the ground, sparking fire as the rider let out a scream in anguish. Quinn was already coming upon her next victim as she slashed and blocked the oncoming attacks. Lost in the haze of battle and blood lust, Quinn found that part of herself she was always missing.

And she embraced it.

"Quinn!" The roar from Lazarus shook her, and she turned her cheek to stare at him just as an arrow grazed the side of her face. A single line of blood slipped down over her chin. The sting of the tip told her she'd been cut, but not killed. Not as she would have been, had he said nothing. She needed to be more careful.

As soon as it occurred to her, two riders rounded on her, meeting her head on. They split, attempting to run down either side of her—boxing her in the middle. She curled her hand around her sword, readying her resolve, unable to stop it from happening, but when they passed her, it wasn't her they attacked.

It was the horse.

Wicked blades sliced down its sides, sending the creature fumbling forward. It jerked so violently Quinn didn't have a chance of holding on as it threw her. Air kissed her skin as she flew from its back and in the moment before she landed, she saw the world in slow motion as the fighting raged.

Lazarus fought with such savageness that she had a feeling—were he alone—he would be the only one to make it out alive. As it was, Draeven and Vaughn had joined the fray and were both facing off against multiple men in blue and white. They were far more skilled than their attackers, but because of the enemy's sheer numbers, they were going to be in real trouble soon. Especially Dominicus who was contending with seven riders on his own, but had Lorraine huddled into him and holding on for dear life—though her expression was not one of terror.

She saw all this in the blink of an eye before her

body hit the ground at a bone-rattling intensity. She rolled, trying to lessen the momentum, but the stabbing pain below her abdomen was stifling. The spot that had plagued her for the last week or so, ever since they left Cisea, was burning. Quinn grit her teeth against the pain and spat the dirt from her mouth. Ignoring the spittle tinged with blood, Quinn rose back to her feet.

Horses surrounded her instantly, their riders seeking her out, assuming that because she had fallen, she was weak.

"Neiss!" she called out. Lightning slashed across the sky as her serpent answered.

The creature slid from her skin as the riders neared. Its mauve-colored scales near black under the moonless and sunless sky she'd created.

"What is that?" She heard one of them call out, his voice tinted in panic.

"I think it's—"

Neiss' body expanded, the width of his length forming to half her height. Realization seemed to echo through their ranks. They knew. "Basilisk!" they shouted, scurrying back as they tried to run, to escape the creature. It was too late.

Neither the horses nor the riders stood a chance when Quinn whispered her command, "Kill them."

"*With pleasure*," the serpent hissed as it took to the fight. Arrows rained down upon him, cracking and shattering into splinters on impact. Swords clashed uselessly against his near impenetrable skin. It was only after two of the riders died from simply being too close to the basilisk as he moved, crushing them under his massive size, that the others got the hint and truly began to retreat.

"Oh no, you don't," Quinn spat. Neiss slithered around, lowering his head as he did. The tip of his nose hit her, and she fell back between his eyes.

"*Kneel on me,*" he told her. Quinn scrambled back, struggling with the smooth surface of his scales, but managing to stay on as he opened his jaws and bit an archer aiming for her. She felt nothing but a sick kind of joy coming from him as he swallowed the man— bow and all.

"*Won't that hurt?*" she asked.

"*Tis' a snack, young one,*" Neiss replied happily as they gained ground on the half dozen soldiers that ran from them and headed straight for Dominicus.

"*After them,*" she urged and Neiss dove. This time the momentum threw her too much and Quinn's body slipped away as she lifted and was airborne once more. Not for long, she realized, as the end of Neiss' tail wrapped around her middle, pulling her along. He gained ground, closing in around them when Quinn realized her fault.

Animals, unlike the people that rode them, knew when to run from a greater predator.

That included the animals carrying the very people she was trying to save.

Quinn cursed herself as the steed Dominicus tried to control deemed the basilisk as the greater threat. Quinn saw it all so clearly in that moment. The horse's panicked wide eyes, the shake of his majestic head. The enemy up ahead, turning back slightly as they ran.

"Neiss," she said in a panicked voice. "Put me down." The creature obliged instantly, but the horses kept running, and with Lorraine's back to them—unprotected. Quinn felt something bubble up in her as Neiss recoiled and shrunk. He knew what she needed, even when she could not say.

"*Do what you must, my lady,*" he said, instantly withdrawing and slipping beneath her skin once more.

No one paid her any mind when one of the archer's stopped and took aim.

No one saw what she did as the arrow flew, and this time, there was no errant wind to displace it. A scream tore from her lips as she tried to warn them.

But it was too late. The damage she'd done unknowingly was going to cost her.

The arrow pierced Lorraine's flesh and the white tunic she wore darkened immediately as blood seeped out. Their eyes met over the great distance as Lorraine's face contorted in pain and she cried out in surprise and agony. Dominicus rounded the horse, his instincts picking up on the woman's distress, but it was too late. The action couldn't be undone.

Time slowed. Paused. Stopped altogether.

Quinn felt it then, something dark and destructive boiling up inside her.

She clenched her fists as several attackers finally noticed that she had called the basilisk back and he was gone. Their eyes focused on where Quinn now stood completely alone. Lazarus and Draeven were too far out. Vaughn was engaged in his own fight and Dominicus rushed to aid the wounded Lorraine. They came for her as that whisper of something ancient and very dark awoke.

She knew then, as her side burned and lit her aflame, that she'd been right to wonder.

The attackers turned on her and Quinn lifted her hands. Tendrils of fear flowed from her skin and theirs, twining together. The two dozen or so that still remained took notice as black strands began to twist and turn.

"You hurt her," she whispered to them. The darkness inside her reached its breaking point and she knew there would be no return if she did this. A whip cracked in the distance and Quinn froze.

Time stilled for only a moment. A mere blink of an eye.

The whip cracked again, and she saw it. The riders that chased Draeven, and the cruel smirk they wore as they pulled him from his horse and began to beat him. She saw as Lorraine toppled off the back of the horse as Dominicus came to a stop, scrambling to get her before they did. She saw Vaughn, seasoned as he was, being backed into a corner.

And the last one, she didn't see. Lazarus was to her back and she couldn't look away even as she felt that dark power inside him rise, bubbling forth. She couldn't explain it, how she knew where he was and what he was feeling.

But she felt it, and it was that *rage* that pushed her over.

A final crack split the air and the dam that had been holding her finally broke.

"No one hurts my people," she said darkly.

And Quinn Darkova fully ascended.

Ascension

"When the only thing left to fear is fear itself, you should still run, because she will find you."
— *Lazarus Fierté, dark Maji, heir to Norcasta, soul eater*

E verywhere she went, he knew without needing eyes. It transcended his field of vision as something changed within them both, at once. He didn't know what it was until it was too late.

He didn't see the signs until the cage that held her shattered from the raw strength of her power.

Shadow creatures, beings made of fear and rage and desperation, rose up from the ground and descended on their enemies. Some shot to the skies, forming wings of obsidian that rode on the nonexistent wind. Others formed into mutated creatures that were like nothing he'd ever seen. Their skin was so dark it stood apart from the void she'd dropped over all of them. Those creatures had no souls. No will of their own.

All they were and would ever be were figments from her mind made real.

Somehow, she had twisted the fears of those on the battlefield into tangible beings. They leapt from the ground, ignoring the horses in favor of the men who were already screaming and attempting to flee. The flesh was ripped from their bones and their clothing torn to shreds until only remnants of this enemy remained.

He'd counted sixty souls apart from their own when this started.

Quinn wiped out over half of them in minutes.

Bones and cloth and weapons littered the ground, but no bodies. The beasts she'd brought forward consumed them with a viciousness that mirrored the woman herself. When the flesh they'd been feasting on was gone, an uneasy feeling spread in his chest as they still remained, still hunted. The shadow beasts seemed to know who was friend and who was foe and they never once drifted too close to him. He turned, knowing where she stood, locked inside a rage so cold that the hottest of flames might not melt it.

He'd seen her angry. He'd seen her in the grips of madness.

Never had he seen this woman so deep in the

throes of rage that it consumed her. The creatures she'd brought forward fell to their knees before her and the ones in the sky took to the ground and followed suit as she simply stood there. The veins around her eyes had run black, exaggerating the cut of her cheekbones and planes of her face. Her fists remained clenched at her sides, and he could sense the battle warring within as she tried to pull back the strength she'd only just unleashed.

She'd stolen the fear of dozens to create her army, and that sort of power wouldn't be displaced so easily. He knew it from the souls he'd taken. Each and every one she took into her would cost her as it did him. He had to get to her before the cost was too steep— before he lost her to her own madness and rage.

"Quinn," he said, standing at the edge of her minions. She didn't respond, but the creatures turned at once, parting to form a path straight to her. He took that as permission enough that they wouldn't destroy him, though his steps were slow when he first entered the mass. Their lavender eyes glowed as they watched him with parted lips and equally dark tongues that licked over their teeth, as if salivating for a taste of him as well.

Even as she self-destructed within, she was keeping them on a tight rein. Thorne had warned him of this, that she'd come back different and the sort of violent whims she might have would be devastating in comparison to what he'd dealt with before.

Lazarus hadn't listened then because he thought he knew her better. He was listening now.

The last of the shadow creatures parted and he came to stand before her. She didn't move, didn't twitch as she kept them all in this dark realm she'd created from nothing but the fear in their hearts.

"Quinn," he breathed. Searching her expression for something, anything that could tell him how to do this. "I need you to send them away now, fear twister," he growled, thinking that maybe the command might pull her from it. Her eyes slid towards him, a sort of cold cruelty in them and she wore it so beautifully.

"Who are you to command me?" she asked in a detached voice. Something swirled in her blue gaze; a power that lurked just at the end, so wrathful that he knew commands would not work this time. He needed to tread carefully.

"Not a command, then," he said, "a request." She didn't even blink at his words.

"Why?" she asked, tilting her head to the side then. "I rather like my creatures. They're a part of me. They're ... *mine.*" Lazarus bit the inside of his cheek because he finally understood not only Claudius' vision, but Draeven's and Thorne's warnings. Just as he knew without a shadow of doubt that Quinn had ascended, and if he had to guess at when, it was when she was in the springs. So much made sense now about why she'd almost died. She was already leaking magic, not because she couldn't hold it, but because the Gods were leaching her of it to see if she was strong enough to hold its full might and she'd done it. She survived not just that, but the stone —and all the signs were there if he'd known what to look for then, if he'd suspected.

He hadn't, however, and that was going to cost him if he couldn't bring her back down.

"They are yours," he said slowly. "Just as the basilisk is. Unlike the basilisk, these creatures don't hold a soul, Quinn. They're using slivers of yours to stay like this, and if you hold them too long, they might want to keep those slivers." He spoke in sure, steady hushed words—meant only for her ears. "You need to hold onto your soul, which means you need to take those pieces of it back from them."

Her lips parted for a brief moment as she said, "How do you know?"

"Because I see souls, and they only hold yours." Her lips pushed together as she seemed to think on it.

"Why do you want me to have a soul?" she asked. "Is it so you can take it from me?" Something twisted inside him for a moment, causing his blood to rise and his palms to sweat. It only took him a second to realize it was her, preying on his fears.

Commanding her wasn't working but neither was being kind.

He needed to try a different approach, something she couldn't manipulate.

"I sense your fear, Lazarus. You worry you'll take

it," she said, sounding indifferent to what exactly those words meant. "Don't tell me you don't. *I know.*"

Lazarus took a deep breath and tried to push down the rising panic. *It's not real*, he told himself. *She's manipulating you.*

He lifted one of his palms to the side of her face and her eyebrows drew together, the slightest touch of clarity in her expression. Then his fingers dug into her lavender hair, gripping it tight as he wrenched her head back. He leaned in and whispered a truth he never wanted to give, but that she needed to hear.

"You're right. I do fear losing control with you." His lips brushed along her jaw and he felt her shudder. "Because I *want* you—so much more than your magic." Her breath hitched and he sensed that power backing away as something else pushed forward. "I hate that you hold the same power over me as you do these creatures, because anyone else I would *crush* if they dared act the way you do. You're a cruel, twisted woman." He paused, his lips only a hairsbreadth from hers. "But you're the only one I think that actually understands me. You embrace the darkness as I do. You play with the beasts that no one would dare touch. You are fearless and *magnificent* as you are—and that is why I fear losing control. If I took your soul, you would be none of those things, and that's why you need those pieces back. So you don't become one."

She turned her head just a fraction, but that was all it took for his lips to meet hers. She stayed frozen before him as he pried her lips apart. Lazarus groaned, and the sound seemed to pull her from the brink of no return. Her lips pressed back against his and he fisted his hand in her hair as she kissed him with abandon. One by one those pieces started to come back to her. Still, he kissed her. Unable to stop himself. Unable to pull back from the edge as he breathed in her scent and wrapped his hand around her throat—powerless to deny himself the possessive act—too weak to push her away even when he felt the last pieces of her soul slither back into place.

Her hands grasped the straps holding his weapons and pulled, reeling him into her. Lazarus—careful, calculated, and controlled as he was—threw caution to the wind and let her. Her nails grazed over the cloth of his tunic, scratching too hard to be accidental. She bit his bottom lip, drawing a groan from him. *Gods above*, he cursed himself. Her tongue toyed with his, wicked and maddening as the woman herself. He tightened his hand around her throat just a fraction and Quinn moaned. He wound his other arm around her waist, pulling her closer to—

A horn blasted from the other side of them, coming from Tritol.

The change in her was instant as she shoved with a strength she hadn't previously possessed. "Liar," she growled, wisps coming off her like smoke as she lifted a hand and clenched her fist.

An all-out dread absorbed him. Impending doom

settled in his gut as anxiety clawed its way up his throat, his knees threatening to collapse. "Quinn, I didn't lie to you—"

She pulled harder and the air left his lungs as terror reached its hands for his chest. Images filled his mind of terrible, dreadful things. "You tried to distract me," she said in that same emotionless voice. "I won't make that mistake again."

"Quinn," he groaned as a flash of silver caught his eye. She lifted the dagger above her, poised to strike. "Don't do this."

"May Belphor embrace you, Lazarus," she whispered.

But it was too late. Far, far too late.

Axe

"Everything has a cost, whether you choose to pay it or not."
— *Quinn Darkova, vassal of House Fierté, fear twister,*
Master of Neiss

Her hand stilled, the dagger hovering above his prone form. The darkness rode her, those shadow tendrils of fear whispering sweet nothings in her ears. They told her that she couldn't trust anyone, that it would all end in chains.

And Quinn wouldn't be a slave.

Never again.

She would die before she took that route.

But to kill Lazarus … even as they pushed and pushed, something held her back. Something made her still her hand, even as the clomping of hooves grew near.

She didn't want to stab him.

Kill or be killed, they told her. Those deadly tendrils feeding on the rage within.

Her arm shook from the exertion as she forced herself to remain still and not do as they commanded. Sweat trickled down her temples, tracing the line of her jaw before falling.

Still, she fought. She fought her own demons with all she had.

I will not be a slave to anything. She meant it, and that included fear itself. It was her drug. Her addiction. Fear gave her power, but giving in to it also stripped her power away, and she could not allow that.

"You. Do. Not. Control. Me!" she cried out as the dagger began to slip from her fingers. Her eyes widened just as a hand clamped over her wrist. "Wha—"

The anger drained out of her, leaving her dizzy and light-headed. She swayed on her feet for a moment, her gaze traveling up a tanned arm to meet the violet eyes of the ash-haired man that stopped her.

"D-draeven?" she stuttered as her magic settled instantly when it no longer had the rage to fuel it.

His jaw tensed and the twitch of his eye told her he was struggling as he dropped her hand and backed away. "Drae—"

"Don't," Lazarus breathed. He rolled on his side before climbing to his feet. "He took your rage to stop you from doing something that would end us both, but the demons you faced are now on his back. Let it be." He reached out a hand to still her and she marveled for a moment, staring at Draeven and then to the hand that touched her.

"Do you fear me now?" she asked him. The void she'd created began to shatter into pieces and fall before disappearing entirely, allowing the harsh light of a new day to bathe them.

Lazarus turned his gaze from her to the rising sun and the people on horses that approached them. Quinn tensed for a moment when he said, "I don't think I would fear you even if you killed me, Quinn. There's a lot of things I feel for you, but fear isn't one of them."

She opened her mouth, not knowing what to say. She stood in silence when he started for the half dozen people approaching them. His relaxed gate kept her at bay as she glanced back to Dominicus carrying Lorraine, and Vaughn trailing behind them.

The horses came to a halt before Lazarus, and the group remained tense for a moment before the one at the back came forward. The steed itself was a beast, but the girl on top of it was barely a wisp. If not for the flaming red hair twined in braids with beads and cloth scattered in it, she would hardly warrant notice. Her face was younger, much younger than Quinn, but her gaze was that of someone well beyond her years as she observed their party and the bones that surrounded them.

"You've got five seconds to tell me who in the dark realm you pricks are that thought to start a war outside my mother's city," the young woman spoke in Ilvan, a language Quinn knew.

Though it seemed Lazarus did not as he answered, "We come from Cisea to speak with Imogen. I am Lazarus Fierté, friend of Ilvas." The girl narrowed her eyes and just as Quinn opened her mouth to say something, she smiled.

"Lazarus," she said in far better Norcastan than Vaughn could speak. The accent was nearly indistinguishable. "She's been expectin' you. Thorne of the mountains sent word, but we were dealin' with a small predicament from Norcasta you so nicely chose to handle for us." She gave him an appraising look. "Tell me, who have you brought to the Pirate Queen's city?"

"I am Vaughn," the warrior said before Lazarus could reply, and she could tell it irked him.

"Emissary from Cisea, I presume?" she asked, sucking the air between her teeth as he nodded.

"Dominicus is a guard, and as you can tell, Lorraine—one of my vassals—has been injured and needs a healer immediately," Lazarus said. The girl motioned with her hand and one of the soldiers dismounted to assist Dominicus and Lorraine.

"Patch and Poppet," she said. "You go with them. Make sure she gets the help she needs and let Mother know our guests have arrived." Two of the riders broke away and escorted Dominicus to the city in the distance. "What about these two?" she asked, waving an axe that Quinn hadn't noticed before in her and Draeven's direction.

"Draeven is my left-hand and second-in-command," Lazarus answered tightly.

"Not right?" the girl asked.

"He's too kind to be the right," came Lazarus' reply. The girl considered that for a moment before nodding.

"And you?" she asked. "You come from the self-righteous bastards over the border, do you not?" Her dislike of N'skara clear from the grim set of her lips.

"She's with me—"

"Obviously," the girl replied, cutting him off.

Quinn stepped up, storing the blade she held before turning her attention to the girl. "I'm Quinn, his right-hand," she answered.

Overhead, a bird, black as the void she'd created, spread its wings and cast a shadow over her. Quinn squinted, putting a hand over her eyes as the beast turned its head and let out a caw so loud the Gods must have heard it. Quinn frowned as a single silver feather drifted on the wind before it turned to the west.

Towards N'skara.

Towards her home.

Quinn looked back to the red-headed young woman who only blinked and then smiled with swagger. "I'm Axe, adopted daughter of Imogen the Pirate Queen," she said. "And I look forward to hearin' all about how you came to be with the next king of Norcasta."

To be continued …

Quinn and Lazarus story continues in :
Blessed be the Wicked
Dark Maji Book Two

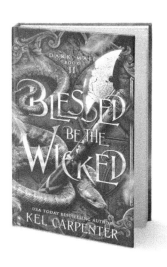

Also by Kel Carpenter

Ongoing Series:

—Adult Urban Fantasy—

Demons of New Chicago:

Touched by Fire (Book One)

Haunted by Shadows (Book Two)

Blood be Damned (Book Three)

—Adult Reverse Harem Paranormal Romance—

A Demon's Guide to the Afterlife:

Dark Horse (Book One)

Completed Series:

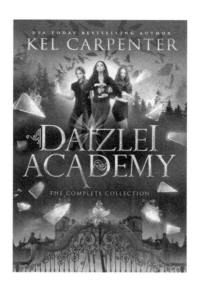

—Young Adult +/New Adult Urban Fantasy—

The Daizlei Academy Series:

Completed Series Boxset

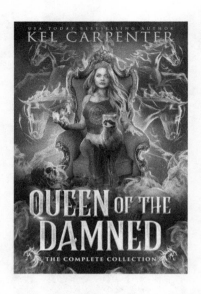

—Adult Reverse Harem Urban Fantasy—

Queen of the Damned Series:

Complete Series Boxset

—New Adult Urban Fantasy—

The Grimm Brotherhood Series:

Complete Series Boxset

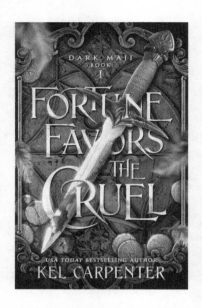

—Adult Dark Fantasy—

The Dark Maji Series:

Fortune Favors the Cruel (Book One)

Blessed be the Wicked (Book Two)

Twisted is the Crown (Book Three)

For King and Corruption (Book Four)

Long Live the Soulless (Book Five)

About Kel Carpenter

Kel Carpenter is a master of werdz. When she's not reading or writing, she's traveling the world, lovingly pestering her editor, and spending time with her husband and fur-babies. She is always on the search for good tacos and the best pizza. She resides in Bethesda, MD and desperately tries to avoid the traffic.

Join Kel's Readers Group!